Poisoned

Dawn's End Book 2

ISBN 978-0-9921037-0-5

Revised February 2014

This book is a work of fiction and any resemblance to persons, living or dead, or actual events is purely coincidental. The characters are products of the author's imagination and used fictitiously.

Dedication

For my big sister, Virla, who is always on my side and loves me just the way I am.

Acknowledgments

Thanks to Robin for rescuing my inaccessible computer files and to my husband Fred for enlisting Robin when he couldn't rescue the chapters himself.

Forward

Holding on to anger is like grasping a hot coal with the intent of throwing it at someone else; you are the one who gets burned.

~ Buddha

Prologue

Nicole Newman pressed the bracelet against her feverish cheek. The whisper of nurses' crepe-soled shoes passed by in the hall. Her husband, Jamail, had brought her the bracelet earlier. She had insisted on holding it one last time.

"Don't say that," he said, frowning.

But Nicole knew she was fading like a Valentine left too long in sunshine. Jamail slept on the cot by the window, spending every night with her since her admittance to the hospice. She had given up trying to convince him to sleep at home.

"The bed is too empty without you," he said, finally, his voice choked.

Sweet Jamail, if only she could spare him this pain. He'd had so few years to spend with her strong and healthy.

She wanted to remember when she was young and vital, before they had even met. Back to a time of murky forests with droopy, dank leaves and sun-filled meadows with hidden royalty. Was it disloyal to remember another man? A man as powerful as the bracelet's embossed panther with its glittering eye? No, Jamail would understand. She knew he sometimes thought of his first spouse, just as she still missed hers.

Morrel, Morrel . . . . Was he still alive? With the difference in time, it seemed impossible. But Nicole also remembered the panther people's unusual longevity. Who knew for sure? Dawn's End had been filled with the unexpected.

What of the threat of darkness? Paradise had been reborn when she returned to Dawn's End, pregnant with Anastacia. She could not imagine a more beautiful place to birth and raise her child. Soon after her return to Dawn's End, she realized the black stones in all the bracelets had turned clear, with a faint pink tinge. As well, her band had turned in color from copper back to gold. She had used her bracelet twice, once to stop a poisonous snake from striking and again to stop a house fire. For almost three years, her life had been blissful. But then illness had struck, and she had to leave and return to Thunder Bay. It seemed so long ago, more dream than memory.

Nicole shifted; the bed creaked. She adjusted the I.V. cords and fingered the button that allowed her to control the morphine drip.

She would never know if Nightfall had ever returned to Anastacia's birthplace. Nicole wished she had found a way to visit one last time. She wished she could have shown her daughter the wondrous place they had shared with Morrel. She had kept too many secrets.

Nicole shivered as a chill emanated from the now copper bracelet. It had dulled again when she left Dawn's End for good, but still she clenched it tightly. It was all she had left. Perhaps Dawn's End had cost her everything, but had it not given her everything as well? Especially little Anastacia.

Chapter One — Arrivals

Kaie rubbed the embossed panther with her thin, knobby fingers. Her gnarled hands protruded like bleached bones from the ragged, black sleeves of her cloak. Her cracked nails, lined with dirt and flecked with white spots, traced the gold panther shape. Its black stone eye glinted against the shimmering, gold bracelet. She sensed another bracelet, beyond the door. But, through spells and the power of her own bracelet, she was drawing it closer, drawing it to her reach like a beltfish to a shimmer worm. That bracelet was worn by an innocent. Soon Kaie would hook both fish and owner, reel them in, smash and slice and devour their strength in order to fuel her own.

While she waited, Kaie would prepare. She had accumulated most of what she needed and set up a laboratory in the abandoned mine. There were those who plotted against her, who challenged her power. Kaie smiled thinly. If they only knew the extent of her plans. If they could imagine the scope of her terrible ambition, they would despair. But then surrender without challenge — where would be the amusement in that? Perhaps this new innocent would provide some distraction. She sensed a silent strength there. Women often did not realize their own power.

"Riva." Kaie croaked the name.

A shapely woman entered through the left cave tunnel. She wore a black G-string, ankle-high black boots, and a thin, black harness crossing under and above her full breasts. In the harness rested a small dagger. Her red, transparent tunic was open to her navel, allowing access to the weapon. Long, blonde hair hung down her back. She moved with the churning rhythm of a woman of desire.

"Yes, mistress," Riva said. Her voice was honey, laced with belladonna.

Kaie's thin smile revealed her gapped and decayed teeth. Her inflamed gums oozed. "Have Lachish bring me one male captive. The rest are his to do with as he pleases. The male should be of a virile age, but neither of you is to touch him. I have special plans."

As Riva left, Kaie absentmindedly yanked the loosest tooth from her mouth and spat blood and pus onto the cave floor. She tossed the brown incisor into a bowl of grisly treasures, fuel for her dark magic.

When the airplane rose, Anastacia Larina Newman was magnetized by the beauty of the clouds, their variations as endless as a northern landscape. Deep piles of white textured the sky with lights and shadow. As the Boeing 747 elevated, levels of strata were revealed. Below was a bright, billowy carpet, above stretched wisps of cotton, and between them renegades of fluff. The layers ran their individual races. She stared until her eyes ached.

She had asked for the window seat, wanting to see as much as possible. However, her lengthy legs were cramped in the smaller space. Anastacia pulled back her long, coffee-black hair. Her lovely, latte-brown skin felt dry. She rubbed her tired, blue eyes and pulled down the window shade.

As she traced the embossed panther on her bracelet with her fingertips through her shirtsleeve, Anastacia again felt a tingle. She had not noticed any odd sensations when her mother gave her the band. It was antique, unique, and made from a strange, soft copper. She hadn't intended to bring it, but it compelled her to take it. Every time she put it away, she was unable to stop thinking about it. Her arm felt naked. She could no more ignore its siren call than she could pass up the last chocolate in a box. Like her mother, Nicole, Anastacia wore the bracelet only on very special occasions.

Anastacia hid the bracelet under a long-sleeved shirt. Her stepfather would not want her traveling alone with expensive jewelry. He would say she was asking for trouble, and he would be right. But Anastacia wanted to wear it to Julie's wedding, a way to bring part of her mother to the family celebration.

When her mother was again diagnosed with cancer, she had given the bracelet to Anastacia. They were sitting in the living room, the filtered sun streaming through the sheers in the bay window. Outside, a cold wind raced across the crisp snow, the sunshine contrasting with the frozen landscape.

"It looks like a beautiful day," Anastacia said. "Until you step outside and the wind tries to freeze your eyes shut and snap off your ears."

Her mother's appearance was deceiving as well. No one would realize, upon first glance, that Nicole was being besieged from the inside. Nicole sat in the stuffed armchair, a cream and mocha comforter tucked around her waist, legs, and feet. Her daughter sat on an adjacent chair.

The living room was decorated in what Nicole called "multicultural Canadian" — a patchworked, sequined wall-hanging from India, a statue of a dancing woman from Nigeria, blown-glass lamps from Venice, gleaming, maple Shaker furniture from Quebec, and a white, leather couch and chairs from Toronto.

"I want you to have the panther bracelet," said Nicole. "I meant to give it to you when you were older anyway." She held it out, her thin arms insubstantial in the large housecoat sleeves. Anastacia realized the bracelet would fall off if her mother lowered her arm.

"Are you sure, Mom?" said Anastacia. "I know this is the only thing you have to remember Dad by." She leaned forward and took the bracelet, studying her mother's expression.

"I don't need a bracelet to remember Morrel. He is always with me." Her mother smiled.

"I wish I could remember him," said Anastacia.

"Don't you remember anything at all?" Nicole adjusted the ocean-blue scarf wrapped around her head. Her blue eyes looked huge in her thin face. The same color as her daughter's. Nicole tugged a little too hard and the scarf shifted sharply, revealing her bald scalp. Anastacia flinched, remembering the shock of her mother's lovely, auburn hair coming out in clumps from the chemotherapy.

Deliberately, Anastacia tried to lighten the mood. "I was three, Mom. Come on, I forget crying the first day of Kindergarten, which you insist I did, hanging on to your pant leg and refusing to let go."

Nicole laughed softly. "Goodbyes are difficult for the both of us, I think."

Anastacia swallowed the lump in her throat. She sat back, silently studying the bracelet. The workmanship was exquisite. Her mother had told her it was handmade. The jeweler must have been a master craftsman.

After a pause, Nicole said, "That's too bad you can't remember your father. He was such a wonderful man. You have his glossy, black hair and his height, although he had a few inches on you. He was a huge, powerful man. Stunning, really."

"And his skin?"

"He was much darker than you. I guess you're halfway between us." Nicole glanced at the back of her pale hand. "You're lucky not to have my overly white skin. I always burn so easily."

Anastacia bit her lip and looked away, trying not to think of the melanomas hidden beneath her mother's quilt. She listened to the growl of wind as it shook the large maple tree, the bare branches groaning and cracking, fighting to hang on. On days like this, she worried the tree was going to crash through their front window.

"Put on the bracelet, honey," said Nicole. "Let me see how it looks."

Anastacia nodded and clasped it on to her left wrist. The metal was cold.

Nicole smiled. "It's beautiful on you. It was made in Dawn's End, the place where you were born in Africa. The bracelet suits your skin tone much better than mine."

Anastacia wanted her mother to stop talking about skin. She changed the subject. "I wish we had pictures of my dad."

"So do I, dear. It was such a tragedy when the moving company lost everything, including my photo albums and my laptop with the digital images."

"How come no one else in the family had pictures of us? Didn't you send Grandpa or your brother any pictures of me?" asked Anastacia.

Nicole looked startled for a minute. She reached for a glass of water on the side table and took a small sip. She stared into the glass thoughtfully. "Um, well, my father and I weren't on the best of terms at the time. I hadn't kept in touch with anyone, really, when I was in Africa. Then he died before I returned and my stepmother took what she wanted and left."

"How come you never talk about Africa? I would think you would have lots of stories."

"I've told you stories about you and your father and me."

Anastacia frowned. "Yeah, but they could have taken place anywhere. I mean, you don't talk about elephants and crocodiles and, you know, African stuff."

Nicole chuckled. "You could learn that stuff anywhere. It's the stories about your father that I want you to remember."

"Sometimes, when I'm just about to fall asleep, I can almost see him. He had different eyes. Almost black, but bright somehow." Anastacia closed her eyes, remembering.

"Hmm."

Anastacia opened her blue eyes and met Nicole's. She touched her cheek.

"And he had a soft, black beard that tickled my face when he picked me up. But I'm not sure if I remember that or if I think I do because you told me," said Anastacia, her face puckered in concentration. "Sometimes, I almost remember the three of us. But then I get this image of cats, and it's gone again."

"Cats!" said Nicole. "Oh." She waved her hand dismissively. "That's probably because of the bracelet. You connect it to him in your mind."

"I guess so." Anastacia frowned. If only she knew what was real memory and what was her imagination.

They didn't talk about her father again before Nicole died. The morphine had been increased; Nicole had been unable to eat for a week. She slipped into a deep sleep. Anastacia's stepfather never left Nicole's side. When the doctor said Nicole would not make it through the night, he telephoned Anastacia and Ali, her older stepbrother. Anastacia had insisted on being there, even though Jamail wanted to spare her. The three of them waited together, not talking, just listening to her weakened breathing. It did not seem real, even when the breathing stopped.

Her friends had felt terrible for Anastacia, losing her real dad when she was a toddler and then her mother at fourteen. She knew they were trying to be supportive, but everything they said annoyed her. She spent a lot of time alone, avoiding the sympathy of others.

She became closer to Jamail. He had lost his first wife and three children to a bomb in Iraq. He grieved deeply at this second loss, the death of Nicole, but insisted his children go on with their lives. Ali became even more overprotective.

Jamail had a single photograph of his first family, the only thing he grabbed when they fled. He had a picture; Nicole had a bracelet. Jamail had a son; Nicole had a daughter. Anastacia wondered if their similar losses had been one of the things that connected her mother and stepfather.

Neither Nicole nor Jamail had family in Canada. Perhaps that was why Jamail allowed Anastacia to go alone on this trip to a family wedding in Switzerland. Family was a precious gift, not to be taken lightly. Her cousin, Julie, would pick her up at the train station in Lucerne. Anastacia wondered if she would meet other long lost relatives of her mother. She wondered if they would notice the bracelet.

Anastacia shifted in her flight chair and rubbed the glistening stone. A prickly sensation traveled up her arm like a wooly caterpillar on bare skin.

She twitched her nose. She sniffed something that smelled at first like burning hair and then like decomposition. Airplanes were stuffy, but this was disgusting. She glanced at the middle-aged man beside her. Was he responsible for that stink? It reminded her of when a woodchuck died under the shed. The male passenger pushed his glasses up his nose and continued reading his magazine. He seemed oblivious. How could he not smell that? She looked past him to the woman in her thirties in the aisle seat. She typed steadily into her laptop, equally unaware.

The bracelet itched. Anastacia unbuttoned her shirtsleeve and scratched her arm. The male passenger glanced over and smiled. Anxiously, she pushed up the bracelet and tugged her sleeve over the top of it. It was stupid for a sixteen-year-old, flying alone, to be wearing such a treasure, but it was too risky to pack it in her luggage. Why had she brought it? Why not just wear a sign saying *Rob Me?* Wanting to show it to her mother's family, those who had not made it to the funeral, seemed a pretty lame reason.

Her cousin, Julie had invited Jamail and Ali to the wedding as well. Julie was five years older than Anastacia, the daughter of her mother's first cousin. The families hadn't been very close, but, when Nicole died two years ago, they connected at the funeral. Jamail had informed them of the death since they were Nicole's closest living relatives. He had not expected them to fly from Switzerland, but they did. Anastacia had the feeling they wanted to be sure she was safe and loved. Julie had taken a numb Anastacia under her wing. Anastacia was doubly grateful for their concern, now that she knew what a long, boring trip it was to cross the Atlantic.

She hardly slept on the plane. Her sinuses and eyes itched, and her mouth tasted like a dog-chewed slipper. She felt brittle and drawn when they landed in Zurich, Switzerland. She staggered through customs before changing to a train bound for Lucerne.

She stumbled on board, barely nodding at the smiling porter, and sank into her seat. Traveling through the countryside wasn't as exciting as she expected. When the click-clack of the rails became a steady rhythm, her eyes closed. Sounds faded. An image of the panther on her bracelet filled her mind. Sadness washed over her. The feline face grew larger. Suddenly, the beast roared; its fangs dripped blood. Non-human faces flashed in her mind, and she heard a shrill laugh. Anastacia's eyes flew open. She looked around quickly, but the passengers continued with their affairs. Her dreams were strange lately. One of the times she had missed her mother most was when she woke up screaming from a nightmare.

Her mother would have been glad Anastacia had decided to attend the wedding even though her stepfather and stepbrother couldn't. Julie would take care of her, like a big sister. She asked Anastacia to come two weeks early, so they could spend some time together. Julie would be leaving on her honeymoon the day after the ceremony.

It didn't seem annoying when Julie fussed over her, not like Ali, who acted like she could break any minute. Anastacia was tough, athletic, and competitive, not at all a fragile china doll. It was one of the things her mother admired about her.

"Don't let anything, or anyone, destroy your zest for life, my daughter," Nicole had said after receiving news of her second cancer. They were hiking together through Sleeping Giant Park, Nicole keeping pace the whole way. It was difficult to believe her mother was seriously ill. "Not even my disease. Your stepbrother is far too serious. It wouldn't hurt for you to be a little more understanding of him though. He's been through more than you can imagine."

Anastacia stopped and tugged her mother's sleeve. Nicole paused, standing on a slightly higher rock on the trail, and turned to face her daughter. Anastacia looked up. The sun lit her mother's hair, fringing it in gold. "Are you going to die, Mom?"

"I hope not," said Nicole. She smiled and squeezed Anastacia's shoulder. "I beat cancer when you were little, and I'm going to try my best to beat it again. This is a different kind, though, and it'll be tougher."

"I don't want to be an orphan." Anastacia bit her lip, fighting back tears. Nicole rubbed her shoulder. The sharp cry of a jay broke the silence.

"You wouldn't really be an orphan," said Nicole quietly. "Jamail loves you deeply. You're the only daughter he has now."

"I know, but . . . . " Anastacia's voice choked off.

"I've always admired your gutsiness and your enthusiasm," said her mother. "Whatever comes, I know you can handle it. Remember Jamail and Ali will be there for you, just as you will need to be there for them."

Anastacia nodded, wiping the tears with the back of her hand. The jay screeched as it flew over their heads. Nicole followed its flight with a smile. She nodded to herself and then looked back to her daughter.

"Don't be afraid, Anastacia. You'll land on your feet. I know you will."

"Lachish!" Riva called out as she entered the lower cavern. She held her knuckles against her nose trying to filter out the smell of body odor and urine.

"Thquirt off," Lachish said, his fangs creating a slight lisp in his guttural speech.

"Die before morning, you fat pig," said Riva.

She stopped in the entrance, her eyes watering from the smell. Lachish turned, clenching his enormous, hairy fist.

"Kaie wants a male captive," Riva said.

"Not now," he muttered, turning back to the lady chained to the stone wall. "I'm not done."

The woman's expensive robes were torn into strips, while Lachish wore his usual grimy, brown overalls.

"Shall I tell her you said that? The stinking pig turned disobedient."

Lachish snarled, but then said, "No. No, wait."

He knew better than to make Kaie angry. He gripped the back of the lady's neck, twisting her pale face towards his mottled orange and black one.

"High and mighty," he growled, "you'll hath ta wait for my return. I'll gif you somesin to remember me by."

The woman shuddered as his wild, orange-brown hair, matted with dirt fell onto her cheek. He rubbed his black nose down her jaw and onto her exposed shoulder, drew back his lips, and sank in his fangs. Riva laughed throatily as the victim screamed.

The short nap left Anastacia disoriented, like Alice in Wonderland after too many potions. She stroked her fingers through her black hair, adjusted the overnight bag on her shoulder, grabbed the handle of her suitcase, and then strode toward the train station.

Julie bobbed up and down on the platform, waving, smiling, her blue eyes bright and welcoming, her blonde hair bouncing. Anastacia thought with a jolt, *Her eyes are like Mom's and mine. I'd forgotten.*

"You made it!" Julie cried.

"Yes, but I won't be very good company for a while. I'm wiped," said Anastacia. "I thought I'd sleep on the plane, but I didn't. Then I fell asleep on the train just long enough to drool all over my shirt."

Julie hooked her arm into Anastacia's. "Poor girl. Come with me; my car isn't far."

"What time is it?" asked Anastacia as they followed the crowd toward the exit.

"Three o'clock in the afternoon."

Even though the train ride was less than an hour, Anastacia had nothing left for the twenty-minute drive to Julie's. It seemed to take forever; she struggled to keep awake. Julie gave her a tour of the house, ending in the guest bedroom.

"Is it okay if I have a shower?" asked Anastacia.

"Of course. But let's eat first. I just got a frantic text from one of my bridesmaids about her dress not fitting properly."

"Oh, oh."

Julie shrugged. "I'm sure it's not as bad as it sounds. You're welcome to come with me, but I'm afraid it will be pretty boring, and she can be shrill and annoying when she's upset. Probably not someone you want to be around after your long trip."

"Probably not," said Anastacia.

"I promise tomorrow will be much better."

"That's okay." Anastacia yawned. "I think I'm going to turn in early anyway."

"I thought you might. There are several English channels on the television and a few magazines on the desk." She set the TV remote on the nightstand. "You know where the kitchen is." She took both of Anastacia's hands in hers. "Please make yourself at home if you get hungry."

After Julie left, Anastacia showered and finished unpacking. Julie had pushed the few items in the closet to one side and left plenty of empty hangers.

Heavy wooden furniture filled the room. There were shutters on the window, which Anastacia closed, blocking out light and sound. The massive four-poster bed seemed inviting and cozy. Anastacia stretched out and fell asleep, still in her robe with her hair wrapped in a towel. She woke two hours later, brushed out her hair, slipped into her pajamas, and crawled beneath the sheets.

She punched the pillow and sighed. Even though she was exhausted, her mind would not quiet. She recalled waiting in the Toronto airport. She had been sitting near a broken door watching travelers attempt to exit. It had fascinated her that she couldn't identify with any of them. So many different people on so many different journeys and all reacting differently to obstacles. Where did she fit in?

Two teenagers, in black clothes, one sporting a Celtic tattoo on his shoulder, pushed relentlessly, exchanged shrugs, and then used the alternate door. A young couple discussed the problem as the male shoved with increasing frustration. In bewilderment, they wandered off to find a new exit. Anastacia was intrigued by the man with the tool belt. She assumed he came to do repairs, but instead he pounded and shoved with increasing fury, before using the other door.

She wondered how she would have handled the door. Probably like the teenagers. She smiled. Her stepbrother, Ali, would find another exit. Always cautious. He'd had a million reasons why she shouldn't come alone to Europe. She wished he could stop playing big brother for five minutes. Anastacia yawned and willed herself to sleep.

Kaie shook the vial again. Still not right. Damn. There could be no margin for error. This mixture must have the lure of cocaine and the kick of crack, and be more addictive than either. Yet, it must hide her subtle surprise. Her special touch that made this new, potent drug more lethal, more threatening than any from the outer world.

A tremor in her bracelet brought a smile to her gaunt face. The other bracelet was closer now. She felt its power. There was purity to this other one; it was different than hers.

Kaie stood the vial in the wooden stand. She placed her hand over the bracelet and concentrated. Pain, sweet pain, surged through her mind as she summoned gold to gold, panther to panther, crystal to crystal. Soon, it would be within her reach.

She sighed, opened her eyes, and picked up the mixture. Kaie clasped the vial in tongs, held it over the flame until it bubbled, and then stirred it again.

Subtlety is all, she thought. Subtlety in both cases. Mustn't scare off the bearer of the bracelet. Mustn't scare off the customers. Before the contents of this vial were produced in bulk and distributed to the trusting idiots in Dawn's End, she must be sure it behaved exactly as she wanted. Nothing less than perfect.

"Perfect, perfect, perfect," she muttered.

Kaie smiled and reached for the blue powder.

Anastacia snapped awake. A weird dream about chemistry class that morphed into a nightmare. Her heart pounded. She sat up. She couldn't possibly sleep until morning. She dressed and went downstairs. Sunlight trickled through the curtains.

A set of keys hung by the front door. Anastacia tested them on the front lock. They worked. She slipped on her hoodie and decided to explore the neighborhood. She had been sitting for so long; her body needed exercise before she would be able to sleep.

She walked for half an hour, enjoying the well-kept yards and clean streets, but then her surroundings changed. She wandered along the waterfront. The beach crowd thinned. Lights pulsed on. Still, her body ached to be moving.

She entered a wooden pedestrian bridge that spanned the river leading into the harbor. Tourists examined religious paintings on the ceiling.

That's Adam and Eve at creation, she thought. *Moses. Possibly St. Patrick. One must be a martyr. What are they doing to him? Oh, God! They're cranking his intestines around a pole! Eww!*

Anastacia shuddered and looked around. Absently, she scratched at the bracelet. The bridge was now empty. The few bare light bulbs cast thick shadows. She hurriedly exited.

Mmm, what's that heavenly smell? she thought. *My body is so screwed up from the time change. I don't know how I can be hungry again.*

From a sidewalk cafe, she purchased tea and a spicy sausage on a bun. She ate as she continued on along the cobblestones.

When she finished, Anastacia stopped to watch a white-haired woman and a bearded young man playing an oversized game of chess. The squares were inlaid with stone under a pillared roof. Carved, wooden chess figures, half as high as Anastacia, were manipulated about the small courtyard. Clusters of onlookers leaned against the wall or sat along a concrete ledge.

The woman, playing black, was merciless. After sweeping through her opponent's pawns, she took the young man's bishop with her knight. The young man picked up a knight with his own, but, when he tried to attack the castle, his other bishop and queen fell in rapid succession.

The lady slid her queen into the final move of the game. The audience applauded and entered the playing area. Anastacia's bracelet tingled as she examined the face of the black queen. Its lifeless eyes, locked in frozen beauty, held hers. She heard a woman snicker by her shoulder and turned.

Who was *that?* she thought, but no one was near. She looked again at the weather-worn queen, its face cracked and splintering. *That's one ugly queen,* she thought. *Nasty. Evil.* She shivered.

Darkness had swept over Lucerne during the chess match. Anastacia zipped up her hoodie and decided to call it a night. She followed a wide cobblestone path between the buildings that led to another courtyard.

I hear water. She squinted and made out the shape of a fountain. *Lovely,* she thought, drawn to its soothing splashes. *I think if I go this way and turn left on the other side, I'll be back on the street I took into town.*

The courtyard was filled with enchanting statues of mythical figures. Two of the three streetlights were broken. The noise of the city became muted as the darkness intensified.

A male face loomed out of the darkness. *A centaur! He looks like he's breathing,* she thought. Her footsteps seemed loud as she crossed the stone tiles. *A Pegasus with huge terrified eyes!* She flinched. *What was that?*

Anastacia glanced back at the centaur. She swallowed and clenched her fists. *It moved!* she thought. *No, no, of course not. I'm just tired. Jet lag, that's all.*

She moved on to a dryad. So lovely, but it was too dark to make out the face. Uncomfortably cold now. Creepy quiet. She turned to leave. Perhaps it was better to go back the way she had come. There was a hedge where the walkway should be. *Was this bench there before? And that bush, where did it come from?*

She saw a narrow path that appeared to lead to the street. She took a deep breath; she straightened her shoulders and stepped between the buildings.

The bracelet tingled as she walked through. Anastacia pushed her sleeve above the wide band and clasped her right hand over it. The eye flashed. Warmth surged up her arm.

"I need to get out of here," she muttered. She focused on exiting the courtyard, getting away.

A bright arch of light flashed over and around her. Her strength poured out like water through a funnel. Her head pounded. She staggered and fell, knees slamming painfully into stone as she collapsed face down. She tried to stand, but her body would not respond. Stunned, she fought to gain control.

Then she heard voices. A bobbing light spread around her, and a woman spoke. "It's a girl."

Two people crouched beside her. Anastacia struggled to turn her head.

"No," a man contradicted. "It's a young woman. And look at her clothing."

Anastacia peered weakly up at the man. Unruly light hair fell into his face. He stared intently into her eyes with a concerned expression. Everything closed off as she fainted.

Chapter Two — Potions and Passions

Anastacia held the cool cloth draped across her forehead and sat up on the bench. It had a sloping back made of spindles, and a large beige handmade cushion embroidered with flowers had been tucked under her head. She was in a white-washed room with wooden beams, carved wooden furniture, and a gray rock fireplace.

"Easy, miss," said a man as she wavered to her feet. He gently held her elbow, steadying her. Sunlight shone through the thick, uneven glass of several small windows.

"What happened?" Anastacia wobbled, trying to gain her balance.

"You fainted," he said. "Please, sit down until you're a bit steadier."

He sat her back on the bench, stepping on her foot as she stumbled. "Sorry."

Anastacia suppressed an urge to rub the scuff mark off her shoes. "That's okay. Where am I?"

"We brought you to our home," the man answered.

Anastacia looked up. It was the man she had seen before she fainted. He was in his mid-twenties and a little shorter than Anastacia's five-foot-eleven, with large blue-gold eyes. Numerous cowlicks taunted his short, blond-brown hair. His long, rectangular face ended in a square jaw. He smiled hopefully.

"Your home?" Anastacia repeated the words. *It looks like a museum,* she thought.

"My name is Canice Durward. Please address me as Durward."

"I'm Anastacia Newman. Have I walked into another suburb? I think I got my directions twisted." She fingered the coarse fabric on the cushion.

Durward looked bewildered for a second and then said, "You came here accidentally?" He pulled up a wooden chair and sat in front of her.

Anastacia nodded as she regained her equilibrium." I was trying to get back to my cousin Julie's."

"But . . . you wear the bracelet!" He pointed.

"The bracelet?" Anastacia peered at the golden leopard on her arm. *Why is it a different color?* she thought.

Durward extended his arm, pushed up the sleeve of his white shirt, and revealed a duplicate, minus the stone.

"Wow!" she said. "This was my mother's. But it usually doesn't look like this. It was copper, but now it's gold. Where did you get yours?"

"Do you know nothing, then, of the bracelets?" asked Durward.

"No. I don't understand any of this." She looked around the room. There was nothing that did not appear handmade. "This room looks like older Switzerland might, but your clothes . . . ."

Durward straightened his garments self-consciously. He was dressed in a silver tunic, breeches, and brown cape, with a white shirt and short, brown boots. A sword was thrust into an elaborate scabbard that hung from his belt; its point rested on the floor.

"What is wrong with my clothes?" he asked, his brow furrowed.

"Not a thing." A warm, reassuring voice came from the doorway. A woman, around thirty years old, entered carrying a tray of food. She placed it on the table beside Anastacia's bench and then stood with her hands on her hips. She wore an ankle-length dress made of dozens of different colored threads sewn in a floral pattern. A reed pipe was attached to her waist with a thin, silver belt. On her feet were sandals made of animal skin.

Anastacia was hypnotized by the woman's gown of flowers which seemed to move and transform as if alive. Anastacia gaped at its beauty before looking at the even more unusual owner of the dress.

"I heard you introduce yourself," said the gray-haired woman. "I am Canice Misty, Durward's wife. Please eat while we talk."

Misty's almond-shaped, gray eyes blinked lazily. She had high cheekbones and a small pug nose that twitched when she spoke. Her smooth skin had the same gray tinge as her hair. She smiled softly, showing small, gleaming, white teeth. Anastacia had an odd sensation of déjà vu.

Don't stare! Anastacia admonished herself. *You're in a foreign country. People are bound to look different.*

While the couple sat on wooden chairs and smiled encouragingly, Anastacia ate the unusual bread and cheese. Misty, the strangest looking woman Anastacia had ever seen, reminded her of a contented housecat. Gray, but young. Gray! Her clothes were even odder than Durward's.

"Your dress is mesmerizing." Anastacia blurted the words out.

Durward looked at her in surprise. "Misty would never use such devious tactics as hypnotism," he said.

Misty laughed. "That is not what she means, dear," she said to Durward. She turned to Anastacia. "You mean it looks nice, don't you?"

Anastacia nodded, puzzled, as she bit into coarse-grained bread studded with an unidentifiable fruit. Misty continued. "I understand that you have come to our world by accident, but I would like to know how you came by that bracelet."

"Yes," said Durward. "The only outworlder we know of to have a bracelet is the Esteemed Nicole Newman."

"That's my mother's name! Except for the esteemed part. This was hers."

"Your mother," said Durward, as he stroked his pointed chin. "That could be. Time flows differently in your world. Does your mother have auburn hair and blue eyes?"

Anastacia swallowed. She held the bread in her hand without taking another bite. "My mother died two years ago, but, yes, she did." She leaned forward eagerly. "Did you know her? Did she come to Lucerne?"

Durward and Misty exchanged glances.

"Not I," said Durward. He stood up, untied his dark brown cape, laid it over the back of his chair, and sat down again. "Alaric Morrel quested with her generations ago."

Nicole straightened. "Generations! Then it couldn't have been my mother. She was thirty-four when she died."

"How tragic," murmured Misty. "Everyone hoped she had lived a long and happy life after leaving Dawn's End." She reached out and squeezed Durward's hand. They exchanged a poignant look.

"I don't understand any of this," said Anastacia with a frown. "Who are you people? Where is this place?" She glanced around the room. Everything was made of natural materials. There wasn't a piece of electronics or item of plastic in sight. Had she stumbled into a Mennonite community?

"I will explain," said Durward as Misty withdrew her hand. "Firstly, you are no longer in Lucerne." He cleared his throat. "Our world occupies a different space and time from yours—"

"You're nuts." Anastacia interrupted him as she put her food down on the tray. "Are you trying to tell me I'm in some kind of Twilight Zone?"

Durward and Misty exchanged looks of bewilderment.

"Twilight Zone? Why does she think she's in a cave entrance?" asked Durward. He shook his head and turned back to Anastacia. "Had your mother never spoken of Dawn's End?"

"I imagine this is difficult to believe," Misty said, "but our world exists and you are in it." She smiled, showing her small, pointy teeth. "Just as your mother was. You used the bracelet to get here, although I don't see how since you're so uninformed."

Anastacia examined the bracelet carefully. It pulsed against her skin. It had felt strange since she put it on yesterday. When she was tiny, her mother said the bracelet had a bit of magic. But that was when Nicole still told her fantastic tales about talking bears and fairy queens.

This is crazy, Anastacia thought. *I must be reacting to the exhaustion form the plane flight. Or something I ate. Maybe I'm hallucinating. Maybe I'm asleep in Julie's bed and dreaming this. Or lying unconscious in the courtyard.*

She crossed her arms. "This is some kind of dream, because I fainted."

"Does it feel like a dream?" asked Durward.

Anastacia looked around the room. It reminded her of Fort William Historical Park. Everything was made of wood and iron. The tin lanterns held candles. An empty stone fireplace dominated the room. The walls were constructed of coarse, horizontal boards roughly covered in a white paint. The floors were unvarnished wooden planks. There were shutters and plain, white, muslin curtains, on the windows.

Time travel? she thought. *Everything feels normal, except for the increasing itch under my bracelet. Am I having an allergic reaction? Ah, maybe that's it. I've gone into shock or something.* She stared at the bracelet, wondering how it could have changed color and why it felt so odd.

"That bracelet was given to your mother by the Alaric," explained Durward. "Among its powers is the skill to open the door to our world. It also enables you to communicate with us. The odd thing is that your crystal is pure, not black. The odder thing is that you found and opened the door unintentionally. When we saw the flash of light and went to investigate, we found you."

Anastacia clasped her hand over the bracelet. "I was lost in the courtyard. I felt a tingle from the band. I placed my hand on it and wanted to find my way through. I felt this surge, and a light arched over me. I fainted, and then I heard voices."

Durward nodded. "That was us. We carried you here."

Anastacia stared at the square of sunshine on the wooden floor. *Sunshine! It should be dark!* She leaped to her feet. "How long have I been here?"

"Not long," said Durward. "We saw the flash of light, found you, and brought you here."

Anastacia clenched her hands, and her heart pounded. "Are you for real? This isn't a joke?"

Misty stood up. "We wouldn't trick you." Gently, she touched Anastacia's arm.

Anastacia jerked her arm away. "I don't know what's going on, but I have to get back before Julie returns. Oh, cripes!" She pressed her hand against her forehead. "She'll be worried. I'll cause a huge fuss just before her wedding."

"Calm yourself," Misty touched Anastacia's shoulder while Durward looked on in alarm. "You can go back anytime you want," said Misty softly. "The same way you came."

Anastacia breathed a deep, shaky sigh. "I'm so disoriented. I thought flying was rough." She pressed her hand to her stomach.

"Flying!" said Misty and Durward in unison.

"Then you do wield the magic," said Durward hopefully. "You will be of enormous help."

"Magic? I have no magic." Anastacia flopped back onto the bench. Misty sat down as well.

"But you said you flew," he said.

"Obviously, I flew in an airplane. I'm not Criss Angel. I just want to get back to Julie's." She absently picked up the bread, broke off a small crumb, and popped it into her mouth.

"Oh," said Durward. "I hoped you would wield the power to change nature, like your mother."

Anastacia stopped chewing and frowned. "My mother wasn't magic."

"No," said Durward. He ran his absently over the hilt of his sword. "But she could use the power of the panther. She cared deeply for our world and peoples and did her best to help us."

Anastacia studied his face. The tousled cowlicks, pale skin, and large, blue eyes flecked with gold gave him an innocent demeanor. She wondered if it was genuine. "Was she married to my father then?" she asked. "Morrel?"

"No," said Durward. "She was single when she arrived. This is where they met."

"Wait!" Anastacia's eyes widened. She raised one finger. "Durward, you said 'Had your mother never spoken of Dawn's End?' It didn't register with me. You said 'Dawn's End."

He nodded. "Yes, we're in Dawn's End right now."

Anastacia sat back, her face paling. "Mom told me I was born in Dawn's End, but I could never find it on a map. She said it was extremely difficult to get to and she could probably never return."

"She was right," said Misty. "But, somehow, you have returned in her place."

"Well done, my savage." Kaie croaked as Lachish threw his captive to her feet. Her praise was his greatest joy.

Lachish was descended from a mixed noble lineage: panther people, mountain dwellers, and bruins. But these honorable bloodlines had twisted abominably in producing him. His mother had died in childbirth. His father, repulsed by his bestial offspring and corrupted by the growing avarice in Dawn's End, had sold Lachish into slavery.

Lachish had been trained to fight for his master's sport. His master won small fortunes betting on his incredible strength and skill in combat. When the opportunity arose, Lachish killed his owner, plus others who challenged his departure, and fled with his master's latest purse.

Rape and pillage became his lifestyle. He had intended to rob and kill Kaie, as he had many travelers, but she subdued him with magic. She showed no fear or repulsion of his appearance.

"I find your appearance honest," she said, staring at him with her eerie, unblinking eyes. They contained black diamond pupils and no irises.

Kaie caged him where he could witness her own acts of cruelty. She recognized his potential as a minion. Her utter evil and limitless power seduced him into allegiance. He was, now, her most devoted servant.

As both a reward and a test, the first assignment Kaie gave him was to kill his father. She didn't know how easy it was for him to obey. Lachish fulfilled her command in an ecstasy of vengeance, dispatching his parent with gory finesse. He brought Kaie a symbolic offering—a human heart.

The only other woman who aroused his passion was Riva Pike. Riva was forbidden; to touch her meant death. It would be unnecessary for Kaie to kill him if he disobeyed and harmed Riva. She lorded her sensuality over him, taunting him with her movements. He hated her for this torment, and she detested him for his maleness. Frustration spurred on his cruelty. If he did not serve his mistress with such devotion, Lachish would have crushed Riva's skull against the cave walls.

Lachish wondered why his mistress had requested the male prisoner, but he did not ask. He threw the dazed victim down and kicked him in the ribs. The captive stumbled to his feet in challenge. Lachish punched the side of his head, and the man crashed to the stones, unconscious.

"Do not damage him overmuch, my great beast," said Kaie. "I have plans for him. I believe an elite lady awaits the caress of your claws. I shall bask in the echo of her screams. Leave now." She gave a dismissive wave of her bony hand.

Lachish grinned and hurried off to his entertainment.

Kaie looked down at the unconscious body. Her head ached again. Probably because of the dreams that ravaged her sleep. Dreams of a familiar young woman. Someone she knew and did not know. Dreams of innocence. Confusing, frustrating images that left her yearning for something she did not understand.

She knew she should be working on her drug. It held the most potential, but she was in no mood for the tedious, exacting work. She needed a distraction.

Anastacia searched her memory. "But my mother said they met in Africa."

Misty shrugged. "I've never heard of Africa."

"I was born with a midwife who failed to register my birth," said Anastacia. "My mother said she had a lot of trouble getting a birth certificate for me. She had to hire a lawyer so I'd have full Canadian citizenship."

"The stories say you were born here," said Misty. "Nicole left with you when you were three."

"That's the right age," said Anastacia. "My father had died."

Misty and Durward exchanged a look.

"What?" asked Anastacia. "Isn't that true? Is he still alive?" Her eyes widened with excitement.

"No, no, he's not." Misty leaned forward and patted her hand. "But we were told Nicole left because she was ill. Morrel was afraid the food or water was poisoning her. She had signs of cancer of the bowel."

"She did have cancer when I was little," said Anastacia. "I thought she found out when she returned to Canada. She had surgery and treatments and beat it. Then she got skin cancer when I was older." Her voice dropped. "She didn't beat that."

Misty pressed her lips together and shook her head slowly. "So tragic."

"But," said Durward, "we do not know for sure that Dawn's End made her ill. It could have been from anything."

"Perhaps I should take that," said Misty as she reached forward.

Anastacia looked at the bun in her hand. She held it out for Misty to take and then wiped her hands on her jeans.

"Her father died of cancer," said Anastacia. "So it might just be genetic."

"That doesn't bode well for you either way," said Durward.

Misty nudged his foot.

Anastacia remembered watching her mother while she slept. Nicole had muttered about the bracelet and a door — drug-induced dreams. Anastacia sat up straight as the meaning of her memories clarified. She glanced from Durward's boyishly earnest face to Misty's exotic one.

"She was *here*!" Anastacia cried. "Dawn's End is not in Africa. Damn!"

Her hosts nodded.

"You have gray skin," she said. "I keep trying to figure out why."

Misty laughed good-naturedly, "Because I have gray skin. You'll see stranger than me in Dawn's End, my dear, if you choose to stay for a while."

"Yes. I have so many questions." Anastacia rushed her words, moving her hands for emphasis. "I need to find my roots. Talk to people who knew my father."

"I'm sorry," said Misty. "That's impossible. Time moves quicker here than in your world. Anyone who knew Morrel is gone. But there are stories you may learn and places you can see that you would have seen as a child. Your parents were heroes. Their quest saved Dawn's End."

"Thank you," said Anastacia. "There is so much I want to know."

"But, we have much to ask in return," said Durward. He jumped to his feet, knocking his cape to the wooden floor. He paced, running his fingers through his sandy hair, increasing his bed-head look. "If you are your mother's daughter, you are exactly who we need to save Dawn's End."

"There is no Meeting now," said Misty. "What do you mean?"

"Don't you see?" He stopped and gestured toward Anastacia. "She can be the catalyst. With the daughter of the Esteemed Nicole Newman and Alaric Morrel on our side, anything is possible."

He stared at Anastacia, his eyes large.

"Well," she said. "You helped me when I fainted. I owe you." She took a deep breath. "And it seems your people are my people too. This is my birthplace. My history! Wow! I'm totally pumped. What can I do to help?"

"We face a great evil and have little magic to defend Dawn's End," said Durward.

Anastacia's brow furrowed. "I'm not sure what I can do then. I'm deadly on the soccer field, basketball court, and the hockey rink. I can high jump like a kangaroo and run like a gazelle and climb like a cat. But as far as I know, I don't have any magic."

Durward raised his arm, bracelet shining. He nodded toward her arm. Anastacia lifted hers in response and drew her band toward his. A soft glow of light danced between the two imprisoned felines.

"Well, damn," said Anastacia.

Green vapor rose from the pewter goblet Riva held in her elegant hands as she approached the captive, a muscular man with a moustache. They were in Riva's chamber. Lachish had carried the man there and deposited him on a stone bench. The room was clean but Spartan: a wooden bed, two trunks, the stone bench, a wooden chair, and a circle of stones which held a fire in cold weather.

"This is for you, handsome traveler." Her voice was charming. "My mistress mixed it to help heal your bruises. Drink it straight to the bottom." She set it beside him.

The trembling man brought the goblet to his face. His nose twitched at the smell.

"You are very lucky she has agreed to your release." She sat on the bench and ran her fingers through his blond, curly hair. "It seems you were unfortunately mistaken for someone else, a vicious enemy. She is most distressed that you have been injured and wishes to make everything right." Riva smiled, arching her body as she urged the goblet toward his lips. The tall man hesitated, and then drained it quickly.

"Thank you for your kindness," he said as he wiped his mouth on his sleeve. "But I need to be on my way."

"No need to rush," said Riva. She sighed and lowered herself beside him on the stone bench. "I do hate a man who rushes."

He licked his full lips, turned his face toward hers and fell forward, unconscious again, into her lap. Riva rolled him off. He thudded to the stone floor.

"Boar dung." She wrinkled her nose. "Men are so easy to manipulate. They are controlled by their own lust. I would have infected him in minutes." She called to the back of the cave, "He's unconscious."

"He must stay healthy to serve my purpose," answered Kaie as she stepped out. By her side padded an enormous, white panther. He looked from one woman to the other, but his eyes, red with a white diamond-shaped center, did not blink.

"Lachish will carry him into the woods where he was first captured." She turned to the panther. "Goar, you will guard him from harm until he regains his senses. Follow him while he accomplishes my task. Do not be seen, but be available should he need you."

Goar's voice rumbled. "When the potion wears off, won't he betray you?"

"I have a small surgery to perform on him before he leaves. Then he could no more betray me, than you could."

Kaie reached to stroke the animal's white head. Goar swayed to the right, and her hand dropped to her side. Her eyes narrowed at this small gesture of rebellion.

"It disturbs me that my pet should even think such a thing," she said. "Do not think distance will matter, Goar. No matter how far you might go from me, as long as he and you are in Dawn's End, I can sear you both. Like this."

Kaie closed her eyes. Under the hood of her ragged, brown cloak a light glowed for but a second. Goar roared in pain. His legs shuddered; he collapsed and writhed on the floor. Kaie opened her eerie eyes and smiled at his seizing body. Slowly, Goar relaxed, lying in his own urine. He staggered to his feet with a zombie-like expression on his noble face.

Goar gasped as he rose. "Yes, my mistress, I understand."

Kaie nodded absently, unconscious of her own nails cutting into her palms. She did not speak. Her eyes became blank, staring. Her hood fell back.

Riva had seen that look before. She coughed. "The surgery, mistress."

"Surgery?" Kaie reached under her hood for a matted clump of hair.

Riva pointed to the body. "To alter the male."

Kaie looked at the fallen man as she twisted several strands of hair around her finger and tugged until they jerked free creating another seeping bald spot. As she unwound the hair from her fingers, her eyes cleared.

The tall traveler awoke on the forest floor where the colossal man had clubbed him. Carefully, he touched his head. There was a painful lump and dried blood in his blond hair, and his entire body ached.

He must have dreamt the encounter with the half-naked woman. She was too voluptuous to be real, he thought as he sat, rubbing the circulation into his legs. Those full breasts underneath that silky tunic, those long, sexy legs, and the way she moved like— a pain stabbed in his groin. He gasped.

"Augh, what in crystal's power was that? I don't remember being kicked."

He examined himself gingerly while the searing heat subsided. There was blood and a small cut. He must have been wounded during the fight.

The pain subsided and did not return that day, as he traveled southwest to the village. He headed toward a tavern and a meal. Considering how ragged he felt, the beer would be as welcome as the food.

Chapter Three — Past and Future

"Are you sure you want to drink this?" asked Misty as she filled three pewter mugs with a hot, clear, lime-scented drink.

"Yes," said Anastacia. "I can't starve while I'm here, and I intend to stay for a while."

"But not too long," said Misty.

"Just long enough to help us," said Durward. He took a drink.

"I really don't see how I can help," said Anastacia. "Tell me about this 'great evil.' That sounds ominous. Where did these bracelets come from? What *is* Dawn's End?"

Anastacia, Misty, and Durward sat on wooden chairs with woven thatch backs and seats around a wooden table. The small home was cool in the early morning, but the liquid warmed them.

"When your mother left Dawn's End," said Durward, "our world entered a period of growth and happiness. Life was as it should be. The wizards had accidentally brought us to the edge of disaster. Your mother stopped it. The wizards then used their powers and knowledge in safer, simpler ways. They no longer lived in isolation, but instead mixed freely with the various peoples in our land. It was a renaissance."

"Wizards? Like magicians?" said Anastacia.

"People of hidden and great knowledge. Their skills were passed to their children and apprentices. Novices attended their ceremonies, learning of medicine, potions, science, white magic, and the powers of the large crystal and the smaller crystals within bracelets. Those with the most potential inherited the bracelets. Only supremely talented and highly ethical wizards possessed one; there were four in our village."

"Are you one of these wizards?"

"I should be." Durward stopped, bent his head, and picked at the lint on his breeches.

Misty continued. "Durward's father, Canice Osmen, was a great magician. He wanted his son to be one, too. When Osmen became terminally ill, he insisted Durward take the bracelet. Durward wore it for his father's sake, thinking to pass it on to one of the other apprentices later." She turned toward him. "He had no interest in magic. He's a smithy." She stroked his shoulder.

"When my father died," said Durward, "my uncle wouldn't allow me to give away the bracelet. He charmed it so it could not be removed and then pressured me to attend the ceremonies and learn the craft. I often disappeared when they held a meeting. My uncle said I was failing in my responsibilities to the people. He wanted me to live according to his plan. Behave the way he thought I should." He traced the rim of his mug with his finger.

Anastacia nodded, thinking of Ali, her bossy older stepbrother. He was always trying to direct her life. Even before her mother died.

"I was resentful. In anger, I did a foolish, terrible thing," said Durward. He sighed and stared into his mug. "I tried to smash the bracelet from my wrist, but, instead, I scratched it and smashed the crystal in the panther's eye. It was destroyed. I didn't succeed in removing the bracelet, but the damage was serious. The power of this panther bracelet was greatly weakened."

The room was silent after Durward's confession. He set down the mug and trailed his fingers despondently across the bracelet.

"Can't the wizards fix it?" asked Anastacia.

He shook his head and looked mournfully toward Misty. She continued. "The magicians were killed by an enormous explosion at one of their meetings. The entire building collapsed, crushing them under the marble slabs."

"My God," whispered Anastacia.

"We don't know how it happened, but we have our suspicions. Durward was not in attendance. No one there escaped."

"We thought no one escaped," Durward said.

"Yes," said Misty. "Kaie was an apprentice. A brilliant but very young woman. Charming and generous. Her teacher was so pleased with her progress that sometimes he allowed her to wear his bracelet. After the explosion, she disappeared. We assumed she had been killed at the meeting."

"But she wasn't?"

Durward spoke, his voice soft and filled with pain. "It took a long time to clear away the rubble. Two bracelets were found, crushed out of shape, the crystals shattered, utterly useless. The large crystal was never found, only minute black slivers. We believe it was destroyed in some great experiment gone wrong. The wizard's bodies were crushed into pulp. We could not tell how many there were for certain."

Anastacia swallowed. "How horrible. I'm so sorry."

"Not long afterward, strange events pointed to the use of a bracelet," said Misty. "The door to your world was used. We know of no other way to open it than by use of the bracelets. Destructive ideas and materials were imported. Rumor said it was Kaie. I found it difficult to accept that the sweet girl I knew was responsible."

"She may just have her own ideas on how Dawn's End should progress," said Anastacia.

Durward snorted. "Progress! Violence has infiltrated our land. Love is dying. Kaie has gathered a group of deceitful and evil people to waylay travelers, to rob, rape, and murder them."

"Some suspect the bracelet has corrupted her," said Misty. "The wizards had again become secretive about their experiments. I believe, when the large crystal was destroyed, the stones in the bracelets may have been changed. They have always been a power for good before, but we do not know what has been done to them now."

Durward gave his wife a worried glance.

She continued. "If we could just talk to Kaie when she wasn't wearing it, I'm sure we could help her."

"Victims are brought to her for ritual killing, to aid in her growing powers of evil," said Durward.

"Good Lord!" Anastacia's eyes opened wide. "This is the woman you expect me to help you fight. What can I do?"

"The bracelet works for you," said Durward. "That must be how you got here. Combined with mine, we have a chance against her."

"Better yet," said Anastacia, "I'll lend you my bracelet, and then you can fight her with both of them."

"No. We don't know why Kaie has become evil. If you give yours to me, I may become just like her. Then Dawn's End would certainly become an abyss."

"How do you know I won't turn to evil?" asked Anastacia.

"Your crystal is clear. Besides, I sense something wondrous in you, the daughter of Nicole and Morrel, something I lack. I may be tainted, like Kaie, by something the magicians have done. In you, there is a strength of character, an unyielding, a purity. You have been kept separate from all the dark changes. I don't think it would be very easy to make you do anything you did not want to do."

Anastacia smiled. Her family would certainly agree with that. Then her expression changed to dismay. "So is my bracelet safe here?" She held it away from her body as though a poisonous snake had wrapped around her wrist.

"I believe whatever the wizards were doing did not affect your bracelet. Perhaps you were too far away. Your bracelet wasn't even in Dawn's End when the explosion occurred. I think it still retains its original purity."

"That's good." Anastacia dropped her arm.

"But," said Durward, "I still don't understand how it brought you here. The bracelets are not supposed to work outside of Dawn's End. There's a lot we don't understand. We have no idea what turned Kaie into an evil wizard."

Anastacia rubbed the bracelet. She wrinkled up her face, considering.

"There is something special about both you and your bracelet," said Durward. "Misty and I will be with you to ensure your safety. If it starts to darken or change in any way, we will remove it. But you will have more influence if you wear it. To be honest, I don't feel worthy. It is your legacy."

Anastacia squirmed, uncomfortable with their stares.

Durward said, "There will be others who will join us, especially now that we have you to rally around."

"Me!" said Anastacia incredulously.

"Yes," said Misty. "The daughter of the Esteemed Nicole and Alaric Morrel of legend has returned with an intact bracelet of the panther. *The* historic bracelet no less. We will never find anyone better to inspire our group."

Anastacia slumped back into her chair. She drained the last drops in her mug, trying to sort her whirling thoughts.

The traveler drained his mug of beer and wiped his moustache with the back of his hand. The searing pain was forgotten, and his head was pleasantly numb. After the encounter with the orange and black giant, he felt grateful to be alive. Death had paused at his shoulder and then passed on. He cheerfully tipped the keeper of the Bullock Inn before staggering upstairs for an early night's sleep.

A ragged boy watched his stumbling. His big, blue eyes had seen more than their share of drunkenness, villagers, and strangers alike. His small chin and high cheekbones, crowned with an unkempt mass of dark curls, gave his face an elfin look. He picked at the threads on the open knees of his faded, brown breeches. Dirty skin showed through.

This traveler drew his attention. Lights danced in his mind. Bedad felt the familiar pulse in his temples as the images formed. He saw himself speaking to the traveler, laughing. A pretty, tall lady smiled. The large eyes of an animal stared at him. He felt—

"Bedad," a harsh voice bellowed, destroying his premonition. "Get in here and help. Why're you sittin' around when it's meal time?"

Bedad sighed and stood up, suddenly looking much older than his twelve years. He stared at the blond traveler's back, wondering where they would meet. He rubbed his hands on his frayed jacket with the torn pockets. Underneath, he was bare-chested. He pushed his tangled, dark hair back from his smudged face and entered the gloomy hut.

The room stank of sweat, smoke, and beer. A man and woman, faces florid, sat drinking at the rough table.

"Get started on the potatoes." His mother drained her mug, stumbled to her feet, and pulled a sausage down from a rafter. "Stoke up that fire so's I can cook."

"Before or after I do the potatoes?"

She put her hand on her hip and leaned forward. "You smart-mouthing me?"

He began to stammer. "N-N-No, Ma, I just asked."

She mimicked him. "'I just asked.' Do it now. Then do the potatoes. Smart-mouth me, and I'll slap you so hard you'll have ears on the same side'a your head." She turned to her husband. "You hear that boy mock me? No respect."

Her husband nodded, bleary-eyed, and poured another beer from the barrel beside the table. It sloshed over the sides and onto the sticky wooden floor.

Bedad soon had the sticks burning brightly and a pot of water set among them for the potatoes. His mother clumsily sliced the sausage into a greased skillet. Bedad watched out of the corner of his eye, ready to run for a bandage. She finished without an accident and laid the pan over the side coals.

"You keep an eye on them sausages while I lie down for a minute. My head's killin' me. Mind they don't burn, or I'll switch you good."

Bedad nodded.

"I didn't hear you, Bedad. Answer me when I speak to you." She pinched his shoulder.

"Yes, Ma, I w-will."

"Good." She shuffled off beyond the curtain to the disheveled bedroom. Soon, the smell of tobacco smoke filtered through the opening.

It was no wonder they had to share one sausage among three people with all the copper they spent on beer and tobacco. Bedad cursed the traders that brought the evil things to his village.

He absentmindedly rubbed the scar on his temple before pouring the peeled potatoes into the steaming pot. He carefully flipped each sausage coin with a cracked wooden spoon. While they browned, he stirred the potatoes. The heat, steam, smoke, and grease in the stuffy room made his eyes sting. When he stood to wipe them on his sleeve, Bedad realized his stepfather had passed out at the table.

As his mother snored and mumbled, he dished the food into two large bowls.

"Pa, supper's ready. Pa!"

He shook his stepfather. The man's head lolled on the table, like an empty swing. Bedad entered his parents' bedroom.

His mother was sprawled across the wrinkled covers, one hand hanging over the side of the bed. The heavy, white flesh on her upper arm hung in a flab, crisscrossed with blue veins and mottled with the skin sores she continually picked. Her mouth hung open; saliva dripped from the right side. Her eyes were partially open, but Bedad knew she was sound asleep.

He hesitated. If he let the food get cold she would be angry he had not called. But, sometimes when he shook her awake, she slapped him in her drunken stupor and then went back to sleep. Bedad decided to eat in peace.

Careful not to take more than his share, he spooned the meat and potatoes onto a plate. He covered the two bowls with dishes to keep the flies off and, hopefully, keep the food warm. He dumped water on the remaining coals and stirred until the ashes were cool. He gulped two long drinks from the water dipper before leaving.

On a tree stump, near the edge of town, the grass smelled sweet. Here Bedad sat and ate. The plate was empty before his stomach was full.

Bedad stretched out and wiggled his sore toes. More than once, he'd asked his parents for new shoes. When he removed the footwear, he found another blister. There was nothing else to be done. From inside the drawstring pouch hanging from his neck, he took his small jack knife. He snapped it open and sliced the shoe fronts. He pushed on the shoes and flexed his feet. Dirty toes protruded.

"Well," Bedad muttered ruefully, "they won't keep me very warm or dry. I just hope I get a new pair before my feet grow out the end too far and scrape the ground."

He stretched back out in the prickly, hot sunshine and breathed deep into his abdomen. The rich smell of green mullick and razor shoot soothed him. Thickly leaved diplock branches hung lazily in the heat. A small flickerbug whined and repeatedly lighted on his naked big toe.

Closing his eyes, Bedad listened to the village sounds fade as he slipped into sleep. The rising column of smoke failed to rouse him. As the child slept, flames engulfed his home. So, too, slept his parents. The burning tobacco under his mother's bed solved the problem of the waiting meal.

"Can't you just dig up more crystals?" asked Anastacia. "My people make diamonds from graphite with high pressure and extreme temperature."

The hot drinks had been replaced with an egg and vegetable dish that reminded Anastacia of the broken omelets she cooked at home. They ate with three-pronged forks, cutting the food with the edge.

"We do not have the means. We are not as advanced in technology as your world," said Durward.

"Oh," said Anastacia. "Can you make some with magic?"

"It isn't that simple," replied Durward, "and my skill is not great. Besides, the crystals came from one special stone mined centuries ago in a place now covered with water. Earthquakes changed the landscape. We don't have the skill to find another or make another like it."

"Why's it so special?" Anastacia examined a green vegetable on the end of her fork. It reminded her of the stems of broccoli.

Durward swallowed and licked his lips. "So large and so flawless a diamond had never before been found. It was a perfect hexagonal stone as big as my fist." He held his hand up and clenched his fingers.

"A black diamond as big as your fist!" Anastacia paused with her fork halfway to her mouth. "Wow!"

"Not black at first," said Durward. "Even rarer. A pale pink, like a hint of sunset. A few smaller pieces were used in the original bracelets. They looked like yours."

"Really!"

He continued. "With a quality even more stunning. Within its lattices was the power to magnify magic. The wizards claimed it, of course, and used it benignly for some time. Then began The Great Experiment."

"A time of infamy," said Misty.

"What experiment?" Anastacia finished her eggs and wiped her mouth with her thumb and fingers. *I guess they don't use napkins,* she thought.

Misty continued while Durward ate. "The wizards used the diamond to control the weather. At first, it was just to temper storms and mellow the most severe weather. They lengthened the summers, made it rain or not at their will, controlled the wind. The stone darkened with each new demand, but the wizard's either ignored the warning or did not understand it."

"Was it a warning to stop?" asked Anastacia.

"Yes. They didn't though, and so the stone turned black as did the stones in the bracelets. The wizards lost control. The crystal ran amuck."

Anastacia sipped water from a pewter mug, listening carefully.

"First, there were tremendous storms and quakes. Then, it seemed to rest. It took a few weeks for people to realize that the days were getting shorter at the wrong time of year. The crystal was enfolding our world in darkness."

"Did they stop the crystal?"

"At great cost. Temporarily and repeatedly. Your mother and Alaric Morrel of the panther people stopped it the last time. Dawn's End seemed safe for many decades to come, if not forever."

Anastacia shook her head in awe. *My mother. Amazing. I had no idea. I wonder if Jamail knew any of this. No, probably not.*

"The wizards were more careful for a while. But they could not suppress their thirst for knowledge and power. And so, once again, Dawn's End faces destruction."

"How so?"

"Kaie uses the bracelet in three ways," said Durward as he pushed his empty plate to the side. "Firstly, it is a weapon. It kills people and destroys our environment. She must have incredible natural abilities to wield such power. Secondly, she alters others so that they do only her bidding. They commit any barbaric act she wishes. I have no idea how this is possible. Thirdly, the bracelet opens the door to your world. Items of corruption are imported to the detriment of our people."

"What kind of things?" asked Anastacia.

Misty answered, "Alcohol has had a devastating effect on our people. Once they acquired a taste for it, they learned to brew it for themselves. Many of our people seem to have a low tolerance for the substance and are easily addicted."

Anastacia nodded. *That's happened before. Great way to destroy a culture.*

"Tobacco also. The plant does not grow well here, so tobacco is sold at high prices. People debase themselves in all manner of ways to ensure their supply. They have low resistance to this poison and quickly develop health problems."

"That's typical," said Anastacia.

"Pardon?"

"People get addicted and can't quit, even when it's killing them," she said. "There isn't a single part of the body that's not damaged, but they can't seem to stop."

Misty shook her head, her exotic eyes filled with sadness. "Even diseases have been imported. Durward has risked entrapment to enter your world for medicines, but, unfortunately, not all are effective. The worst are those illnesses which mutate into new forms. Your medicines are then worthless."

Anastacia was appalled. "I feel for you. But can't your people be educated against the influence of alcohol and tobacco?"

"Does that work in your world?" Durward asked.

Anastacia grimaced. "Not well enough."

Misty continued. "There are subtler forms of corruption as well. But the damage is extensive. Greed has become common. People care more about unnecessary acquisitions than they do about each other. Possessions were of little value in our society. Kaie imported attitudes and items from your world. There have been murders over trinkets and worthless substances."

"One idea of Kaie's did partially backfire," said Durward. "She distributed magazines filled with pictures of costly possessions, extravagant houses, and even lurid sex and violence. People were seduced by these images.

He smiled. "But some people became interested in the symbols of your writing. For the first time in our known history, people joined together and devised an alphabet."

"You didn't have writing?"

"No," said Durward. "Now, the history of Dawn's End has been recorded for future generations. Our traditions have been oral and pictorial, but with the widespread unraveling of our society, we feared much would be forgotten. When Kaie's power is destroyed, people may read of our happy past and attempt to restore our wholesome society."

"That is how they will learn of your mother," said Misty, as she licked her lips and pushed aside her empty dish. "The storytellers in our village have been murdered, but Nicole Newman's importance in our history has been recorded. Books are few and carefully cherished. They are painstakingly written. Durward has copies well hidden."

"And you want me to help destroy Kaie," Anastacia said, sighing. "As evil as she sounds, I don't want be to part of some magical execution. I only have your word for all of this. They're two sides to every story, and my mother taught me not to judge people on the basis of gossip."

Misty answered, "Well said. Your mother was wise. We hope not to cause Kaie's death. Our plan is to subdue her long enough to remove her bracelet."

Anastacia laughed. "How can you ever 'subdue' her?"

Durward and Misty exchanged worried looks. Durward stood, collected the dishes, and carried them to the counter.

"I don't know," he said as he walked back. "But we have to try. There is a new consideration that I have just learned on my journey. Our time may be limited."

Misty touched his arm as he sat down beside her. "What is it?"

"I met an older man who had been brought to her caves about a few months ago."

"He escaped!" Misty said.

"No. He was released."

"Unheard of." Misty frowned. "Why would Kaie let anyone go?"

"He had a sexual disease. He suspected one of her servants infected him."

"What good would that do? He wouldn't deliberately infect others."

"Not if he knew, but he thinks she tried to make him forget. The servant gave him a drink after they—" Durward stammered, glancing at Anastacia as a blush spread over his face. "After they were intimate. It made him unconscious. He thinks it was supposed to erase his memory."

Misty crossed her arms, thinking. "Why didn't it?"

"A woman hidden in a long, hooded red robe and long gloves woke him by trickling water into his face. She warned him not to touch her. Then she ordered him to vomit into a bucket so he 'would remember.' He did. She left with the bucket. He passed out again, and, when he woke, he was alone in the forest."

"So, Kaie is responsible for the spread of the disease." Misty nodded, considering.

"Yes, but that's not what I was most troubled by." Durward rubbed his thin eyebrows, making them as disheveled as his sandy hair. "Before he fainted for the second time, he heard Kaie talking to someone."

"What did she say?" asked Anastacia, leaning forward.

"She said she would soon be able to shatter the doors without a second bracelet. She said her experiment was successful, and the barriers to chaos would be gone within the year, forever."

"What doors?" said Anastacia.

"The doors to your world."

"Oh, no!" cried Misty. She gave Anastacia a startled look.

"I don't understand," said Anastacia.

Misty replied, "Imagine what would happen if the doors to your world were shattered."

"People couldn't come here anymore," said Anastacia. "That might be good. No more imports."

"No. She said the barriers to chaos would be gone forever. The entrances would be open. To anyone."

Anastacia paused, considering.

"Think what would enter," said Durward. "Pollution, illness, damaging insects, and plant and animal diseases. People would come. They'd crowd into our land bringing violence, political ambitions. Many of our people would be treated like freaks. Hunted. Some might be enslaved or caged. Our lives —
"

Anastacia interrupted him. "Oh, come on! My world isn't exactly hell on earth."

"Hell? Some words do not translate well in my mind. Hell? Wait, I think I understand. A place of pain and horror, an eternal punishment."

"You got it." Anastacia crossed her arms.

"Perhaps not Hell," said Durward. "But it isn't exactly paradise. Before Kaie's terrors, we had a chance to regain our idyllic world. If she shatters the doors, everything is lost."

"The end of Eden, eh?"

"Will you help us?" asked Misty.

"Maybe. But I think it's too late to put the snake back in the basket."

Durward and Misty exchanged confused glances.

Wouldn't Ali just have a fit if he knew, she thought. *It's almost worth doing just to make him crazy. But I probably won't be allowed to tell him. Mom kept everything a secret.*

"Please, say yes." Durward's long face resembled a sad hound dog's.

This is nuts, Anastacia thought. She examined her bracelet. *Mother wore this to save a world, and none of us knew. She always said I was the gutsy one, but she was really brave.* The others were quiet, waiting. *Imagine if I can wield magic. What power! More control than I've ever had in my life.*

Anastacia remembered how powerless she had felt kissing her mother goodbye for the last time, before they upped the morphine drip so Nicole could sleep until the end. She had wanted to *do* something, but all she could do was watch. She had felt as though part of her was dying with every weakening breath of her mother's.

She felt most alive when she was moving, doing, overcoming, winning. *Anastacia could imagine what Ali would say, just like when she started ice climbing.* "I don't see the point of risking your life for an adrenaline rush."

He just didn't get it. Anastacia never felt more alive than when her heart was pounding and her muscles quivering with strain. It was exhilarating to refuse to acknowledge the possibility of death or injury. She never felt more in control than when she was white-water canoeing, when a slight mistake of balance could send her crashing against the rocks. She never felt more powerful than when she faced a bigger opponent on the ice and slipped the puck right past him and into the net.

She looked up and nodded. "I'm in."

Chapter Four — Allies Assemble

A scratch on the door interrupted their talk. Misty smiled and went to the door. Anastacia gasped when the visitor entered.

"This is Sacha," said Durward. "She will help us in our venture."

Anastacia stood, her eyes huge in wonder, her heart racing. It was a large leopard with a pure white coat. Their eyes met. Sacha's were a shocking red with white, diamond-shaped pupils.

Anastacia whistled appreciatively. "She's quite an ally. What a remarkable creature. Is she yours?"

"She doesn't belong to anyone. She comes for her own reasons."

Sacha crossed the floor and stretched out on the stones on the cool hearth. Anastacia ventured a timid smile in Sacha's direction. The large feline licked her paw with her enormous, pink tongue and solemnly cleaned her ears.

"Well," said Misty. "We'd better get organized."

The morning passed slowly. Durward sharpened and polished his sword and readied the weapons. Misty prepared and packed food for their journey. Sacha dozed. Anastacia explored the area around the house. She kept expecting to discover a Lucerne landmark.

The exterior of the small house was constructed of wooden beams and mud-brown bricks. Window panes appeared smoky, due to their varying thickness.

While exploring, Anastacia discovered a square, wooden well with a pitched roof behind the house. Beyond it, she saw an extensive garden containing familiar looking plants as well as vegetables unique to Dawn's End. Farther on was forest.

Anastacia peeked inside a small outbuilding and saw a type of forge, presumably Durward's smithy. She assumed he made farm tools and weapons. She didn't see any horses so he wouldn't make shoes.

Feeling useless, she went back inside to ask Misty again if she could help.

"You *are* persistent, Anastacia. Take the water bags." She pointed to two collapsed sacks. They were made of a tightly woven, oily material and the size of a sofa cushion. "Fill them from the well."

"No problem," said Anastacia as she picked them up by the cloth strip handles.

When Anastacia approached the well, she froze as a yellow and red striped snake slithered out from the shade. It flicked its tongue in her direction, smelling for an enemy or prey. Anastacia didn't move. She stood still, waiting, wondering if she should frighten it away or try to be invisible. The snake stretched out its head and flicked its tongue warily. It dropped back down and wriggled away, disappearing into the garden.

"Well done, Anastacia," said Misty.

"How long have you been there?" Anastacia turned as the gray woman approached with a basket on one arm.

"Long enough to know you're not afraid of wineplant snakes."

"Is that what it is?" asked Anastacia, glancing over to where it disappeared into the garden. "Is it poisonous?"

"You don't know!"

"No. I've never seen a snake like it before."

"I'm impressed. You were very calm for someone who could have been facing a killer."

Anastacia shrugged. "Thunder Bay doesn't have poisonous snakes, so I guess I assume the best. Besides, snakes in my world won't attack unless you startle or threaten them. "

Misty nodded. "Same in Dawn's End. Still, some people would kill just to be sure."

"It might be important to the local environment. Maybe it hunts rats or something?" Anastacia's brow wrinkled. "Should I have killed it? Is it dangerous? I really prefer to live and let live."

"Excellent philosophy. Don't worry. The wineplant snake won't harm anyone. It's not poisonous. In fact, it helps by eating garden pests. That's probably where it went, and I'm heading that way as well." Misty padded to the garden, her basket swaying smoothly.

Anastacia pulled the wooden cover from the well. Underneath was a square hole with a beam across the middle. A rope was looped over the beam and knotted in place. A wooden bucket hung from a metal hook tied to the end. She untied the rope from the beam and lowered the bucket. Although she was in strong physical shape, Anastacia found pulling up the rope hard on her hands. *Doing this once is no big deal, but if I had to fill a bathtub, I'd get blisters,* she thought.

She carefully poured the well water into the first water bag, trying not to spill too much. It took six buckets to fill the bags. Durward approached as she was retying the rope onto the crossbeam. He was carrying a heavy burlap bag.

"Why don't you make a pulley to help raise the water bucket?" she asked him. "You do use pulleys here, don't you?"

"Of course," said Durward. "We are not that primitive. But why would we need a pulley just to lift a bucket of water?"

"Because it's heavy and the rope is rough on your hands."

He glanced at the well. "Heavy! But you seem a strong girl."

"I am. As strong as several of the boys in my class," she said, setting the bucket down on the grass and lifting the cover back onto the well.

Misty approached, her basket filled with root vegetables. Durward turned to her, frowning. "Anastacia says the buckets of water are too heavy to lift without a pulley. Do you find them heavy?"

"Durward, darling, you forget," said Misty. "Just because she has Alaric blood does not mean it gave her power."

"Oh, right," said Durward sheepishly.

"Because Durward's great grandmother was of the panther people, and my father also, we have more strength and speed than most humans. We do not know what qualities you inherited from Alaric Morrel, if any," said Misty as she stopped beside Anastacia.

"Is Sacha a panther person?" asked Anastacia as she lifted the water bag. She flinched under the weight of the second one. Durward stepped forward and took it from her as though it was an apple.

I could have carried it, she thought. *The handles are just awkward.*

The three of them walked side by side toward the house.

"No," answered Durward. "Sacha is a panther-who-once-was, descended from the same ancestors, though."

"I don't understand," said Anastacia as she adjusted the handle.

Misty said, "In Dawn's End, there are humans. There are creatures like Sacha, and there are other beings like the panther people. They have characteristics of both humans and panthers. They may have skin and hair that is black, brown, rust, gray, tawny, white, orange, or even mixed colors. Your father was one."

"What!" Anastacia stumbled and dropped the bag. It thumped, and then sloshed back and forth with shifting water. Puzzled, Durward slung the burlap bag over one shoulder, and then bent down and picked up the water bag with his other hand.

"Alaric Morrel was a panther person." Misty studied her expression. "Oh. I guess you didn't know that."

Anastacia's stomach did a flip-flop. "No, and I'm a little freaked out by it."

"Why?" asked Misty. "You look completely human. I thought Nicole and Morrel's daughter would look more like me."

Anastacia looked her up and down. "With gray skin?"

"Alaric Morrel's skin was black, and his cousin Aubin's was pure white, so who knows? They were both large, powerful men, even for panther people."

"Holy shit. Is that why I'm so tall and strong?"

"Strong?" said Durward as he looked at the bag he had picked up.

"I *am* strong. Those were just awkward." Anastacia pointed toward the bags Durward now carried.

"I'm sure you are," said Misty soothingly as they reached the door. She opened it and held it while the other two went through.

"In my world, I'm a pretty impressive athlete," said Anastacia as she sat on the wooden bench.

"Of course you are," said Misty. "Durward just expected you to have more panther blood."

Durward set the water bags down behind the door and looked from Anastacia to Misty, uncertain what to say. Anastacia sat, resting her chin on her fist, and thought. Misty poured water from a bag into a sink and washed the vegetables. Durward took out a knife and peeled what looked like a purple orange. They worked in silence, allowing Anastacia to absorb this new information.

Anastacia sat up. "How do you keep all the kinds of people straight? Are their names for each race, or whatever you call them?"

"None other than what I've said," answered Misty. "Terms only stress differences. We are all of the same soil in Dawn's End. There is no need, or desire, to differentiate. Occasionally, a panther person will join with a human. Durward has a touch of the cat blood in him, although you cannot tell by his appearance. In me, it is much stronger, as you pointed out when you commented on my gray skin."

"Amazing," answered Anastacia. "I feel kinda dull in comparison. The only plain, old human. Well, at least, plain, old human-looking. On the inside, I guess I'm something else. I'm not sure what."

At lunchtime, Misty explained that the passage of time was much quicker in Dawn's End and they would probably have her home before anyone noticed she was missing.

"I hope so," said Anastacia. "I don't want to do anything to upset Julie two weeks before her wedding. Couldn't I just go back and tell her?"

"Tell her what?"

Anastacia considered. They would think she was crazy. There would be a huge fuss.

"Besides," said Durward, "we don't have the time. And going back and forth may not be such a good idea. We still aren't sure how you got here."

"Then how can I get back?" cried Anastacia.

"Don't worry," said Durward. "Once we get the bracelet from Kaie, I can bring you home."

There was another scratch at the door. Anastacia sat erect in anticipation of some form of panther person, but when Misty opened the door, a handsome, blond, but clearly human, male entered. Durward stumbled to his feet grabbing the back of the chair before it fell over. The man, in his mid-twenties, gripped him by the shoulder. Durward returned the gesture.

"You should have been here day before yesterday." Misty scolded the young man. "I suppose you were delayed by a lady but will insist it was a debt of honor." She waved away his attempt to protest. "No matter, you're here now. In fact, your tardiness was a blessing. If we had left earlier, we would have missed the arrival of Anastacia Newman." She presented Anastacia to the newcomer with a flourish.

As the tall man bent to kiss Anastacia's hand, Misty said, "The daughter of the Esteemed Nicole Newman and Alaric Morrel. Anastacia, this charmer is Kent of the Lake."

Kent's gaze shot up in surprise at the mention of Nicole. His large smile spread over white, even teeth, highlighting dimples in a sun-browned complexion. He wore a short, sparse, blond-brown moustache. His blond hair fell in long, soft waves around his jaw line.

"She is going to join us on our quest," said Durward.

"Indeed," said Kent. "Is it not fitting that the daughter of the Esteemed Nicole and Alaric Morrel should not only be beautiful, but also brave? Where did you find her?"

"She found us," said Misty.

"Remarkable," said Kent.

Anastacia was conscious of firm muscles beneath his tight-fitting shirt. Although Anastacia was tall, he stood taller. She smiled up into his eyes, a twinkling shade of robin's egg blue, framed by untanned laugh lines.

Well, she thought. *He's hot. And, he knows it. Things are getting interesting.*

Kaie shrieked. "Lachish! Come!" She pounded her summoning bell furiously. The black diamond iris was vivid in her bulging, colorless eyes.

Lachish lumbered in as quickly as his bulky legs could carry him. He bowed to the wizard.

"I know why the potion is not working exactly as I wish. I have been concentrating on chemicals and proteins and crystals and other foolish scientific dung. I forget myself. I am Kaie, the greatest wizard who ever lived. I am more powerful than all the simpering, cautious wizards in this stinking land. How could I downplay my best asset?"

She glared at Lachish, who fidgeted, nervously unsure whether to respond. He decided the best safety was silence and simply nodded.

"It's magic, don't you see? That's what I should be binding the drug with. Magic. And I know the perfect spell. Lachish —" her voice lowered threateningly — "have you killed the female captive?"

He twitched, realizing how close he had come to snuffing what life was left in the savaged woman. "No, mithtreth. She liveth."

"Good. I have no time for you to search for another. Now, tell me. Has she still her eyes?" She pulled her hood forward.

"Her eyeth?" He rocked nervously from one foot to the other.

"Her eyes, fool! Can she still look upon your hideous face or have you nibbled them from their sockets?"

"Yeth, I mean no. She hath her eyeth, misthreth. I like her to thee what ith happenin'." He sniffled and then rubbed his stubby, black nose.

Kaie chuckled. "Of course." She chucked his sweaty, black and orange jaw. "We are of the same spirit, you and me."

Lachish's blood quickened at the compliment and the unusual physical contact.

"Unfortunately, my faithful servant, I must deprive you of this simple joy. I want her eyes. They are exactly what I need to bind the drug."

"Of courth, my majethtic mithtreth." Lachish stumbled over his words, his lisp worsening in his eagerness to please, his excitement at following her command knotting his tongue.

"But," Kaie said firmly, "You must follow my instructions. They must be removed properly."

Lachish nodded quickly, his eyes shining.

"You must remove them with your bare hands. No metal must touch them."

"Yeth. Yeth." Lachish flexed his powerful fists and felt the long nails press against his palms.

"She must, of course, be still alive when you do it." Her head tilted to one side.

Her servant shifted impatiently from one foot to the other, his breath increasing. He leaned toward his mistress, her words heating his bestial brain.

"It is important that you do not crush the eyeball." Kaie raised a finger like an admonishing schoolteacher. "It must be intact. Afterward, you may do with her what you wish, but bring the eyes to me immediately. They must not dry out. They must be fresh."

"Ath you command." Lachish fell to his knees and kissed the hem of her dirty, black robe.

"Now, go." She kicked him away, her lip curled in distaste. No one was allowed to touch her unless asked, not even her clothing.

Lachish stumbled to his feet and hurried away. He could not move fast enough. His blood was pounding in his ears at the thought of fulfilling Kaie's wish. He steeled himself to do it properly. He must not crush the eyes in his excitement. He must steady himself. It would be difficult to tear himself away from the woman when she felt the pain, knew the horror of blindness. But he would hurry, hurry, to deliver the treasures to his mistress, hurry, hurry, back to the chained lady. It would not do to miss her cries of anguish. Lachish panted as he ran. He knew today she would cry her last cries of anguish. He knew his excitement would push him over the edge.

The allies assembled at the Canice home and checked their weapons again before traveling. Kent oiled, dried, and polished his sword and knife. From a distance, his eyes were a peacock blue, framed by thick, blond, child-soft lashes. His complexion was smooth, lightly tanned. Anastacia admired the bone structure of his face, high, yet masculine cheekbones, straight nose, well-formed jaw, and a hint of a dimple in his chin. His curly hair was blonder than his moustache, with one rebellious lock breaking free to twist above his left eye. His lips were a delicious bow shape, yet everything about him exuded sensual masculinity. His soft handsomeness was set off by a tall, strong body. Women would adore him.

Anastacia had shown little interest in boys since her mother died. It was easier to lose herself in sport than try to deal with all the emotional baggage that came with having a crush. She had enough emotion in her life, dealing with the death of her mother. Someday, she hoped it would get easier, and then maybe she'd feel differently about boys. The guys she hung out with saw her as one of them, and she preferred to keep it that way. Besides, this guy was about a decade older than she was. Still, he was so *freaking hot*!

Trying not to stare at Kent, Anastacia closely examined the dagger she had been given. Her brow furrowed at the thought of actually pushing this into someone's flesh, cutting their skin, veins, muscle.

Kent watched her expression. "Rest assured. We will protect you. You'll probably never need to use that.

"I'm having second thoughts about this," said Anastacia. "It seemed like an exciting adventure at first. But I don't want to die for the problems of strangers, nor do I want to kill anyone. I'm kind of a pacifist at heart. I prefer to outskate my opponent rather than muscle them. Peace out, and all that."

"None of us want to kill," said Misty. "The weapons are mostly to protect us against robbers and bandits. Usually, a good show of arms is enough to frighten them off."

Anastacia looked doubtful.

Kent patted her shoulder. "Don't worry. You think anyone's going to get near you with Durward's sword and mine at the ready, Misty with her crossbow, and Sacha being a panther?"

Anastacia managed a smile. *I guess I'm safe,* she thought. She looked into his gorgeous eyes and thought, *I wonder if he's married. Does his family know he's off on a crusade? I guess I shouldn't talk. What would Jamail do if I disappeared? He's already lost so much. And Ali. He would be frantic if he knew where I was. The best thing is to get this done quickly and get home.* She glanced at Kent, who helped Misty pack food into parcels. *There's no reason why I can't enjoy this crazy expedition, though.*

Sacha yawned, showing her large, pink tongue, black lips and mouth, and wicked sharp fangs. The hair on the back of Anastacia's neck rose.

"I still don't understand about Sacha," said Anastacia. "Why is she here if no one controls her?"

"Because I choose to be," came Sacha's rumbling reply.

Anastacia's dagger clattered to the floor when she realized it was the panther speaking.

Kent walked over and picked it up. "I gather from your reaction that panthers don't speak in your world."

Anastacia shook her head, dumbfounded, as she clumsily replaced the dagger.

Sacha sniffed, stretched like a house cat, and padded away.

"I have a feeling there are many things in Dawn's End you will find interesting," Kent said with a mischievous grin.

"I'll bet!" said Anastacia. "I wouldn't miss this for anything."

"Great," said Kent. "It seems we are all ready. I believe it's time to go. I do love a woman of spirit."

He winked, and Anastacia tried to remain cool.

As they traveled, the countryside reminded Anastacia of Southern Ontario. Less rock and fewer conifers than Northern Ontario where she lived, but plenty of streams and ponds. The landscape was dotted predominantly with tall, pink and short, white flowers. The air was fresh and clear, as though she was far away from any industrial pollution. The only sounds were the calls of birds, the occasional gurgle of water, and the buzz of insects. It reminded Anastacia of camping in Quetico Provincial Park, one of the quietest, cleanest places on earth.

The paths were wide and well used, occasionally rutted with wheel marks and dinted with hoof prints. Anastacia wondered why her group didn't ride horses but, thinking it might have something to do with their panther blood, didn't ask.

Misty and Durward walked closely together. They often touched hands or talked privately. Sacha generally kept to herself. Anastacia found Kent a comfortable companion.

"They're a devoted couple," she said when Durward helped Misty over an enormous fallen tree.

"There is no one in Dawn's End — or any other land — for Misty like Durward," answered Kent as they followed. He bit his lip thoughtfully.

"He seems to feel the same," said Anastacia. She jumped onto the log and off the other side.

Kent followed. "He depends on her, but I don't know if he has her depth." Kent absently fingered his moustache.

Uncomfortable with the turn in the conversation, Anastacia shrugged. "Is there someone special in your life, Kent of the Lake?"

"Yes." He adopted a lovesick expression.

I'll bet there's more than one, she thought. *Guys like that play their looks for all its worth.* Aloud, she said, "What's she like?"

His blue eyes sparkled; he grinned. "Tall. Beautiful. Hair the color of coal. Lovely eyes, blue, but more . . . . What color would you call them?"

"Pardon?"

"Your eyes." He grinned. "What color would you call them?"

Anastacia blinked and then laughed. *What a smooth mover.*

At the house the group inhabited on the first night, no one could be convinced to join their cause. Anastacia felt her influence as Morrel and Nicole's daughter had been overestimated. After all, it was a long time ago to these people.

Durward did not tell the farmers of her bracelet. With the widespread corruption, people could no longer be easily trusted. He did not hold this village in much esteem. Someone might decide to steal the bracelet and use it for their own purposes. A key to the door of the other world would be priceless.

As Anastacia stood outside for a breath of evening air, she watched Misty bring water to Sacha. The panther preferred to sleep outdoors. Anastacia suspected their hosts were more comfortable with this arrangement as well. When the wind shifted, she caught snatches of their conversation.

" . . . smells different."

"No, I hadn't noticed, but your sense of smell is keener than mine," replied Misty.

The voices faded away again. Anastacia arched and rubbed the small of her back, stiff from the heavy packsack.

" . . . his lip . . . ." said Sacha in a rumbling voice.

"He's probably as nervous as we are about all the changes. Your grief has increased your sensitivity."

Not wanting to eavesdrop, Anastacia entered the farmstead for the night. *Last thing I want to hear about is grief,* she thought.

The third day they journeyed through brush interspersed with trees. The small band had not been disheartened by the lack of volunteers. Anastacia began to form friendships with the odd collection of travelers.

"How long have you and Durward been together?" she asked Misty when they entered an open area.

"Seems like forever." Misty sighed.

Durward's thin eyebrows shot up. Misty laughed and nudged him. He smiled, hesitatingly.

"We have been married for six years, but I have loved him for twenty-three."

Durward chuckled. "I'm only twenty-five years old."

"Doesn't matter." Misty shrugged. "I loved you the first moment I saw you, in your mother's arms, as I played with my dolls."

Durward reached out to hold her hand. Ahead, Kent rolled his eyes over his shoulder at Anastacia.

"And you, Anastacia Newman. Is there a special man in your life?" Kent asked.

"There are fourteen special men in my life."

"Ambitious!" said Kent. "It must be hard to juggle them all."

"You should know." Misty laughed, having been listening in.

Kent shook his head in astonished denial.

Anastacia smiled slightly. *It figures. A girl in every village, I bet.*

"Anastacia wouldn't be like that," said Durward.

Anastacia nodded, smiling. "They're my ice hockey teammates. I'm the only girl in the city who still plays on a boy's team, and I'm every bit as good as they are."

"So, you haven't found anyone special," said Kent.

"I'm not looking," said Anastacia.

"It'll happen when you're ready. I had to wait until Durward was ready, and I was glad I didn't get involved with anyone else," said Misty.

"Maybe," said Anastacia. "But he'd have to be someone who understood me, and I don't think that's very easy."

"Like Durward understands me," said Misty. "But he is a diamond among a river of glass." Misty squeezed her husband's hand.

Anastacia noticed the back of Durward's neck and his ears turned bright pink.

He coughed and changed the subject as they entered a more wooded area. "Kent of the Lake, did you see or hear anything during your travels that might help us against Kaie?"

"Help us, unfortunately no, but I did see evidence of her handiwork. An ugly blight spreads over Dawn's End. I have traveled for a dozen years now, since I was fourteen, and I see our world change with each journey."

Twenty-six, thought Anastacia.

"There is drunkenness, poverty, and violence where none before existed," said Kent. "People are mistrustful. True friendships are rare." He nodded at Durward and Misty. "Love—such as yours—is even rarer. The forest and the mountains have dark and dangerous places. "

"Then it is good we are together," said Sacha with a growl.

The deep voice still startled Anastacia. She smiled nervously at the huge beast as it trotted up beside her. Falling in step, Sacha gently nuzzled Anastacia's hand with her powerful, white head. A thrill tingled through Anastacia as she scratched the giant cat between the ears.

"There have been many times when friends have made the difference," said Kent. "I remember when I went to Whisper Rapids with Aravene. Now there's a man who thought on his feet. We had been walking for three days—"

Sacha halted and rumbled a warning. "Silence. I sense . . . . Danger!"

Chapter Five — Sisters

Among the imprisoned captives was another potent man who was given over to Riva's talents. The male was about thirty-five, thickening around the middle, but still in fair shape. His wife had been the elegant lady murdered by Lachish.

Riva enjoyed destroying people of this class. They were her enemy, and she would never forget how it began.

The Pike family had been prominent in the community, since her father was a respected storekeeper. Her mother was a quiet woman, often ill. No one had suspected, or appeared to suspect, what went on in that comfortable house.

Nightly visits by her father began when she was four years old. She was too innocent to realize his actions were immoral. As she grew in age, so did his demands. One night, she voiced her doubts about their behavior.

"Don't start acting righteous with me, little doxy," he said angrily. "You like it as much as I do. You've been using these visits to get presents and favors you wouldn't otherwise get. If you weren't doing it with me, you'd be doing it with somebody else."

He towered over her, a large finger jabbing near her face. Riva wept.

"Don't get any ideas about telling anyone either. It would kill your mother to find out her daughter was nothing but a drab. You just do what I say, and keep your haughty mouth shut."

She did. The only way to assert herself was to make increased demands for toys and sweets. Pike readily complied.

"Why does Father give you so many toys?" asked her little sister.

"Don't ask, Carlie, and I'll let you play with them anytime you want."

"Okay. But why doesn't Father like me?"

"You silly twit. Be glad he doesn't. I'll share my candy and everything. Just be glad you don't have to . . . . "

"Have to what?"

"Shut up, will you!"

Carlie sniffled.

"Don't cry. You're my best friend. Just stick with me, and stay away from Father."

"I like Father."

"You're hopeless. Let's not talk about it anymore. Let's just play dolls."

The seeds of rebellion were planted the day Riva heard someone in the hall when Pike was with her. The next morning, she asked Carlie why she had been listening in the hall.

"I wasn't in the hall. I didn't wake up last night."

At breakfast, Riva's mother avoided meeting her eyes. She realized her mother knew.

"Father," she said the next night he came to her room. "You better not come anymore. I think Mother heard you last time."

Pike snorted. "You don't think she notices me gone? She hardly sleeps, just moans and complains all night."

"She knows!"

"She's not stupid. I'm not bothering her anymore. Everyone's happy all around. Don't worry your little head, Riva, just move over."

When her younger sister began to attract his attention, Riva felt a mixture of fear and despair. Carlie usually looked up to her for help and advice. This time, Riva felt powerless.

When Carlie cried to her about the pain, Riva's despair turned to fury. She protected her sister the only way she knew, by attracting her father's advances with verbal promises, suggestive movements, and provocative clothes. She made sure Pike left her bed too spent to bother Carlie. Her little sister began to act like her old self, and Riva felt the debasement was worth it.

Then their mother died, and Riva's father flaunted his power over them. He forced them to visit his bed together. He brought home glossy pictures from outworld magazines and insisted they imitate the sexual activities portrayed. Riva and Carlie acquiesced until, one morning, Riva saw him carry something new to his room. She raced to her sister's room.

"Carlie, quick, get up!" She shook her sister awake.

"What? What is it?" Carlie rubbed her sleepy eyes.

"We've got to leave. Hurry." Riva pulled open drawers and pulled out her sister's clothing.

"What's the matter?" Carlie sat up in bed.

"It's father. He's got a new toy for our 'games.'" She stuffed Carlie's clothing into a large canvass bag.

Carlie hugged her knees and rubbed her chin on them. "He scares me, Riva. Those pictures he showed us."

"Those pictures have given him a new idea. We've got to go. Strike out on our own. We should have left before. Nothing could be worse than this." She threw open the closet and selected clothing for the bag.

"How? Where could we go?" Carlie flung back the sheets and twisted her legs over the side of the bed.

"I've got money saved. We have to leave. Now." Riva laced up the bag. She threw clothes at her sister. "Get dressed."

"I'm scared, Riva." Carlie pulled off her nightdress.

"Not as scared as I am. Father just brought a whip up to his bedroom."

Riva and Carlie walked to the nearest tavern. They entered the dusty establishment, blinking in the dark as their eyes adjusted.

"Well, well, what have we got here?" One of the men inside shouted. There followed various catcalls and imitations of sexual noises.

"Come on," said Riva urgently. "Father wouldn't dare challenge us with them around. They can protect us."

"Who'll protect us from them?" asked Carlie.

"Can't be worse than home."

Carlie nodded and forced herself to smile as they joined the travelers.

The men paid for the food and drinks, but when the girls asked to join them on their journey, they shook their heads.

"We can pay." Riva tossed the biggest man a silver coin.

When the valuables ran out, the girls paid with themselves. Then the girls moved on to a new group and began to charge for their company. When they launched their new careers, Riva was sixteen, and her sister was twelve.

Within a year, Carlie contracted the new disease sweeping through the prostitutes, and then Riva contracted it. By youthful strength and luck, Carlie recovered quickly. Riva had a more difficult time.

Carlie nursed her sister during the feverish, pain-wracked illness. She earned money for the medical care by soliciting in the village, unaware that she was now a carrier. Whomever she copulated with became infected. The disease had an incubation time of seven to ten days.

Before Riva was fully recovered, a wealthy merchant in town became ill. His sickness was traced back to Carlie. The man publicly accused her of spreading infection. His wife was spared the infection since she had just returned from a trip. The day her husband died, she persuaded the villagers to storm Riva and Carlie's hut.

The woman screeched. "Send her out! Send out the doxy who killed my husband."

"Don't go," whispered Riva, trying to sit up.

A man shouted. "Send her out, or we'll set fire to the place."

"Don't worry," said Carlie, her face pale. "I'll settle this and send them away. You rest." She sponged her sister's face once more before leaving.

Riva heard an upsurge of voices, closer to the hut, the thud of feet on the step.

A man jeered. "Strip the drab. Let's see if she's hiding any sores."

The voices surged again. Trying to steady her swirling head, Riva crawled to the window. On her knees, she clutched the ledge and peered out the window. Carlie was standing, naked, arms crossed, head down. The mob circled her.

The merchant's wife shrieked. "She killed him. If I hadn't been away, it would have killed me as well. How many others has she murdered? We have to stop her."

Carlie pleaded with the crowd. "Let me go. I'll leave town. I'll pay for your husband's funeral. You can have everything I have."

The merchant's wife spat. "Drab's money."

"I didn't force him."

"She'll kill others," a man shouted.

The merchant's wife hissed. "The gauntlet."

The cry was taken up. Two men grabbed Carlie as she tried to escape. Riva fainted as the crowd formed two lines.

She was not allowed to see Carlie's body. It was carted to the village dump and burned as refuse. The community felt generous after their bloodletting. Riva was ordered to leave or die since she was now a carrier. Riva suspected the pleasure they had taken in violence embarrassed them, made them uncomfortable. They wished to purge any traces of shame by allowing Carlie's sister to escape. Riva had fled, carrying only her anger and hatred with her.

The travelers stood motionless, listening. Misty touched Durward's shoulder. Kent chewed his lip and fingered the hilt of his sword.

With a thunderous roar, Sacha leapt to a large, overhanging branch. "Beware! They come."

The attackers appeared, a band of eight men who had felt the odds were in their favor. They scanned the group.

They said we wouldn't need the weapons, thought Anastacia. *Those men look determined and deadly. Other than Sacha, we look a pretty harmless group. What have I gotten myself into?*

"The panther skin will fetch a good price," said one.

Another snickered. "The others look as though they have a few things worth taking. We'll kill them first, of course."

"Except the girl," said a third. "We can sell her after a bit of fun."

They plunged into the battle with all the confidence of well-seasoned bandits. Durward pushed Anastacia behind him. Kent stood on her left and Misty on her right. Kent drew his sword, while Misty loaded her crossbow. Anastacia clutched her dagger.

Durward stepped forward, held his bracelet aloft and commanded, "Stop!" The bracelet sparked and crackled. The others paused to watch. Worms of light gyrated around his wrist. Then . . . nothing.

"Boar stench," he muttered as he drew his sword. Under different circumstances, Anastacia would have laughed aloud. Kent chuckled softly and edged forward. The two men plunged and dodged, slicing through the oncomers. Misty loaded, fired, and reloaded in a blur of speed. Sacha leapt here and there dealing deadly blows.

The bandits soon realized they had underestimated their enemy. When three had been slain, they regrouped and fled. Sacha followed their retreat, ensuring they would not return. Anastacia heard a scream as the white panther claimed one last victim.

Durward stood panting, resting on the hilt of his bloodied sword. One hand held the grip while his other arm lay over the pommel. The point dug into the earth. Misty straightened her back and flexed her hands, stretching like a roused cat. Anastacia sheathed her dagger, shuddering at the carnage.

"I've never seen anyone killed before," she whispered.

"Better them than us," said Durward. "They picked the fight."

Anastacia nodded. "I wasn't much help."

"This battle was unimportant. We must keep you safe for the one that really matters," said Durward.

Sacha returned. "Everyone alright?" she asked.

Anastacia looked at everyone one by one, stopping at Kent. He swayed on his feet, white-faced. His left hand clutched his abdomen below his ribs and blood ran through his fingers.

Aimlessly, Riva had wandered, begging and stealing to survive. Lachish had captured her and brought her to Kaie. His mistress had sensed deep rage within Riva and, after questioning her at length, made her an offer.

"Would you like to revenge Carlie's murder? Enact your vengeance on every man who touched you? Teach the righteous rabble a lesson in pain?" she asked Riva in her grating whisper.

Riva wore rags, her face was filthy, and her shoes were worn through. She had nothing to lose and nowhere to go. "And what do you want in return?" she asked.

"Your total obedience." Kaie's eyes narrowed." But, I assure you, my requests will be greatly to your liking. I can also use my magic to make your beauty more powerful. I can enhance your voluptuousness until you are irresistible to any man who sees you. I can protect you from harm and see that you want for nothing. We do not live in luxury, but you may have anything Lachish pillages, and I think you will be satisfied."

Riva had been more than satisfied. The jewels and trinkets Lachish brought were amusing, but her real enjoyment came whenever a sexually potent male was given to her. Husbands sank into her arms while their wives were manacled in the cave prisons. Spiritual men tore the robes from their backs. No one ever resisted.

Once fornication was complete, Kaie provided two potions. One caused amnesia; the victim forgot all that occurred between his first encounter with Lachish and his release. The other made the virus dormant until the next sexual encounter.

The man was then freed far from the caves. When the contaminated male infected his mate, he developed the symptoms of the virus. Using this method, Dawn's End was contaminated far and wide. The few survivors became carriers. A vicious circle began, and Riva was doing her best to keep it cycling.

Her newest, confused victim sat on the end of the bench. He had heard his wife's screams and waited in vain for her return. The hideous giant brought him to this erotic woman, then left. She poured him a glass of beer and sank down beside him.

"Don't look so worried," she whispered huskily. "I'm not going to bite you. That is, unless you want me to." She laughed softly and ran her fingers down his thigh. The man shuddered and felt an involuntary response in his loins. She stroked him again and licked her lips.

On the anniversary of their first year together, Kaie offered Riva a "present." It was the storekeeper, captured by Lachish while exiting a bawdy house. The usually cool and detached Riva was wild at the sight of her father.

She screamed at him. "Now we'll see who feels the whip, Father." She ordered Lachish to tie Pike's hands to an overhead beam. Lachish was spellbound by her impassioned fury as she flogged Pike into unconsciousness. Panting, she threw the whip to the floor.

"Don't touch him! No one touches him but me."

She left him hanging for over an hour, while the blood clotted to his shirt, as she considered.

"Why do you pace so?" asked Kaie.

"I can't decide how to kill the slime-faced dung-eater. I have wanted this for so long. Ached for it. I would stare at the ceiling after he left, hoping he'd be killed in an accident. When I was older and he hurt Carlie, I used to plot his death. If I'd stayed any longer, I would have killed him. Now I can. But, once it's done, it's done. He can't be killed again."

"It depends what you had in mind," purred Kaie. "I have the power to destroy and restore."

Riva looked into her mistress's uncanny eyes. They stared back, lacking an iris, the pupil a black diamond. A tingle went through Riva's body. "Do you mean I can kill him more than once?"

"As long as I am alerted within a minute after his death, I can probably revive him to his full senses. Otherwise, it's no fun torturing a vegetable. Of course, if you cut out his heart"—she smiled at Lachish—"then there is nothing I can do. But, if the damage isn't too severe, I may revive him a half-dozen times before he's beyond my reach."

Riva Pike threw herself at Kaie's filthy feet and showered them with grateful kisses. Kaie flinched and stepped away.

Anastacia winced as Kent swayed, his blood threading through his fingers. "I'm afraid I didn't do too well," he muttered.

Durward held him still while Misty examined the deep stab wound. When Kent released his hand, the blood gushed out, and his face turned even paler.

Anastacia gasped. "Kent! Oh, Lord, so much blood."

She'd seen plenty of blood on the hockey rink, broken bones, skate blade cuts, and mashed-in faces from fist fights, but the deaths of the three bandits and Kent's severe wound left her shaken.

"Help me ease him down," said Misty.

They lowered him to the grass.

Misty unpacked bandages, a curved needle, thread, and ointment. "Chew this root. It'll ease the pain."

Kent took it gratefully. Anastacia turned away when they removed his shirt. It was less ragged than a skate blade slice, but who knew how deep it went?

Kent gave a suppressed scream when Misty probed the injury.

"No organ damage," she said. "I'm going to have to sew the muscle together though, and then the skin."

Anastacia turned away. Her eyes fell upon a bandit with an arrow in his throat. She had seen death before, but never murder.

Better him than us, she thought. *They attacked us first.* She bit her thumbnail when the stitching began, and Kent groaned loudly.

"I smeared some infection thwarter under the bandage," said Misty as she finished wrapping him. "It should also help ease the burning." She stretched a bed roll over him. "Anastacia, would you bring my water canteen."

Anastacia came to her side. Misty took it and gave Kent a drink. Water dribbled town his trembling chin. Misty wiped it, took the canteen, and patted his shoulder.

"How're you doing?" Anastacia asked Kent.

Lips pressed tightly together, he gave a small nod.

"Stay with him," said Misty, as she gathered up her medical supplies.

Misty, Durward, and Sacha stood together, speaking in low tones as Durward wiped his sword repeatedly on the grass. Kent tried to sit up.

"No, lay back." Anastacia knelt down beside him.

"I'm cold," he whispered, his teeth chattering.

I hope he's not going into shock, she thought. She helped him sit up, gathered him in her arms, and tucked the bed roll tightly around him. Anastacia held him carefully against her shoulder and smoothed back his blond hair.

"Thank you, Kent of the Lake," she whispered. "For protecting me. I feel so bad that you're hurt."

"My own fault," he muttered. "I'm always caught off guard when they're left-handed." He smiled thinly. "I guess I haven't made much of an impression as your protector." His voice came in harsh spurts as he tried to suppress the pain.

"You were very brave, Kent."

His trembling fingers wrapped around a strand of Anastacia's black hair. She tried not to flinch, hoping his fingers weren't bloody. He drew the hair to his face and smelled.

"Like wildflowers. I thought it would be." He smiled, his dimples causing Anastacia's heart to do a little flip.

"Lie quietly," she said.

"How can I lie quietly in the arms of the most beautiful woman in two worlds? Anastacia. Such a lovely name. But I would like to call you something special in private, a shorter version, if you would honor me so."

Please, don't say Stacey, she thought. *That's what Ali always tries to call me. Like I'm Barbie's little sister.*

"Ana, for private side of you."

"Okay." She placed her fingers on his lips. "Shh, now rest."

He kissed them, winked, and then closed his eyes. *I should probably tell him how old I am*, she thought. *But maybe it doesn't matter in Dawn's End. Yikes. What am I thinking? I must be in shock myself.*

Anastacia held him while the medicine worked. She suppressed the rising shakes in her own body. She was very vulnerable here. She felt the sense of otherworldliness she felt when SCUBA diving, only ten times stronger. She was out of her element. Once, after emerging from a deep wreck, she became disoriented and unsure which way was up. For a few panicked seconds, she thrashed about, trying to spot something familiar, before she remembered to watch the direction of the bubbles. There were no bubbles in Dawn's End. She listened to the others as Kent dozed off.

"It doesn't look good," Misty said. "He's lost a lot of blood. The wound is very deep and will take a long time to heal. Much longer than we have. We will have to find someone to care for him while we continue on."

"The lilyvern grow west of here. Perhaps they could help," Sacha said.

"The lilyvern were destroyed by Kaie," said Misty.

"I have a feeling, an intuition," said Sacha. "Perhaps some seeds escaped her notice. We should go to the Pond of the Lilyvern. It will only delay us by one day, and it is worth the chance if there is anything left."

"No," said Durward. "It's pointless. There is nothing there. I've seen it myself."

"Wait," said Misty. "I trust Sacha's instincts. I think we should go."

"If you wish" said Durward. "None of us want to believe such innocent beauty has been slaughtered completely, but I fear we are chasing smoke."

Chapter Six—Pond of the Lilyvern

Goar didn't react to the stroking of his sleek, furry head.

"What is it, great panther?" Beora asked, her voice a soft strain. "What are you watching?"

"Death," he replied.

Past his head into the cave beyond, they watched Riva laugh as a man tore off her flimsy tunic.

Beora flinched. Although Riva's baseness disgusted them, Beora and Goar both ached for the touch of another of their kind. Riva's movements mocked them.

"I wonder where Clayton is now," Beora murmured. "How long did he search for me? Does he still wear my garnet pin? Does he know I survived?"

"Someday," said Goar, "if Kaie is defeated and a new council of wizards formed, they could help you."

Help her. Who was he kidding? She would be punished for supporting Kaie, as would he. There would be no mercy for the servants of evil.

"I hope he never sees me," she said. "He would be as repulsed by my actions as by my appearance. He was such a gentle man. I hope he thinks I am dead."

Goar turned his massive head toward her, "How is it, Beora, that I do not burn when you touch me?"

"I don't know," she answered. "Perhaps because of your own fire within. Perhaps because Kaie holds us both. I don't understand much about magic."

Goar nodded.

"Kaie has cursed me to burn anything with a heart whether I want to or not," said Beora. "I can control the amount of fire, but that's all."

"I know," said Goar. "At least you don't burn everything you touch."

Beora scratched his head. "Yes, heartless things are my choice to burn or not. But come, Goar." She turned away. "Don't stay to watch this act that brings death instead of life. I saw an owl in one of the front caves feeding her fledglings yesterday. They are all gawkiness and noise. Perhaps they are learning to fly. Come and see."

Goar nodded. "Yes, Beora. I would like that."

He padded softly beside the small woman. Her ravaged appearance contrasted sharply with Riva's perfection. They were as different as ice and fire. Internally, Riva was twisted and disfigured. Beora's scars were external, for all Dawn's End to view.

The white panther had found her lying among the remains of her home. She was his friend in the time before Kaie. They had hunted together, more for companionship than necessity. Beora's family had always been kind to Goar.

On one of his meaningless rampages, Lachish had set fire to their modest dwelling, burning the occupants in their sleep. Unaware that Goar had watched everything from a thick wimpole tree, Lachish threw his torch into the flames and left them all for dead. When the flames cooled to ash, the great panther heard moaning.

It was slow work digging Beora from the ruins. He repeatedly leapt back after touching a hot coal. His paws were singed and sore, his white fur smothered in black ash.

Goar dug in constant fear. If Lachish returned, he would have to kill the last victim in order to spare himself the wrath of Kaie. She did not approve of mercy.

The woman was burned beyond recognition. Her skin was crusted black, with bleeding wounds and blisters. Her scalp was bald with small clumps of singed hair matted to the skull. Goar realized she had not long to live.

The woman croaked. "Goar?"

"Beora?"

"My family? Did any of them escape?"

He shook his great head sadly.

"What happened? Father is careful with fire." She choked. "I was asleep. Smelled smoke. No window in my room. Tried to leave through kitchen. Filled with flames. Tried to shout, wake my family. Smoke so thick, I couldn't breathe. Trapdoor."

She stopped for a moment, coughing painfully. Goar could see the exposed chest muscles contract where the skin had been burned away. He didn't tell her of the arsonist.

"Cellar," she whispered, her strength failing. "Still so hot. Oh, Goar, the pain. Help me."

"I can't help you," answered Goar. "You need care beyond my abilities. I think beyond anyone's. I'm sorry."

"Please, stay with me." She tried to clutch his fur but the muscles in her hand would not respond. She slipped into unconsciousness.

Goar sat patiently by her side waiting for an end to the raspy breathing. Time slipped by until the silence was broken by the sound of Kaie approaching. He raised his paw to kill Beora.

"Don't!" Kaie's voice was harsh.

Goar froze with his powerful paw in the air. He retracted his claws.

"What have we here?" asked Kaie.

"Just a girl on the point of death," said Goar. "I was about to finish her off. No use leaving her alive. Someone might come and decide to help her."

Kaie examined the blackened body. "No healer could help her, that I know," she replied. She paused in thought. "But I think I could."

Goar started in surprise. "You?"

Kaie laughed. "I want to use her. My magic may be able to enhance what the fire has begun."

They brought Beora to the caves where Kaie worked her spells and brewed her potions. Beora's body partially healed. Most wounds closed, but her skin remained black and blistered. In spots, it was so thin it appeared translucent; arteries, veins, and muscles could be glimpsed beneath.

The pain was overwhelming. Kaie's magic intensified the fire within until it became a weapon. Now, Beora burned whomever she touched. Tables, dishes, plants, and rocks were safe, unless she chose to submit them to fire. But anything with a heart would start to burn regardless of her wishes. Her body never healed, but neither did those with whom she came in contact. And so Beora became another tool of the evil wizard.

Kaie ensured Beora's dependency and obedience. Each morning, she gave Beora a potion. It stopped the pain without rendering her unconscious; there was no medication like it in Dawn's End. Without this drink, Beora would be driven mad with agony. But the soothing liquid must be earned. Kaie commanded the girl to burn at her bidding. Any sign of resistance, and Beora's potion would be withheld until she begged for forgiveness.

Goar and Beora developed a deeper friendship. They avoided the others, but obeyed Kaie when compelled. She held the power to inflict agony on both of them. Each understood the other's frustrations, fears, and deep, dark shame.

They kept themselves separate from the other three. Beora chose a chamber farthest away from the lower tunnels. Goar slept in a tree outside the cave entrance. Still, neither could completely escape the horror.

"I wake in the night," Beora told Goar. "I can hear the faint, echoing shrieks of Lachish's victims even here."

"I know," he said. "I hear them no matter where I go. Plug your ears with wax."

"I do, and I hum a tune I used to sing to Clayton. Sometimes, I cry, and my tears hiss instead of falling."

Beora never shared her feelings with Riva. The other woman looked on Beora with obvious disdain. She called Beora a soft and dependent fool. She mostly ignored the panther.

In turn, Goar and Beora found Riva disgusting. Riva could escape at any time, yet she chose to stay. This was beyond their comprehension.

Lately, Riva had been egging Kaie on to more frequent acts of violence. Beora was dependent on Kaie for the painkilling drug, while Riva seemed committed to the horror. Like an addict, Riva's appetite increased steadily. Beora and Goar ached for freedom, but Riva cherished her wicked life.

Beora wore gloves and a red, long-sleeved, hooded gown that trailed the floor. Wearing it, she was able to move around with some safety. Occasionally, the small animals brushed against Beora's enchanted clothes and were safe. Any creature that made contact with her skin was instantly burned.

The first time she unintentionally touched Goar bare-handed, she screamed and jumped back. The panther tensed, expecting to burst into flames. But nothing happened. At least they could touch each other.

Goar tried to help Beora ease her miserable life. She delighted in the wild creatures that sought the caves and hid them from her violent mistress. Although Goar was carnivorous, he ranged far from where Beora's little friends might abide. Generally, he consumed fish from the river, reluctant to kill another mammal. There were rules for those of the panther lineage.

Kaie tolerated Beora's affection for the forest creatures, as long as she obeyed a direct order to kill. Periodically, Kaie tested her by demanding the death of a night bird or animal captured by Lachish. After these encounters, Beora was withdrawn and depressed for days. Her green eyes — bare of lashes or brows — mirrored her desperate sorrow. Goar sat quietly by, hoping his presence brought some comfort.

Kaie didn't order the death of a human without cause. She knew not to push Beora too far; the girl was unpredictable. As a guard against attack while traveling, Beora was invincible. Flying arrows turned to ash before they could strike. Swords became too hot to hold. Anyone foolish enough to try hand-to-hand combat quickly died screaming. Beora would fight anyone to keep Kaie alive.

If it had only been him under Kaie's control, Goar would have risked killing the wizard. But he knew that, without Kaie, Beora's life would be agony. Kaie had assured her servant would not die without the potion. She would simply writhe in an eternal inferno of agony.

Durward paused and then turned to his companions. "If you both wish that we search for lilyvern, then I agree."

The trip took the rest of that day and part of the next, with Kent moved in a litter. Anastacia insisted on doing her share of the carrying. It was slower when she helped, but not much, and they understood her need to contribute.

"Tell me about the lilyvern," Anastacia said when they stopped for food.

"The Pond of the Lilyvern is — or was — one of the wonders of Dawn's End. The lilyvern are part human, part plant," explained Misty as she passed out chunks of cheese.

"Get out!" Anastacia wrinkled her nose.

Misty looked startled but then realized Anastacia was using a colloquialism. "I make them sound homely, but they are incredibly beautiful people. They mature at three and live for only sixteen years."

Anastacia paused with the cheese partway to her mouth. "Oh, that's my age!"

"Really?" said Durward. He unwrapped a flatbread, tore off pieces, and passed them around.

Misty paused, studying Anastacia. "Sixteen is young."

I guess they thought I was older, thought Anastacia as she chewed.

Misty continued. "Their roots have incredible healing power, which they generously share with other species." She held out a bag with dried apple slices. Anastacia took a fist full.

"And the songs," said Durward.

"Yes, the songs." Misty paused, a faraway look in her eyes.

"What about the songs?" Anastacia had an odd image of sunflowers holding microphones. She suppressed a laugh.

"Their roots heal the body, but their songs heal the mind," said Misty. "It is like music in the wind. No words, but never quite the same. The Pond of the Lilyvern was the place to go to recover. No one ever left without their pain diminished."

"I see why they would be a target of Kaie."

When they arrived, the Pond of the Lilyvern looked like an ordinary marshland to Anastacia. Despondently, she examined the green, filmed surface.

"I'm sorry," said Durward. "But there is nothing here. Kaie was very thorough. She will not be easily subdued."

A voice bubbled up from the water. "You aim to subdue the evil wizard?"

The group broke into smiles. "I knew it," said Sacha. "I could smell her when we approached. She's over here somewhere."

Everyone followed the leopard along the shore. Misty gasped with delight at a small, white bud on the water's surface.

"We come in peace. I am Canice Misty. This is my husband, Durward, my friends, Sacha and Anastacia Newman, and Kent of the Lake who has been severely injured. We need your help."

The flower trembled. It rose out of the water, attached to the lilyvern underneath. She had white hair, green skin, and yellow eyes. She stood with the water around her waist. Anastacia could not tell if there were legs below. Leaves hid her naked female torso from view.

"I cannot be of much help," she said. "I am but two years old and can give only a little root. Your friend will recover in time without me."

Durward interrupted. "But where did you come from? When last I saw the Pond of the Lilyvern, there was no sign of life."

"I am Sida," she answered. "I was spared as a seed by being encased in a string of frog's eggs. I escaped Kaie's notice. Since then, I have grown quietly, hiding from passersby. I do not want her to know I exist."

"We will not betray you." Misty said. "We need some root to heal our friend so that we may continue on to Kaie's caves. We seek to subdue her."

"Help us," said Anastacia. "And we will avenge the destruction of your kind."

The others looked at her in dismay. *Yikes,* she thought. *I guess I said the wrong thing.*

"I do not seek vengeance." Sida began to sink below the surface. "I only wish to be left alone."

"Wait," said Durward. "We won't harm you, but Kaie will. She is sure to learn of your existence as you grow."

Sida stopped. "It matters not." She sighed. "I am the last of my kind. Without a male, my species dies when I die."

"All the more reason for you to live your full sixteen years," said Misty, "but, if you care so little for your life, why will you not run the small risk of helping us?"

"True," Sida answered, once again fully surfacing. "You want my root to heal the wounded man?"

Misty nodded. "His name is Kent of the Lake. He is a solid friend and a brave man. He travels with us to Kaie. We hope to remove her bracelet of power and return Dawn's End to peace."

"Peace. I should like to see peace in my lifetime, even if I can have no children to enjoy it."

"Neither can I," said Misty softly. "I had an illness that has made it impossible to bear children. But I care for all the children of Dawn's End and want them to grow in joy."

"We are sisters in our loss, but you remind me to see beyond my own pain. He is a beautiful man, like moonlight. I will heal him."

"Thank you," said Misty, pulling off her dress to reveal a short white tunic and underpants. She waded into the water to the lilyvern, took out a knife, and dived below the water. She arose with a thick, white, stringy root the length of her hand.

"Goodbye, noble travelers, and good fortune." Sida smiled sadly and sank from view.

"Goodbye, Sida," they responded, "and thank you."

Misty cut open the root and scraped out the soft interior. She unraveled Kent's bandages and spread the yellow-gold substance in the wound. She quickly rewound the cloth before the blood could wash away the medicine.

"We will rest here tonight. By tomorrow, he will be fit to travel on his own," she said to the others.

"Tomorrow!" said Anastacia. It was the first she had spoken since her awkward comment on vengeance. *This I gotta see,* she thought.

Mornings were the hardest for Beora. She lay there, postponing the day. Thinking about her life with Kaie made her chest ache, heavy and hot. She felt crippled within. The weightiness threaded its way through her body. She sank onto the rock, unable to move.

Was life really worth so much when it was merely existence? Was she worth so much when her life brought only pain to others? If only she could find a way out of it all.

"Beora!" The wizard's screech stabbed through her lungs, raking her stomach.

Beora rolled onto her side and hugged her knees. Kaie was calling. No one could ever refuse her summons. Willing or unwilling.

Beora exaggerated her own importance as a way of coping with the wizard's unpredictable temper. But Beora knew, if she rebelled, she would be killed. Kaie, like everyone else, would continue on in the same path with or without Beora. Her own existence was unimportant, meaningless.

"Beora!"

Kaie's voice sounded closer. She resented having to come to her servant's quarters. Beora had convinced her she could not hear the bell from her cavern. That way she hoped the wizard might summon her less frequently, although she usually sent Riva or Lachish to fetch her. That was worse. Riva's hatred burned like Beora's own fire. Lachish, himself a hideous abomination, cringed at her freakish appearance and abilities.

Beora moaned. The tips of her fingers and toes were burning with pain. Pain only Kaie could stop. Taking a deep breath, she answered the summons.

"Sida." Kent called the name softly, not wanting to wake the others before the sun rose. Birds twittered in the trees, and a soft breeze carried the heavy smell of pond water.

The flower stirred, but did not rise.

"It's Kent of the Lake. I want to thank you. Please let me see your face." He held his hand above his eyes, peering into the pond.

The lily rose, revealing a delicate green face lit by moonlight. Water streamed down her skin. Her face was oval, topped with little mats of wet white hair. Her lips were tiny, shaped in a pout. She stopped when her shoulders broke the surface.

Kent blinked. "You're lovely."

She gave a small smile and rose out of the water to her waist, leaves protecting her modesty.

He kneeled on the bank in front of her. "Thank you for saving my life."

"You weren't in danger," she said in her sweet, high voice. "Misty could have healed you." She shook her hair, water spraying from her hair. The mats separated into strands, some fluffing up in the breeze.

"Not in a few hours. It was urgent that I recover quickly."

"Are you so important?" She gestured with her tiny hand.

Kent laughed. "Not really. But I *must* be with them when they confront Kaie."

Sida shook her head sadly. "You will be killed, and my root will be wasted."

"No. I know that I won't." His voice was firm, confident.

"You will all be killed," said Sida. "The wizard is powerful and quite insane."

Kent gave a crooked grin. "Cheerful little weed, aren't you?"

The lilyvern began to sink.

"Wait! I didn't mean to insult you. Please. I was only teasing. Making a joke. I do that with my friends."

She stopped when the water lapped her chin. "Being alone so much, I have become depressed and see the world clothed in mourning. I find nothing humorous."

Kent put one fist on his hip. "Life without humor isn't life at all. You can't close yourself off like that."

"It has been so long since I had someone to talk with." She sighed. "I have almost forgotten how."

"So talk to me." He sat down on the grass and crossed his legs.

"Sometimes I talk to the frogs or the insects, or even myself," she said. "I would like to listen to your voice for a while. Tell me about yourself, Kent of the Lake."

"My favorite subject." He gave a dimpled grin, showing his gleaming, white teeth. He wiggled his eyebrows. "Settle back, pretty Sida. There's a lot to tell, although a gentleman has to keep some things private."

Chapter Seven — Lupas and Traps

The group left shortly after Kent's conversation with Sida. They were cheered by Kent's quick recovery but disappointed that the lilyvern did not sing for them. Anastacia suspected Kaie had ended the lilyvern's music forever.

They walked all day, periodically stopping to rest or eat the fruit, cheese, and bread Misty had packed.

What I wouldn't give for a hot, juicy hamburger right now, thought Anastacia as she chewed a stringy, yellow fruit when they made camp for the night. *And thick arena French fries doused in vinegar.*

Anastacia kept Misty company during the first part of the evening. She felt too wired to fall sleep. They did not allow Anastacia to be on watch alone.

Like I can't yell for help if someone shows up, she thought.

Durward took the middle watch, then Sacha. The sun was sending its first tendrils of light over the land when Sacha stirred. Anastacia opened her eyes and looked at her questioningly.

"Lie quietly," the panther said.

Now what? thought Anastacia. *More bandits?*

A small shadow flicked across her view. Anastacia tensed. Was it one of Kaie's assassins? The shape reached the side of Kent and paused. It bent. Anastacia saw the shape of a dagger rise into view. Before she could scream, Sacha had crossed the distance and was upon the figure with a mighty roar.

The assassin thudded to the ground with a thin cry, followed by a rush of breath as Sacha pressed on the body. The others rose, and Misty lit a lantern. The panther dwarfed the small person under her front paws.

"She sends midgets to murder us in the night," said Durward.

"No," Misty said. "It's a child." Her voice caught. "I can't continue if she is going to make us fight children."

"Children with knives can kill the same as adults," said Sacha as she stepped off the boy. He rolled over with a whimper.

"I w-wasn't g-gonna kill nobody." The boy stammered as he sat up, his legs splayed in front of him. "Honest. I d-don't even know who you are."

"Then why were you standing over Kent of the Lake with a dagger in your hand?" asked Anastacia.

"I was gonna st-steal it. It's worth mo-money. M-Maybe I could use it to get game. I was lookin' for-for food too."

Misty lowered her lamp to look more closely at the prone child. She picked up the fallen dagger. "Step back, Sacha," she said. "He can't hurt us now."

"I wasn't gonna hurt no-nobody," the boy said, sitting up and rubbing his knees and chin. "By the cr-crystal, you didn't have to drive me into the ground."

Sacha growled. "You're lucky I had my claws velveted when I landed."

The child looked at her sorrowfully with large, brown eyes. His clothes were in tatters, his hair was a knotted mess of dark curls, and his toes protruded from his shoes.

"He's as thin as a skeleton," said Misty.

"And as tattered as a scarecrow," Durward said.

The boy pulled his ragged vest around himself protectively. "My n-name is B-Bedad," he stammered.

"This little sapling couldn't hurt me." Kent laughed.

The adults looked at each other.

"I don't know," said Durward. "Kaie can be very devious."

Kent teased the boy. "So, do we run him through or let him go?"

Bedad's eyes widened in fear. He clenched his fists and stumbled to his feet.

"Neither," said Misty as she touched the child's shoulder. Bedad jerked away.

"He's a lost little soul in need of our care. What do you think, Anastacia?"

Bedad swallowed nervously as Anastacia examined his face. "I agree with Misty. He needs our help."

"It seems we accept your story," said Durward.

"We were just about to start breakfast," said Anastacia. "Perhaps you would like to join us, if you promise not to run off with any of the utensils."

Bedad sighed with relief. "I promise. I can help. I'm a pretty good cook with simple stuff."

Anastacia punched him lightly on the shoulder. "That's good, 'cause I'm not."

Bedad saw the lights dance in his mind. His temples throbbed as he stared into Anastacia's eyes.

"Come and help me make the gruel, then," said Misty.

Bedad shook his head at the strange faces, now resonating with familiarity. Especially Kent. He was sure he had seen him before, but where?

It took four bowls before Bedad finally lay back, satiated. Anastacia smiled and collected his bowl for washing, "That is, if you don't want another helping."

Bedad smiled, tempted to take one just to watch her reaction.

As Anastacia collected the dishes to take to the stream, Bedad heard her whisper to Misty, "We need to put some weight on those bones, get him some decent clothes, and clean him up."

He was happy with the food. Anything else would be paradise.

Misty donated a gray shirt, and Durward gave brown pants. The clothing had to be cut to size and was still roomy. He felt like the last potato in a burlap bag, but he didn't complain. It was clean and comfortable.

Durward fashioned simple moccasins from a leather ground sheet. Bedad was ecstatic with their soft warmth.

"You better take them off before they get soiled," said Anastacia. "You need a proper wash."

"Wash. How?"

"Well, we could ask Sacha to lick you clean." Anastacia said, teasingly. "But, how about in the stream."

"Not me." He crossed his arms. "It's too cold. I don't mind a little dirt."

"We do," said Kent as he pinched his nose. "And you have more than a *little* dirt."

"At least I'm not a sissy like you two." He glared at Kent and Durward.

"These men are far from sissies," said Anastacia. "They fought off eight bandits without blinking an eye. They, and I, don't believe dirt has anything to do with manliness. Of course, if you're afraid of a little cold water, we could heat some for you. You know, if you're delicate."

Kent laughed. "Sure. The ladies will give you a sponge bath right by the fire."

Bedad was horrified. "All right, all right." He held his hand up in a stop gesture. "I'll wash."

"What a foolish lad." Kent chuckled. "I would have taken the sponge bath."

Bedad put up a small protest when they passed him a lump of herbal-smelling soap.

"Either you scrub, or I'll scrub you myself," Anastacia insisted.

"No!"

She laughed. "All right, then. Kent, will you supervise him?"

"Yes, ma'am." Kent gave a bow.

"Help him wash that tangled hair. I'll be checking after so you'd better sparkle, Bedad." She handed him a soft drying cloth and pointed upstream. Bedad gave her a baleful look and trudged off, shoulders drooping.

Misty struggled not to smirk as he shuffled past.

Anastacia caught Kent's sleeve in passing and whispered, "Check for lice."

He nodded and grimaced.

"If this is what it's like to have a big sister," Bedad said, "I'm glad I'm an only child."

As she packed up, Anastacia said, "That boy's been neglected. He's so thin and ragged. His teeth are a mess. He looks like something the cat dragged in."

"What cat?" Durward looked confused.

"Just an expression. What kind of parents let a child get in that condition? That is long time neglect."

"Perhaps he has no parents," answered Durward. "Or they don't care what kind of shape he is in. This is an example of the decadence now spreading in our society. He needs good food, proper hygiene including a dentist, and the support of a loving family."

"You have dentists?" asked Anastacia as she fastened her pack.

"Of course. Don't be fooled by our lack of technical dependency. We are not backward." Durward stirred the coals, throwing dirt on any that still burned. "We simply hold different values than your people. Until recently, a child in this condition was unheard of. We will find someone to care for him."

"Couldn't we?" asked Anastacia. "If he's lost his parents, we can't just dump him. I don't think he'd be any problem."

"You sound like Misty." Durward shook his head. "And I'll tell you what I told her. Do you want to be responsible for delivering that child into Kaie's vicious hands?"

"Of course not." Anastacia undid the tie in her braid, ran her fingers through her hair, and started rebraiding.

"Then the sooner we find him a safe home, the better," said Durward.

Anastacia smiled welcomingly when Kent and Bedad returned.

"He is as clean as a dog-licked plate," said Kent boastfully.

Bedad held his arms out at his sides, displaying himself to her appraisal.

"Great job," said Anastacia.

Kent gave another little bow. "I'm fun to be with and fatherly, too. What more could you want in a man?"

Anastacia snorted. "Modesty wouldn't hurt."

"It was sure cold," said Bedad, "but I feel kinda tingly and good all over."

"Well, you look brand new," said Anastacia. "I figured there was a pleasant boy under all that dirt, but I didn't realize how handsome."

She raised her arm, fist forward. Bedad looked at it, confused. She laughed. "Lift your arm, and make a fist like me." He did. She bumped her fist against his.

"What's that?" he asked.

"That's what I do with my teammates when someone does something great."

"Okay." Bedad gave a self-conscious laugh. "What's to eat?" he asked.

Everyone groaned.

"I can't help it. All that scrubbing in cold water made me hungry."

"I think I've got something in my sack to stop that insatiable appetite for a while," answered Anastacia.

"What's insatiable?"

"It means always wanting more, never satisfied."

"I get satisfied. It just don't last for long."

Bedad devoured what was left of Anastacia's bread.

As they traveled, he plagued everyone with questions about themselves, the countryside, their venture, and anything else that crossed his mind. Whenever one adult tired, he moved on to a new target.

"You live alone?" he asked Anastacia as he fell in beside her.

"No, I live with my stepbrother and stepfather."

"No mother?"

"You need to develop some tact," interrupted Kent from behind.

"It's all right. My mother died two years ago. She had been sick for a long time."

Bedad pressed his lips together and nodded. "Too bad. My mother died last week."

"Good heavens!" Anastacia stopped walking and put her hand on his shoulder. "You poor kid. Is that why you're alone?" She dropped her hand.

"Yep." He nodded, matter-of-factly, and then started walking. Kent and Anastacia exchanged looks, and then she fell back in beside Bedad.

"Don't you have any relatives?" she asked.

He shrugged, one-shouldered. "They kinda disowned my mom before she died. She'd been sick for a long time too, but not like yours. Was she nice?"

"My mother? She was wonderful. I feel bad about the fights we had before she got sick. I was pretty stubborn. The last months, she was in the hospital a lot too."

"That's no good. How about your father?"

"My father died when I was three. Well, that's a long story, I'm told." She gestured toward Candice and Durward walking in front. "My stepfather, Jamail, is a good guy. He's been my dad since I was ten. He's quiet, quieter now. I think he still misses my mom."

Bedad raised one hand, palm up. "Why don't he get married again?"

Anastacia laughed. "It's not like picking out vegetables. Besides, he's lost two wives. Maybe he doesn't want to risk losing a third."

"So, what happened to your first dad?"

"He died in Africa. Oh, wait, that's not right. He's from Dawn's End, I just learned. And apparently he was a black panther man named Alaric Morrel."

"*The* Alaric Morrel!" Bedad's dark eyes widened, and his mouth dropped open.

"It would seem so," said Anastacia. She lifted a branch that protruded out into the trail and ducked under.

"Wow!" He digested that for a moment, studying her face. "So I guess you get that black hair from him."

"Yes."

"I like it," said Bedad. "But you must get your beauty from your mother."

"Smooth, kid." Kent put in.

Anastacia chuckled.

"What's it like, having a brother?" asked the boy.

Anastacia hesitated. "I love my stepbrother, and I know he loves me, but he's such a pain sometimes. Bossy." She made a face.

"He orders you around? I hate that."

"Not really," said Anastacia. "He's more subtle. He just tells me what I should do in such a way that I wind up feeling guilty if I don't do it and angry if I do. He's always worried I'm going to break my neck or something."

"Why?"

Anastacia shrugged. "I guess I take a lot of chances."

"Like coming here?" he asked.

She lowered her voice. "That wasn't really by choice."

He nodded. "So why *do* you take so many chances?"

She shrugged again. "When I figure that out, I'll let you know. I think it's time you quizzed someone else for a while."

Misty was also patient. Durward was a vast storage of fascinating information. Sacha was kind, but her answers were short. Kent told exciting tales of his many travels. He spoke of battles with bandits, gambling with rich and famous characters, and meeting beautiful women. Bedad soaked in every word, although the others raised their eyebrows occasionally. Anastacia indulged him the most. But, when he circled back to her for the third time, she exclaimed, "No more questions!"

"I can't help it," he said. "My appetite for learning is insatiable."

Kaie paced, her black robe twisting and flapping around her skinny frame, while Goar related his report. She screeched.

"How can this be? I destroyed the lilyvern myself two years ago. Now, you tell me a survivor has aided my enemies. I will not allow this!" She punched her tiny fist into her palm.

"Who knows what cures it may hold to thwart my plans? My door crystals are complete. My drug is aging well and will soon be ready for testing. Nothing must interfere." She halted abruptly and turned to Goar. "Ready the others! We leave in fifteen minutes. This last survivor of the lilyverns will be no more." She clenched her hands into fists, her eyes wide.

Riva added a bow and arrow, warm shirt, and breeches to her attire. She quickly packed food and water and joined Kaie.

Lachish was there before her. He had brought his sword, club, water bag, and pack of dried meat.

Goar reappeared. They waited impatiently for Beora.

"Where is that stupid ash head?" asked Kaie.

The others shrugged nervously.

"Find her," she told Goar. "She has five minutes, or you will both feel my anger."

Kaie rubbed her temples. Dreams of the young woman had haunted her again last night. The woman in white, smiling, eager, happy. She hated that woman. If she could remember who or where she was, Kaie would move mountains to reach her and rip those sweet lips from her face.

The leopard bowed and departed. Like lightning, he leapt from boulder to boulder following Beora's scent. Lying on her stomach, she was watching the mother owl feed her young on an adjacent ledge.

"Why are you not ready?" asked Goar. "This time wasting has made Kaie angry."

"I don't want to march on the lilyvern," she whispered. "I'm glad one has survived. I won't slaughter the last of a beautiful species." She turned back to watch the owls, resting her chin on her folded hands.

"You will come right now, or we may be slaughtered ourselves."

"No." She set her jaw stubbornly and refused to look at Goar.

Goar roared, leapt to the owl's nest, and crunched the mother in his powerful jaws. He swept the nest of owlets to their death. "Come, *now*, or you will be next."

Beora looked into his red eyes for a second, then stood and turned away.

She filled her water bag and threw supplies into her pack. Kaie was waiting with Riva and Lachish at the cave entrance. She hissed when Beora approached. Beora gave a small bow in return.

Kaie turned and strode away, followed by Lachish, Riva, and then Goar. Beora took up the rear. She did not speak to Goar as they traveled toward the lilyvern.

Kaie was cross with her throughout the day, mistrustful, testing her. Beora had to ignite her mistress' dinner, a treehare, while it was still alive.

Then she was ordered to travel point, ready to take the impact of any enemies they might meet. It was a surprise to Kaie that they encountered danger from the rear.

Bandits, not realizing with whom they were dealing, attacked Lachish, who had traded places with Beora. They had assessed him as the most dangerous and so planned to take him out first. When he was killed, the women would be at their mercy. Goar, now traveling through the trees, had not been sighted.

With a battle cry, Lachish faced his adversaries. Wielding his club in one hand and his sword in the other, he dealt easily with the first three men. Others surged from the woods, hoping to take the women hostage. Lachish knew Kaie could take care of herself. He planned to kill as many as possible before they realized their stupidity and retreated.

With a resounding roar, Goar leapt from the trees onto a sword-wielding robber. The seasoned fighter sank to his knees within seconds, a fatal wound in his throat from the fearsome teeth. Goar whirled and, using his claws, disemboweled the man coming to aid his comrade.

Riva was most vulnerable. She stood between Kaie and Beora, loading her bow and letting fly the arrows with cool precision.

On her left, Beora intercepted incoming arrows, turning them to ash. She suppressed the urge to ignore a missile headed for Riva's heaving breasts. A courageous man approached her, and then went screaming into the woods, a rank tower of flame.

Kaie was in her element. Her arm raised, she laughed devilishly, flashing light from the bracelet to her targets. The first she turned to a pile of sand. The second became a small insect. The third melted into a puddle. The fourth came within arm's length before she turned him into a caterpillar which she ground underfoot.

The gang of bandits had rapidly diminished to three, who were attempting to escape with their lives, if not their sanity. Goar selected the quickest runner and pursued him with efficient leaps.

Lachish cut off a panting, muscular bandit and caught him in his grasp. He gripped him in his vise until bones began to snap.

Kaie selected the last, imprisoning him in a circle of electricity while she pondered his fate. No one was ever allowed escape. No one lived to tell the tale, unless Kaie chose to maim him and send him out to fill others with fear.

The wild-eyed bandit fell to his knees. "Great wizard," he cried. "We did not know who you were. We would never have attacked one as powerful as you."

"My name is Kaie, you stupid beast." She hissed. "Say it when you address me."

"Kaie. Majestical wizard. Kaie. Please have mercy on my worthless life. I surrender my sword."

"Blasphemer! Kaie gives no mercy." Spittle flew from her mouth as she shouted. "A pathetic creature like you deserves to die the death of your nightmares."

The man looked around at the carnage and shrank within himself. He shook his head and moaned. "No, no, please."

"What is it you fear most?" asked Kaie as she circled him. "An animal?"

His eyes widened. She raised her arm, and a creature, half-lizard and half-bear, appeared beside her. The man lurched back.

"Even a big, brave boy like you has an inner fear. The kind that makes you flail in your sleep and wake screaming. Perhaps, it is bugs?" Instantly the man was covered in millions of wasps. He froze in place, not daring to disturb them. Beora fought the urge to vomit as one climbed into his ear.

"No, not that," mused Kaie. She tapped her foot in thought. "What is it then?"

She waved the wasps out of existence, watching him carefully for a clue, and he granted it. An involuntary glance in Beora's direction gave him away.

"Oh." Kaie sighed. "How disappointing. It's fire, isn't it?"

"No! No!"

"I shall have Beora toast you for a while," she said, grinning crookedly. "Make sure you really enjoy it. Not many men get to die the way they yearn to."

"No!" The bandit screamed, trying to breach the electric ring.

"Beora, start with his fingers. Burn them to stumps."

Beora looked at the quivering man, then at Kaie.

"Mistress, please. You can control fire. Why don't you do it?"

"I said I want you to do it." The wizard raised her arm towards Beora.

Beora recoiled, then raised her hand and brought it close to the victim's. The heat radiating from her body singed his fingers while Kaie held him rigid in a spell. The man screamed hideously.

"Now his feet," said Kaie. "A nice toasty brown, if you please." She giggled shrilly.

Beora hesitated.

"Now!"

Beora complied, tears flowing so quickly that they sizzled partway down her cheeks. Her hand shook violently as the man's screams became guttural.

"His hair," said Kaie.

Singing inward, the bandit's hair dissolved toward his skull. Beora leaned forward and touched his forehead. Instantly, flames shot through his nose, mouth, and eyes.

Kaie raised her arms, stopping the fire. Her gesture was ineffective, for the man sank to his knees in death.

Kaie screamed. "You boar dung, you did that on purpose!" screamed Kaie.

"No, mistress." Beora lowered herself into a deep bow. "It was an accident."

"Liar!" Kaie slapped Beora's left temple. "You think to disobey me?" She slapped her right temple twice as hard, and then stepped back, panting. "We shall see whether a day without my potion heals your clumsy hand."

"No, mistress, please." Beora fell to her knees. "It was a mistake."

Kaie snarled. "You bet it was. We will return to the caves." She whirled away from Beora, who had fallen forward on her hands, whimpering. "My enjoyment has been spoiled by this treachery. The lilyvern can wait. I must root out all disobedience before I continue."

When the forest assumed the ruggedness of the Canadian north, Anastacia felt in her element. Coniferous trees, similar to those in her world, but of a darker green, filled the air with their heady Christmas scent. Their feet were cushioned by the layer of needles on the forest floor. Anastacia paused to collect a cone of unusual spiral shape. That is when she heard the moan for the first time. As she turned to her companions, Sacha met her eyes.

"I heard it too," said the panther, before Anastacia could speak.

"What is it?" she whispered. "Is someone hurt?"

"An animal in pain," answered Sacha.

"Where did it come from?" A growl, and then another moan sounded to her left. They nodded.

"Spread out, and walk quietly," said Sacha. "But not too far apart. It may be an injured wild animal. That can be dangerous."

I know, thought Anastacia. *You don't grow up in Thunder Bay and not know about wild animals.*

An unusual silence settled over the forest as the travelers threaded their way. Anastacia was on one end of the line. She tried to move the branches gently, straining her ears.

Ducking under a thick tree, she was suddenly aware of luminous eyes watching her. She rose slowly. Four paces ahead was a powerful canine, much like a timber wolf, but bigger and with shaggier fur. His mouth hung open displaying long, sharp teeth. Anastacia swallowed and wet her lips. The wolf-creature bent its head and licked his right hind paw. He was in a leg-hold trap, the vicious metal teeth cutting into his skin. The earth around the anchor chain was bloodied.

Damn, thought Anastacia. *They have those horrible things here, too.*

The wolf-creature balefully lifted his head and moaned again. The sound hurt Anastacia's stomach. She took a cautious step forward. The animal watched, waited. She took the last three steps and bent beside the animal. Her instinct told her to run but something deeper drove her on.

"Don't be afraid." She used her babysitting voice. "I'm going to help you."

Anastacia held her hand to be sniffed, but the animal turned away to lick his wound. Inching closer, Anastacia touched the trap. The wolf-creature had tugged the base from the earth. Anastacia examined the thickness of the springs.

"That's a good boy," she said in a soothing voice. "You're not a talking animal are you?" She spoke comfortingly as she placed a palm on each upper bow. "Such a good wolf. Such a *good boy*. Steady now. I'm going to push."

She leaned forward, placing her weight on both springs. The animal lurched as the trap eased, and then yelped as it snapped shut again. Anastacia froze, expecting his teeth to sink into her arm. Instead, he licked her hand.

"You understand what I'm trying to do, don't you boy? Even if you can't speak. Damn, I hate these things. I've got it figured out now. I'm going to stand on the bows. It might twist a bit, but it'll open."

Goose bumps rose on Anastacia's skin as the wolf-creature gave a half-moan, half-growl while she pushed with her heels. The bows creaked down the jaw posts and then locked in place. The animal jumped free. It turned to face her; it was larger than she had realized.

"Nice wolf," she said, her eyes widening. "Be a good boy."

The animal whimpered, flopped to the earth, and set to licking.

"He's going to need that bandaged," said Misty. Anastacia gave a small jump at the sound. Glancing around, she saw Misty and Durward standing close by.

Sacha spoke from an overhead branch, "It's a wild lupa, you know. He didn't understand a word you said."

"He must have!" Anastacia looked back at the lupa, intently licking his injured leg. "He let me hurt him to release the trap."

"He understood your tone and your intent," said Misty. "Even so, you took quite a risk."

"Yes," Durward said. "Most commendable."

"What was commendable?" asked Kent as he arrived with Bedad. Misty explained while Anastacia looked awkwardly from the lupa to her feet.

"By the crystal!" said Bedad in an awed voice. "You *are* brave."

"Doesn't surprise me," said Kent.

"I just did it on impulse," Anastacia said. "My brother would say I was stupid."

"He would be wrong," said Sacha. "I arrived the moment you started toward the lupa. You were conscious of the danger and handled it well. It took courage. You didn't know I was ready to leap if he attacked. I'm sure he smelled me; he glanced in my direction. He seems an intelligent animal and understands we are no threat."

Anastacia laughed. "He's bigger even than a timber wolf, so I probably wasn't much of a threat."

Sacha said, "I am proud to travel with you Anastacia, true daughter of the Esteemed Nicole and noble Alaric Morrel."

Anastacia blushed at this. The lupa leapt to his feet and limped off into the forest.

"Wait," said Misty. She spoke to the others. "I have to check that wound. No telling how long he was in the trap. It might get infected."

Durward and Kent nodded and headed west where the lupa had gone. Sacha bounded ahead and followed his scent.

"I don't understand," said Anastacia. "We were already delayed by Kent's injury. No telling how long it will take to catch the lupa."

"Would you have us abandon it after you took such a risk to help it?" asked Durward.

"But reaching Kaie quickly is important." Anastacia ducked and twisted, avoiding branches, stepping carefully through the underbrush.

"Saving a life is important, too," said Misty. "Our journey to Kaie may even be futile. Catching the lupa will not be. Why toss away a chance to be of real help?"

"Then why come at all?" said Anastacia. "There must be plenty of people you could be helping right now instead of going on this quest. Besides, it's only an animal."

The others exchanged glances. Misty clenched her lips in dismay.

"So are we," she said as they resumed following the lupa.

Kent squeezed her shoulder, "Don't worry. People here see things differently than you do. In Dawn's End, most cultures live in the present. We believe it is important to make every action, each day, filled with compassion. It would be impossible for my people to turn their backs on someone in need, in the hopes that tomorrow they might do a greater deed."

Anastacia nodded and fell in line in front of Kent. A moment before, she felt like a heroine. Now, she was embarrassed and irritated. They always held her opinion in disdain.

What am I doing here anyway? thought Anastacia. *Bandits trying to kill me. Handling an injured wolf. Oh, pardon me, a lupa. Off to trap a wizard. And still I'm in the doghouse with these people.*

Misty and Anastacia tried in vain to call the lupa back. Over two hours were spent following it.

"He's running," said Sacha. "I don't know how, but he is."

They sped up the pursuit. Suddenly, Sacha stopped at the edge of a small clearing. The others caught up and paused.

"What is it?" asked Anastacia.

"A shelter," answered Kent. "Not made by an animal."

Chapter Eight — Pack Animals

Lachish and Riva made themselves scarce when Kaie ordered Beora to her chamber. Both would have enjoyed seeing the fool punished, but Kaie had a tendency to get over stimulated when she was this angry and lash out at everyone in the room.

The crazy wizard, thought Lachish. *Someday we'll all turn on each other and end up in a bloodbath.* The thought both terrified and thrilled him. It would be the ultimate battle, and he would triumph.

Lachish headed toward the exit. These screeching women had left him edgy. He needed something to calm his nerves. He'd seen women's clothes on the line of a nearby farm. He had to vent his frustrations, or else he'd start to howl.

When he reached the homestead, he burst in. Subtlety was never his strong suit.

Lachish was forced to kill the husband, not that it gave him any regrets, but it did slow him down. It was near evening when he returned with the woman. She was no elegant lady, but she would do. He'd heard an infant crying in the background and wondered absently if he should take it for Kaie. Then the bitch had clawed his face, and he'd had to pummel her into unconsciousness and carry her back.

Now, she hung limply in shackles, Lachish's twisted needs indulged.

"You cheated me, half-bear." Riva complained as she entered. "You killed the lovely lady without letting me watch."

"Thoo what?"

Riva examined the woman's clothes. Then she lifted a limp calloused hand. "This was no lady," she whispered. To Lachish, she said, "I could tell Kaie you took a woman from the farm. She doesn't like you to raid so closely to the caves. I know that's where you got her. There wasn't time to go anywhere else."

"Maybe I got her from a caravan," he mumbled.

"She's not wearing traveling clothes. I could get you in big trouble," she hissed.

"You won't. You don't want to piss off Kaie today."

"Maybe." She pushed the woman's hair out of her face. "She's still breathing. Did her husband defend her?"

"To the deafth."

"She shouldn't be here. She's not some spoiled lady. She's just a regular girl."

"You getting soft?" He sneered.

She crossed her arms. "No."

"I think you are. Maybe I should tell Kaie you're just like Beora."

"Do what you like, pig." She shrugged. "I don't care."

He threw water in the farm woman's face. She moaned, opened her eyes, and screamed. Lachish laughed.

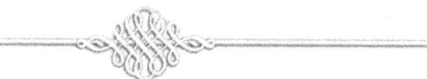

The woman's eyes reminded Riva of her sister, Carlie. She enjoyed watching Lachish with men or the spoiled ladies of leisure, the kind of women who had screamed for Carlie to die, but this woman was a little too close to home for comfort. The best thing to do would be to push Lachish into losing control. Mocking and insulting him, questioning his manhood, she drove him into killing the woman quickly.

"Lachish, you stupid bear spoor, when will you ever learn the value of foreplay?"

Lachish sucked his breath in between his foul teeth. He reached toward the lady's body, hanging limply in chains. His arm muscles tensed as his thumbs dug into her sockets.

"Pathetic," muttered Riva. "She's already dead."

"Don't tell Kaie about her," he said.

Riva sighed.

"I should have took her eyes first," he mumbled.

Riva grimaced. "What the hell are you going to do with her eyes?"

"They're a present, for Kaie."

He carried his treasures away. Riva shook her head. She turned to the dead woman.

"The kind of company I keep these days," she muttered. She stepped forward and pulled the woman's eyelids down over her empty sockets. She sighed and wiped her hands on the woman's clothes.

"You and I," she whispered to the corpse. "We're not much different."

That's when she realized the woman's blouse was wet with breast milk. She swore.

"Too much," she muttered, "too much, too much."

Kent and Durward approached the shelter, hands on their sword hilts, with Sacha between them, Misty and Anastacia close behind.

"You not in danger," said the inhabitant as he stepped into view. Beside him stood the lupa, wagging its tail.

"Griswold show me, you not one who hurt," said the slightly built man. His hair was dark brown, straight and long. A thick scruffy beard hid most of his light brown face. He was dressed in brown and green.

"We found him in a trap," said Anastacia as she stepped around Kent.

Griswold limped toward her and licked her hand. She gently petted his muscular head, a thrill tingling through her. She'd always been attracted to powerful predators. To have that muscle and speed, those claws and teeth, what a thrill that would be.

"You free him?"

"Yes, she did," said Durward. He introduced the group ending with, "Anastacia Newman, daughter of the Esteemed Nicole and Alaric Morrel."

Anastacia felt like she had recently learned she was royalty, but the man quickly deflated any sense of importance.

"Who they?" he asked.

"You are not familiar with the history of the panther people?" asked Durward.

"Little. I keep to self — with friends."

"Friends?"

The small man whistled. One by one, a pack of lupas appeared, materializing without warning.

"I be Randolph of lupas." He smiled. "They not hurt if you mean us no harm."

"That's a relief," muttered Kent.

"I tell them leave. You nervous." He blew a single note, and the lupas melted into the forest. "Sit. Rest. I fix Griswold leg."

"That's why we were following him," said Misty. "I wanted to check his wound. I can heal those who have the blood of beast. I am a piper."

"Know of pipers," said Randolph as he gave her a respectful bow.

Misty unfastened the small reed pipe from her belt. The others watched expectantly. Misty blew a soft note. Griswold whined, came to her and lay at her feet.

A soft, sweet tune filled the air. It spoke of the promise of spring, seedlings struggling to the sun, speckled eggs hatching, and fish leaping upstream to spawn.

Anastacia breathed in the sound like the scent of a wild rose. Then she noticed the flower patterns on Misty's dress were moving, weaving to the music. *They are mesmerizing,* she thought. She remained spellbound until Griswold leapt to his feet with a bark.

The lupa jumped, chased his tail and raced round the waiting people. Amazed, Anastacia realized that his leg was completely healed. There was no trace of a limp.

"You did that?" she asked Misty.

Misty nodded, smiling, as she retied the simple pipe. "I can heal the wild things, mammals and birds, but I cannot restore life."

"Why didn't you heal Kent?"

Kent interrupted. "Hey! Do I look like a wild thing to you? Don't answer that."

Everyone laughed.

Misty said, "Kent is all man."

I'll second that, thought Anastacia.

"He has no blood of the beast in him," said Misty. "The more human you are, the less effect. I would have a small effect on Durward. A bit better effect on people like myself and even stronger impact on someone like Sacha. You, I don't know. Even though you are Alaric Morrel's child, you seem to have mostly your mother's qualities. Griswold was no difficulty at all."

"Why didn't you just pipe to him in the forest?"

"He was too far away," said Misty. "He must be able to see me and hear me. He must sit close to me and listen to the music, be calm and receptive. Then he will heal."

"That's some fantastic ability."

"Yes," said Randolph. "In your debt. What do for you? Must repay great kindness. Griswold closest friend."

"Join us," Durward said.

"Why? What do?"

Over a meal provided by Randolph, they explained the situation.

"I not know. Kaie no hurt me."

"Did people set traps before she gained her power?" asked Kent.

"No," said Randolph. "She do?"

"Not her, but one of her followers," said Durward. "At the very least, it was someone corrupted by her evil influence. There will be more traps and much more pain in the forest if we do not stop her. More people killing for pleasure, trophies, or furs they don't need."

Griswold whimpered and licked Randolph's hand. He then trotted to Anastacia and Misty and did the same. Randolph laughed.

"Griswold answer. Other lupas stay with cubs. Griswold, me, after sleep, we go with you."

The quiet Randolph showed a canny knack for locating trails, campsites, and food. Upstaged by this superior woodsman, Kent told even more remarkable stories of his exploits.

Unaware of his effect, Randolph walked with Griswold, occasionally speaking to him in a combination of words, sounds, and hand movements. The lupa's hunting prowess, combined with Sacha's, kept the travelers in game.

Anastacia was charmed by Griswold's merriness. She socialized with Bedad, Randolph, and the lupa. She copied the man's hand movements and soon had the canine responding to simple commands.

"How do you do that?" asked Bedad as he ineffectively signaled again.

"I don't know. Randolph, why will Griswold follow my commands and not Bedad's?"

"Bedad young. Griswold pack animal. I leader. Dominant in pack. Others must fight to rise."

"But I didn't fight him," said Anastacia. "Why should I be dominant over him in the pack order."

"Not sure. Maybe 'cause you open trap. You powerful. Maybe, he love you. You female. Partner. Maybe 'cos you have panther blood, too. Special."

Bedad asked, "You mean he won't ever obey my commands?"

"If want to. Not command. Favor."

"Oh." Bedad looked crestfallen.

Randolph smiled and picked up a stick. "Fetch for fun. I start."

As they walked through the meadowland, Bedad happily tossed the stick for Griswold. The lupa's energy seemed boundless.

Anastacia laughed when the lupa trotted up with the stick in his mouth, looked Bedad in the eye, and flung the toy over his shoulder a short distance away.

"I think he wants you to fetch this time!" she said.

"Right," said Griswold. "Boy's turn."

Bedad thought it was a great joke. He raced after the stick, mock barking. Then he threw it for Griswold. They continued for some time until the animal carried the stick off and buried it.

"Why'd he do that?" asked Bedad. "We could have just put it away for later if he was tired."

"Plenty sticks. Griswold say 'enough'. Still much walking today. Save feet."

"Yeah, I guess so," muttered Bedad.

"Come Bedad," said Anastacia, "tell us about your village. We really know very little about you."

"Not much to tell," he answered, rubbing the scar on his temple.

"How'd you get that?" asked Anastacia.

Bedad hastily put down his hand and shrugged.

"Remembering pain," said Randolph.

"I didn't mean to upset you," said Anastacia. "I wouldn't want to do that."

"I know," he murmured. "You'd never hurt me."

"Not intentionally," she said, reaching over to hug his shoulder. Bedad started to pull away, then relaxed and allowed the hug. They continued on in silence for a while.

"My mother threw a p-plate at me b-because the p-potatoes were overcooked."

Anastacia gasped. "No child should ever be treated like that!"

"Sometimes I can be really bb-bad," Bedad hung his head. "When I'm v-very angry, I hit things."

"You've probably had good reason to be angry."

"What d-do you do when you g-get angry?" asked the boy.

"Me? Well, I try to control my temper, but I often don't succeed, especially where my brother is concerned. Usually, I do something physical. Shoot hoops, practice shots on net, or work out. Sports keep me sane."

"I wish I c-could. I k-keep it all inside until I get s-so frustrated, I break something. Sometimes, I get c-caught, and then it's twice as b-bad. Isn't that c-cowardly?"

"Try telling people how you feel when you're upset," Anastacia said.

"So, who'd listen?" Bedad frowned.

"I would." She mussed his hair.

Griswold padded up and licked both their hands as though he approved.

Who am I to talk like such an expert, thought Anastacia. *I don't tell people how I really feel. Maybe I should take my own advice.*

Bedad stayed close to Anastacia when they broke camp and prepared their evening meal. He was far more skilled than she at cooking on an open fire. He knew just when to turn the meat, stir the food, and move the pot. Griswold and Sacha left to hunt.

"Durward," Anastacia said, "you never told me why you waited until now to begin this journey?"

"I had to be sure Kaie was responsible for the problems," he said as he added sticks to the fire. "Then it took some time to locate her base. Just before you came, I spent a month trying to marshal support for our endeavor."

"How did you do?" asked Anastacia.

He grimaced. "Not great, but Kent and Sacha agreed to join us immediately."

"I'm a fool for adventure," Kent said.

"A few others were undecided. I'm hoping when they see you and your bracelet they will choose in our favor."

"Did you go too, Misty?" asked Anastacia.

"No. I wanted to preserve food for our journey, take care of the garden, and set things in order. I wasn't sure when we would be back, once we left to meet Kaie."

"If ever," muttered Durward grimly.

"We'll do great," said Bedad. He smiled at each person in turn. The adults exchanged glances.

"Not we, Bedad," said Misty. "You stay behind at the next village."

"No!" he shouted, jumping to his feet. "I'm coming with you."

"Be reasonable, Bedad," Durward said. "We can't take care of a child while we're in the middle of a battle."

"I'm not a child! I'm twelve-years-old, and I can take care of myself! Nobody ever took care of me before." Bedad's face was flushed, and his fists were clenched.

"Well, they will now," said Misty.

"I'm the son of a wizard, you know." He crossed his arms and held his chin high. "Kaie might hunt me down and kill me. Then how would you feel?"

"What are you talking about?" said Misty.

"I heard my parents. My dad isn't my birth dad. He married my mom when I was a baby. My family name isn't really Kamek. My father was a wizard, killed in some kind of explosion."

"Who was he?"

"I don't know." He lowered his voice, dropped his arms and slumped. "That's all I heard." He straightened and his voice rose. "But my mom was afraid Kaie might find out and come for me. She said many of the children of wizards have died mysterious deaths."

"Is that true?" Anastacia asked Misty.

"There has been an uncommon number of wizard's children die since the explosion. We wondered, but we couldn't quite believe Kaie was involved."

"I've heard stories," said Kent, "that make me suspicious."

"Then Bedad is in danger," said Anastacia.

"Only if she knows about him," said Durward, "and, since he uses his stepfather's name, I'm sure she doesn't. He will be safer in the village than with us."

"So, you're gonna dump me off with some jerks who probably need a servant," said Bedad accusingly, hands on his hips. "Well, I ain't staying. I'll run away." He crossed his arms again, looking down his nose at Durward.

"That would be very thoughtless. My sister would be worried about you," said Misty.

"Your sister?" He lowered his arms.

Misty nodded. "Her name is Lissa."

"How do you know she'll want me? Maybe she'll be really bugged to have a stranger in her house."

"She'll be thrilled," said Misty. "Lissa could never have too many children. She has already adopted four. Three girls and a boy. The boy is about seven. I imagine he could use an ally."

"I ain't babysitting nobody's brood of orphans."

"Bedad," said Anastacia, "you're being very unfair. You haven't even met Lissa, or the other children. Why don't you wait and see? If she's as nice as Misty, and I'm sure she is, it will be much better than being alone."

"What do you know? You aren't even staying in Dawn's End. You're an outworlder!" Bedad marched out of the ring of firelight and slumped down in the darkness just beyond. "Leave me alone."

The group quietly finished their meal and cleared up. When Griswold returned, he went to Randolph and then trotted over to Bedad. He sat beside the boy and set his soft chin on the boy's lap. Bedad didn't respond. Softly, Griswold whined to be petted.

"Okay. Okay," said Bedad as he scratched the lupa behind the ears and under his throat. Griswold put one paw on the child's leg, then the other. He leaned forward and gave a sloppy, wet face lick. Bedad chuckled and soon the two of them were rolling and laughing. Anastacia smiled. The boy's outburst reminded her of her own temper. The lupa and the child stood up.

"I'm going for a walk with Griswold," said Bedad.

"Don't go too far," said Misty. "You never know what you might meet in these woods."

"I won't. And I'll stay with Griswold."

Randolph summoned the lupa. He gave quick commands. The animal ran back to Bedad. Together they headed off in the dusk.

"He safe," said Randolph. "Griswold protect cub."

Griswold and Bedad enjoyed a peaceful exploration. They cuddled together on a boulder surrounded by shrubs to watch the night arrive. The apricot moon revealed her gnarled face as the first stars blinked into view. Bedad sighed and rubbed Griswold's head. He was about to speak when a movement caught his eye. Someone was coming from the camp. Savoring his solitude, Bedad edged out of view.

The person passed their hiding spot and stopped a few paces beyond. Bedad knew, from Griswold's disinterest and the height, that it was not Randolph.

The figure began to speak in a low tone. Suddenly, a white shape appeared beside the figure. It was Sacha. Bedad caught the words "Kaie" and "attack."

"It must be Durward with another of his boring plans," Bedad whispered to the lupa. "But I can't figure why they are talking way out here and whispering."

Sacha vanished into the darkness. The man walked back to the campsite.

Bedad stretched out on his back, staring up at the stars. He considered Misty's idea. He wondered what the village was like. Was there as much drunkenness as in his own village?

Dots of brightness danced behind his eyes. A quick image of a drunken, blond traveler crossing his village street formed. His temples pounded. It was someone familiar. Very familiar. There was danger. What did it mean? A sloppy lick snapped him back to the present. Griswold whimpered.

"I suppose I could give her dumb sister a try," he told Griswold. "But if'n I don't like her, I'm gone."

A cool evening breeze ruffled his dark curls. He scrambled from his refuge as the fire beckoned. Griswold went to Randolph and lay at his feet.

"Good. Both need sleep."

"Yes." Misty said. "I'm quite tired too."

Bedad realized that they had waited for him.

"Night, all," he said, heading toward his bedroll. When everyone had settled in, he said, "I'll give Lissa a try, but I ain't promising I'll stay."

"Sounds reasonable," said Misty. "Sleep well, Bedad."

Chapter Nine — Deceptions

A moan drew Anastacia from sleep. She sat up quickly. No secretive figures had aroused her alarm this time. She tossed a log on the fire and listened carefully as the sparks twisted skyward. Someone cried out; it was Kent. He thrashed feverishly about, talking in his sleep.

She threw off her blanket, crept over, and shook him. "Wake up."

Groaning, he sat up. "What?" He ran his hands through his hair and looked around.

"You were having a nightmare," Anastacia whispered. "Take a few deep breaths, and get your bearings."

She waited glancing around. Everyone else was asleep. The fire snapped and crackled. A soft wind rustled the trees. Overhead, the bright stars twinkled in the darkest sky she had ever seen. She asked, "Are you ill?"

"No," said Kent. "Damned embarrassing. I don't usually scream at monsters in the night."

She knelt down beside him, keeping her voice low. "Is that what you dreamt? About monsters?"

"Yeah, monsters and beautiful women."

Anastacia laughed softly. "Well, there's bound to be a beautiful woman in there somewhere. You remind me of James Bond."

"Is he a friend of yours?"

She patted his shoulder. "Never mind. Go back to sleep. Try to think of something pleasant before you doze off."

He placed his hand over hers. "Perhaps I'll think of you."

His hand was strong and calloused on the back of hers. "I'll bet you say that to all the girls." She slipped her hand away.

"Of course, but that doesn't make it any less true. Stay and talk a while, Ana." He patted the ground beside him. "Unless you're too tired. If I go back to sleep right away, I'll probably have the same dream."

"All right, one moment." She put more wood on the fire and returned. "What shall we talk about?" She sat down, crossing her legs.

"I could talk about how your black hair looks almost blue in the sunlight, or how your blue eyes have little flecks of golden brown."

"How can you see all that in this darkness?" Anastacia laughed.

"I can't. I've been watching you ever since we met."

"Why?"

"I like the way you ignore me." He grinned.

"What? I don't ignore you. I treat you the same as everyone else."

Kent nodded. "Exactly. Not what I'm used to."

"You certainly have a high opinion of yourself when it comes to girls."

"Ordinary women. Not exceptional women, like you."

"And how many women have you said that to?"

"Only two—you and Misty."

She gave him a small punch in the shoulder. "Misty! You scum! A married woman."

"She wasn't married then, but she might as well have been. I never understood what she saw in that bewildered tripster." He sounded forlorn.

"I hope you don't mean Durward." Anastacia was indignant.

"The one and the same. Our great leader." He groaned. "The guy is totally helpless without her."

"Kent, I don't like this conversation," she spoke firmly. She hated gossip, one of the reasons she enjoyed the company of her teammates more than her girlfriends. "Misty and Durward are my friends."

"Mine too! Why else do you think I'm here?" He threw up his hands. "I don't want Misty taking an arrow for him because he blunders into Kaie's waiting arms."

"He wouldn't let her do that! He loves her." Anastacia glanced over to where the couple were sleeping, Durward behind Misty, his arm draped over her waist.

"He'd be a fool not to," said Kent. "But that doesn't change his luck. It's like a black cloud follows him everywhere, and Misty is his umbrella. He'd never let anything happen to her intentionally. He's no coward. He just seems to miss the mark, if you know what I mean."

Anastacia had noticed his clumsiness, but it was sporadic, and, usually, it emerged only when he was nervous. She listened to a log shift in the fire and glanced over, watching the sparks soar upward into the dark night. "Maybe, but what would you do differently?"

"Not a thing. We're fighting in the dark, here. We don't know Kaie's abilities, her allies, or even her motives. This is the first time anyone's ever openly challenged her."

"But you're sure it's her?"

"I am, even though she doesn't leave many witnesses to support my opinion. Misty and I had a devil of a time convincing Durward that it had to be Kaie. It's difficult to imagine. She was such a quiet, sweet little thing before the explosion."

Anastacia wondered what could have changed her. It must have been something pretty bad. Still, people always had a choice. She'd sometimes felt like smashing things since her mother died, but she'd focused that anger into pursuing more acceptable goals. "If she's such a powerful wizard, how are ordinary people going to fight her?" Anastacia tugged at a blade of grass.

"Like me you mean?" he said.

"I was thinking more of the villagers Durward wants to enlist," said Anastacia. "But you, too, come to think of it. Won't she just zap you away?"

Kent fingered his moustache, thinking. "Durward's not sure how many ordinary people she has working for her. Someone has to keep them out of the way while he handles her. I think it's for moral support as well. Besides, the more people who go, the more chance someone will be left to tell the tale."

Anastacia cringed. "What a horrid thought!"

"Don't worry." He patted her knee. "I always live to tell the tale."

"I'm not sure if I do," she muttered.

"Ana, nothing will harm you as long as I'm alive, I swear it. I promise I won't be caught off guard again. I was too cocky with the bandits, not concentrating. Someone distracted me." He paused. "That won't happen again."

They sat, lost in their own thoughts. Anastacia sighed. "I guess I'll go back to sleep now."

"Don't go." He clasped her wrist. "This conversation didn't turn out at all like I wanted."

"And how did you want it to turn out?"

He leaned toward her. "I wanted to charm you, like the song of the lilyvern."

"Ah, I see." Anastacia chuckled.

"Unfortunately, my charms don't appeal to you." He sounded wounded.

"I wouldn't say that," she whispered.

His eyes were now a blue-black in the darkness. Anastacia fought the urge to touch the truant blond curl on his forehead.

"Really? What do you like best about me?" He cocked his head and grinned.

"Kent!"

"Come on." He gave an exaggerated pout. "I need some cheering up."

"You're something else." Anastacia covered her mouth to smother her laughter.

"I am not! I'm completely human."

She patted his forearm. "I didn't mean that literally. It's slang. For someone out of the ordinary."

"Oh. Well, then, we're a perfect couple." He continued to hold on to her, now rubbing his thumb on her wrist bone.

"I'm sorry, Kent. I'm really not . . . . "She pulled her hand away.

"I realize you'll be leaving when this is over. It's my fate." He held his hands out, palms up. "I meet someone like Misty, with quiet courage, a warm heart, and beauty to boot, and no matter how I feel about her, she'll soon be gone from my life for good."

Anastacia sighed. She should probably tell him her age, but, there was something flattering about his attentions. "It would be stupid of me to complicate things more by responding to you, Kent. I think you see that. I prefer to be free as a bird."

"Birds are beautiful, and some can be trained."

Anastacia snorted. "I'm not interested in being trained."

"Trained was the wrong word." Kent traced his fingers along her jaw, threaded them into her hair behind her ear and kissed her. His moustache was thick against her skin, little hairs tickling her nostrils. Anastacia opened her mouth for his hot, probing tongue. He held the back of her head with his other hand and drew her closer. A tingle ran down Anastacia's spine. He kissed her cheek, her jaw, and her throat, his lips like a string of pearls.

"Perhaps you've met the right man, but in the wrong place," he whispered.

"Kent, I . . . . "

"Shh. A few kisses in the dark, is it so much to give?"

Anastacia sighed, afraid to trust her voice. She didn't have to tell him her age just yet. She'd never kissed a man before. A boy in grade nine whom she'd liked for a while, but nothing like this. She ran her hand over his strong chest and drew his lips back to hers. Kent responded, capturing her breast. Anastacia felt her nipple tense under his thumb. She wondered if he could tell through her clothes. Kent jerked away, his hand shooting under his blanket.

"What is it?" asked Anastacia, startled.

He gasped. "Oh, cow splot, a pain."

"Your wound?" she whispered.

Kent took a while before answering. "No, a cramp. I saw stars for a minute."

"So did I." Anastacia said teasingly.

Kent managed a thin smile.

"I think you'd better get some rest," said Anastacia. "Does it still hurt? I could wake Misty."

"No, thanks. I'm embarrassed enough. Sleep'll help. I feel totally drained." He collapsed back in his bed roll.

It's just as well, she thought. "Goodnight, Kent." *I could get in a whole lotta trouble with this one.*

The villagers greeted them warmly. Durward and Misty were treated with respect and some awe. Durward's bracelet and history as the last of the wizards had catapulted him into fame. Tales of Misty's piping had circulated ahead of her arrival. Everyone met in Lissa's large common room. Kent, Durward, and Misty sat on benches along a rectangular table relating the events of the last few days to the villagers. Anastacia sat on a chair off to the side, watching Lissa fuss over Bedad.

Lissa began immediately picking fabric for his clothes. She asked his opinion on colors and style, interjecting comments about the other children as she came and went from the adjacent room with bolts of cloth. She held them up against him, nodded, and disappeared for another one, back and forth.

"Bedad, help yourself to some cake in the box," Lissa said, pointing to the counter. "I'll go tidy up the fabrics. I think I know what to make first. Some tough but comfortable breeches."

Bedad nodded and headed for the counter. Anastacia stood and followed Misty's sister into the next room.

"Lissa, I'm glad to see you hit it off so well with Bedad."

Lissa rummaged through a pile of fabric as they spoke. "He has a deep sadness, but somehow he's kept his sense of humor and his ability to hope. We'll be just fine."

"He lost his mother recently," said Anastacia as she fingered a bolt of heavy, blue cloth. "He acts like he's okay, but that's not something you get over easily."

"Oh, the poor child," said Lissa. She stopped unfolding a piece of brown cloth and looked at Anastacia. "You sound like you know something of that."

"Yeah, I do."

Lissa dropped the fabric and approached Anastacia. She gazed into her face and then slowly drew her in for a long, warm hug.

Anastacia felt tears start in her eyes. They embraced for a moment. Then Anastacia stepped back and wiped her eyes. "He's a lucky boy," she said. "I'll miss him."

"Miss who?" asked Bedad, as he entered the room.

"You! You little menace." Anastacia laughed as she hugged him. She quickly wiped her eyes. "And don't give Lissa a hard time about washing," she teased.

Bedad giggled. "As long as she keeps feeding me like this" — he displayed a fist full of cake — "I'm her devoted slave."

They laughed.

"I brought a piece for you," he said, holding one out for Anastacia.

She thanked him and took the cake from his hand. It was enriched with red berries. It was moist and mildly sweet.

"Mmm," she said.

Bedad nodded as he took a second bite, crumbs settling on his chin. They ate the cake as Lissa finished tidying and organizing her fabric.

"But you be careful, Anastacia." He wiped the crumbs from his lips. "I don't want anything bad to happen to you, or Griswold, or any of the others."

"Don't worry. With Durward, Sacha, and Kent around, we'll be just fine." She tucked back an errant black curl.

Bedad licked the corner of his mouth, thinking. "I'm pretty sure I saw Kent before. Maybe he came through my village."

"And broke every heart while he was there, no doubt," said Lissa as they returned to the common room.

The tale of their journey was complete. Now Kent was laughing with the men, answering questions about his exploits, while two women competed to serve him ale and food. Many a promising smile was sent in his direction. Anastacia tried to disguise her irritation.

She fist bumped Bedad goodnight as he headed for bed.

Griswold, Sacha, and Randolph did not come inside. They set up a small encampment close by.

Anastacia felt awkward with the villagers. They all leapt to her assistance, but no one engaged her in a friendly conversation. They did not know how to treat the daughter of two legends, a girl with a powerful bracelet with a pure crystal and an outworlder.

Kent lived the moment to the limit, while Durward and Misty busily arranged supplies and recruited aid as villagers came and went. Anastacia put together a bundle of food for Randolph.

On her way back from their encampment, she saw Kent staggering away with a large-breasted, young blonde. Their arms were around each others' waists, and she was giggling.

I guess I deserved that, thought Anastacia. *If I'd been more encouraging. No, that'd be dumb.* Wistfully, she watched them disappear from sight. *Maybe he'll be thinking of me the whole time and change his mind,* she thought. *There must be a reason women love him. I'd better watch myself, or I'll just be one more notch in his belt.* She chewed thoughtfully on her finger. *Would that really be so bad?*

By morning, a small knot of people had joined, among them Lissa's husband, Ellsworth. He was a short, stocky, but strong, brown man, with dark eyes and the weathered hands of a farrier. He greeted everyone with a crooked smile. Anastacia wondered if he might not be trying to escape the house full of noisy children and give his wife free rein while she mothered Bedad.

Three other men agreed to come; a long-legged hunter named Fulke, who did not like the threatening changes in the forest; a peddler named Steevin — with a hooked nose — who had been robbed by bandits; and a burly, pock-faced farmer named Hugh who had lost his farm to debt.

Isabel, Durward's cousin, a tall, willowy seamstress whose husband had first developed a fondness for drink and then young women, was the only female to volunteer. Anastacia felt only the hunter had anything to offer, but Durward was pleased with their involvement.

"I will not have these gnats showing up and disrupting my work." Kaie spoke in a hissed whisper as she stood behind a long, wooden table covered in materials and containers for her spells. She picked up a dead fly and dropped it into a grimy, stone mortar. She sprinkled a grainy, gray substance from a wooden box and crushed the two together with a stone pestle. It made a dull combination.

"It is time we threw a few hornets into their honeycomb."

She pushed the mortar and pestle away and peered between long strings of her matted, black hair at her followers. "Let's have some fun."

Riva smiled eagerly and nodded. She was dressed in tight-fitting leather pants and shirt, her fingers cluttered with gold and silver rings.

"Prepare for stealthy travel," the wizard said. She paused, picked up a mold-covered beaker, peered inside, and set it down again. "We will strike as lightning." She reached out and swept the beaker, along with several dishes and brass instruments, onto the floor. They clattered and shattered. She stared at the pieces. "Smash, crash, down it all comes."

Lachish shifted from one foot to the other. No one spoke.

She looked up. "I have begun a second batch of the drug" — she smiled at Lachish who had provided the eyes for binding — "and the first will be ready for testing any day now. I will not have meddlesome fools tromping about my caverns upsetting things. I shall clap my hands together and squash these annoying insects." She clapped in the air as though killing a mosquito, clapped again in a different direction, turned, and clapped again. "Clap," she said. "Clap. Clap."

Beora glanced at Riva, but the other woman refused to meet her eyes.

Kaie turned back and thumped the table with her boney fist. "Ready yourselves," she commanded. "We're going for a walky-walky."

Anastacia, Griswold, Randolph, and Sacha did not join in the frequent discussion on how best to approach Kaie. The travelers argued loudly, unable to come to an agreement.

Anastacia, Griswold, and the animals walked quietly at the rear of the troop. She avoided any private conversation with Kent. By nightfall, a rough plan had been formulated. Anastacia realized it was little different than what had been first suggested on the onset of their quest, but she didn't say anything.

Once they reached the area of the caves, Sacha would be sent ahead to scout for signs of occupancy and resistance. Griswold would follow, ready to alert the others should the panther find herself in difficulty.

If the two animals returned safely, Randolph, Kent, and Fulke the hunter would further scout the area and select the easiest entry. Inside the caves, it would be catch as catch can. They would attempt secrecy as long as possible, but, once discovered, would fight until they reached Kaie.

"I think she'll join the fray early on," said Durward. "We won't have to search for her."

"Well," said Isabel. "That's for the best. Get it over with as quick as possible. Though I must admit I'm not looking forward to meeting her face to face. I'm glad I'm good with a bow and arrow. Maybe I won't have to get too close to her. If she's half as terrifying as people say, I'll be lucky to hold my lunch down."

The other villagers agreed.

"The sooner we get this done," said Ellsworth, "the sooner we go home to our families."

"Right," muttered Isabel bitterly.

"Anastacia must be protected from stray arrows and the like," said Sacha. "She is to be kept safe until Durward confronts Kaie."

"Wait a minute," said Anastacia. "I don't want anyone taking an arrow in my place. I can take care of myself."

"I'm sure you can," Durward said as he adjusted the campfire. "But we don't want your skills wasted on the small fry. Your fight with Kaie will be the ultimate challenge. When you meet her, you may wish you had taken an arrow."

"Durward," said Misty. "Sometimes you could use a bit more tact."

"No use misleading her," he said defensively as he poked a coal with a stick.

"I will stay by Anastacia," Kent said.

"She is our most important weapon," said Steevin.

"Also me and Griswold will protect," Randolph said.

Anastacia hoped, when the time came, their courage and faith in her would prove well founded. She still had no idea how to defeat the wizard.

Their first encounter came before they reached the caves. While the travelers slept that night, Sacha and Hugh, the farmer, kept watch, one on each side of the camp. It was a full moon night.

Hugh stepped away to relieve himself in the bushes. He tidied himself and looked up. Someone stood close by, watching. He was so startled by her appearance, he did not even raise a challenge. She was the most beautiful woman he had ever seen, with long, blond hair and tight, leather clothes revealing the body of a goddess. She wore a dagger in a small sheath on her hip. She beckoned, smiling.

He stood. "Who goes there?"

"I've come to join your party," Riva whispered. "I arrived at the village just after you left. I hurried to catch you. I want to be of service."

"Walk slowly toward me."

Riva obeyed, her sultry walk unnerving the man.

"Stop there. Drop your dagger to the ground, and carefully kick it toward me."

"Of course. You can't be too careful." She winked.

When the farmer bent to retrieve the weapon, he did not see or hear Lachish approach to split his skull.

Sacha paused in mid-stride. Something made her hair rise. Stealthily, she slunk to the farmer's spot. He wasn't there. She followed his scent. She saw three shapes. One was lifting a large cudgel. Sacha lifted her head and roared, an alarm to the others and a threat to the attackers. She raced toward Lachish, he turned, swung the club, and struck her on the side of the head. She staggered and fell as the farmer lifted out his axe to defend himself.

Riva shoved him to the ground and shouted. "Come on, you blew it."

Voices approached.

Lachish growled as he lumbered off into the woods. "Later, I will split your skull."

Hugh knelt beside Sacha. She stumbled to her feet and shook her head. "I'll follow them," she said.

"Better not," said Hugh. "I think you might have a concussion."

Everyone was awake now and clustered around the woozy panther, weapons at the ready.

"Stay here," said Durward. "Randolph, can you follow their trail in the dark?"

"Griswold too," said Randolph.

The lupa picked up the scent and led them into the forest. After a few minutes, Durward called a halt.

"It's no use," said Durward. "We can barely see where we're going. Even if we catch up to them, we can't tell where they might be hiding in the forest. They can wait anywhere for us to pass by. We should return to camp."

"Enemy might circle back," said Randolph. "Be there already."

Durward hissed through his teeth and quickly turned.

"How did they get that close?" Sacha asked when he returned. Misty had wiped the blood from the panther's head and was gently coating it with an ointment.

"I don't know," said Durward. "They waited until Hugh had moved further away, for whatever foolish reason." He glared at the hunter.

He nodded to Sacha. "If you hadn't raised the alarm, they might have murdered us where we slept."

"Stupid man." Isabel snapped at Hugh. "Your carelessness could have killed us all." She removed an arrow she had notched into her bow.

"Shut up!" said Hugh. "I had to take a leak. They surprised me, is all. This gorgeous woman coming out of nowhere."

"How did they know you would be alone and male?" said Isabel.

"How the hell should I know?" said Hugh.

Everyone exchanged looks. No one spoke as they returned to the campfire. Since no one felt able to sleep, Misty made a hot drink, and they huddled together.

"Now that she knows we are coming," said Kent of the Lake, "we can forget any element of surprise."

"How did she know?" asked Isabel.

"Kaie has powers I cannot understand," said Durward.

"Powers my ass," said Fulke. "You've been telling everyone in Dawn's End that you were coming. She was bound to learn of a force being raised."

"Some force," muttered Steevin the peddler, his jeweled fingers rubbing his crooked nose.

"It don't matter," said Ellsworth. "Now we just march straight in and don't worry about bein' seen. Direct approach is best."

"I'd still like to know how she knew exactly when we were coming and where we were," said Hugh. "I covered our tracks leading into the camp."

"She also knew who would be easiest to attack," whispered the peddler.

Everyone looked at each other suspiciously.

"Now there is no use making this into something it's not," said Misty, tossing bits of branches into the fire.

"Come to think of it, your husband has the most to gain by all this," said Steevin. "He gets Kaie's bracelet when we're done, and maybe even the one worn by the daughter of the Alaric. Wait a minute. Maybe that's what Durward's after. Anastacia's bracelet. He could be helping the wizard in exchange for a working band of power."

"No!" said Misty and Anastacia together.

"I'd be crazy to do that," said Durward. "No one can trust Kaie. She'd probably kill me and keep all the bracelets. Besides, why would I bother getting all of you to join me? Wouldn't it be easier to just bring Anastacia alone?"

"Yes," Ellsworth nodded. "That's right. It wouldn't make sense."

"We mustn't bicker and doubt each other," said Kent. "That's playing right into Kaie's hands."

"True," said Isabel. "She sent her assassins to unnerve us as much as to reduce our numbers."

"That means we may be unnerving her," Anastacia said. "Why would she go to such trouble if her caves are as impenetrable as people think? Maybe she's worried about us. We may have a better chance at beating her than we thought."

The others nodded, assured by her words. One by one, they returned to their bedrolls to sleep or think their private thoughts.

In the morning, they discovered Hugh the farmer was missing. Anastacia wanted to search, in hope of finding him still alive, until Randolph spoke.

"He not dead. Bedroll gone. Food gone. No fight marks."

"You're right," said Kent. "No one carried him off. He decided to leave on his own."

"The coward abandoned us," said Durward.

Anastacia counted six men—Ellsworth, Fulke, Durward, Kent, Steevin, and Randolph; three women—herself, Misty, and Isabel; a panther, and a lupa. But they were still a stronger force than before they visited the village and the remaining travelers were determined. They ate a hearty breakfast in forced cheerfulness."It can't be far now," said Durward. "The caves are less than a day's journey. Perhaps the attackers were simply on patrol."

"Perhaps," said Sacha. "But it was the strangest thing . . . . "

"What?" asked Anastacia.

"Last night, before the attack. I smelled something. I smelled it a few times before. So familiar, and yet not right. It annoys me that I can't place it." She rubbed her nose with her paw.

"It might have been one of Kaie's allies," said Durward. "Since they don't live right, they probably don't smell right either."

"Perhaps. But I have the feeling I should know it. I'm concerned about what that means."

Chapter Ten — Murder and Sacrifice

The forest was heavy with silence as they traveled east. Every shadow or sound brought the group to a tense halt. Their nerves were frayed by the time Durward spoke. "The path widens here. Let's rest and eat."

"I'm starving," said Isabel.

"Me, too," said Anastacia, "I'm beat. My back—"

A scream cut her off. Durward pulled out his sword and ran back along the path. Those behind joined him. Anastacia crowded together with the others, as Misty examined the fallen man. It was Steevin, the peddler; his gray vest was drenched with bright blood from his torn throat. One of his arms ended in a ragged bloody stump. Griswold growled low in his throat. His nose lifted, sniffing the air, and his ears stood stiffly up, twitching.

Isabel notched her bow, her head swiveling in search of a target.

Anastacia stepped off the trail and vomited. She'd seen hunters gut a moose before, but this was worse than anything she'd imagined. Kent's wounds had been bad enough, but this . . . . She couldn't stop shaking.

That poor man! she thought. *How could it have happened so fast? It could have been any of us. It could have me. What the hell am I doing here? This isn't some video game. I could die, forever, like Steevin.*

She emptied the rest of her stomach, weakly gripping a branch, fighting the urge to run and keep running.

"The killer must be close by," whispered Isabel.

"It's that same smell I caught before," said Sacha. "I'm following it."

Randolph quickly signaled to the lupa. "We follow you. Griswold and me help track."

The three of them disappeared into the forest.

"Whatever killed him wasn't human," said Durward.

"What do you mean? Was it a spirit?" asked Isabel, her eyes wide.

"No." Misty hastened to calm her. "It was an animal."

Kent examined the surrounding area. "I can't find any tracks but Sacha's and Griswold's."

Everyone considered this discovery. Misty voiced the only plausible answer, "Then it must have been either a lupa or a panther. Their tracks would look the same as Griswold's and Sacha's."

"Where was Griswold when Steevin was killed?" asked Fulke.

"What do you mean?" said Anastacia.

"I mean where was *our* lupa, if he is *our* lupa?"

"With Randolph, I presume," said Anastacia. "What are you getting at? You don't think Griswold did it!"

"Why not?" said Fulke. "We know nothing about those two. Those injuries could have been done by an animal. They live off by themselves. No one here has met them before. They could be Kaie's servants for all we know."

"Enough!" said Misty. "We play right into the wizard's hands suspecting each other like this. If you have something to say to Randolph, then say it to his face when he returns." Her little nose twitched angrily. "For myself, I believe no one in our group is responsible for this man's death. Did you never consider that if we have a lupa and a panther helping us, then Kaie may have animals of her own?"

"Are you alright?" Kent asked Anastacia.

She nodded mutely. He squeezed her shoulder. She couldn't stop staring at Steevin, one of his bejeweled hands missing.

Kent, Durward, and Isabel set about burying the peddler.

Anastacia watched in horror; her head pounded. *Of course I'm not alright. Why didn't I say no? I'm scared. My knees feel like rubber. I haven't felt this frightened since Mom told me she had stage four cancer.*

Fulke muttered to Isabel.

Anastacia watched them, thinking, *We would have been better off without the villagers. They're destroying the team. We have to work together, just like hockey. Everyone has to know what everyone else is doing and support them. The last thing Durward needs is his leadership challenged. You have to follow the captain's lead. Everyone knows that.*

Finally, Fulke spoke to the group. "This whole damn thing's too weird for me. Give me a straight-out confrontation, and I'll do my best. I don't know how to deal with these attacks. It's unnerving."

I can't blame him, thought Anastacia. *If I could figure out a way to get out of this without the others hating me, I'd do it.* She looked at Misty, who was surreptitiously wiping her almond-shaped eyes. *Nah, I'd never know how it ended then. Besides, I haven't a clue how to get home.*

They walked for a couple of hours and then stopped to rest. When the group had completed preparing their lunch and was sitting in a circle to eat, Anastacia stopped munching in surprise. "Where's Fulke?" she asked.

Everyone looked at each other. There was no answer. "Oh, no." Anastacia leapt to her feet. "I didn't hear anything. How could they have gotten him?"

"Shh," said Ellsworth. "I saw him slip away. I guess he didn't have the guts to tell us. I thought it best to let him go."

"His balls were the size of peas anyway," muttered Isabel.

"Hell." Anastacia mumbled, sitting back down. "That leaves four men and three women."

"And Sacha and Griswold," said Kent. "A small group, but the true gold in the rock." He flashed his winning smile.

Anastacia nodded, chewing thoughtfully.

"So, why didn't you recruit the buxom blonde from the village?" asked Ellsworth. "We would have four women then."

"She wasn't a fighter," said Kent. He glanced quickly at Anastacia, who avoided eye contact.

"Well, she couldn't be much of a lover either," said Ellsworth, "considering how soon you were back at the table."

Anastacia flinched. Kent shrugged. "A gentleman doesn't discuss such things. Just keep in mind that I believe, if it's worth doing, it's worth doing well."

I guess it wasn't worth doing then, Anastacia thought as she suppressed a smile.

Griswold and Sacha stayed together for the first kilometer of tracking. Again, Sacha felt there was something familiar about the scent, but something wrong as well. She had to know what it was. She picked up her pace.

Randolph, fit as he was, had difficulty keeping up. The larger group fell further behind him. Then Sacha stretched out her sleek, powerful body and broke into a run. Claws extended, she tore up the trail, a white blur racing through the woods.

Griswold barked in protest. Randolph and the others fell further behind.

Sacha shouted back to him. "Stay with Randolph. He'll need your protection. Do not leave him." She didn't know if he understood and didn't wait to see. She broke into a faster sprint. She heard Randolph's voice far behind.

"Come back." Randolph called to Sacha. "Stay in pack. Not safe alone."

She ignored him.

He whistled for Griswold. "We follow your track, Sacha."

Griswold barked in agreement.

Bedad's body jolted; the plate crashed to the floor, smashing to pieces.

"Oh, dear," said Lissa, bending to pick up the debris. She stopped when she saw the boy's pale face. His dark eyes were large and frightened.

"It's just an old dish. You look terrified. Bedad!"

She shook his shoulders, as he stared, unblinking, unmoving.

"What's the matter?" Tears rolled down his thin face. "Bedad!"

He blinked. "Lissa?" His voice was small and timid.

She took his hand. "Yes, what is it? Sit down here, and tell me." She led him to the wooden bench. They sat, and she patted his arm as he licked his lips, turned, and looked at her with sorrowful eyes.

"I saw them," he whispered. "My friends. There was blood everywhere. I heard Griswold howl. It was so mournful, full of pain and loss. Oh, Lissa. Something dreadful is going to happen."

"There, there, Bedad." She put her arm around his shoulder and hugged him. "Not to worry. They'll be home safe and sound in a day or two." She stroked his hair, resting his head on her shoulder. He had finally stopped flinching whenever she touched him and now seemed to welcome her affection.

The poor child. He must have the onset of the gift. It usually came during adolescence. It was always a shock at first, of course, but this was more than she could handle. She did not know if his visions were true. If they were warnings or statements of fact.

Her soft, gray face creased in worry as she gazed out the window, down the trail where her husband Ellsworth, sister Misty, brother-in-law Durward, long-time friend Kent, and her village neighbors had gone. Would she ever see any of them again?

Griswold and Randolph heard the battle before they saw it. Sacha's thunderous roar echoed through the trees. Griswold whined and looked questioningly up at Randolph, his intelligent, brown eyes searching for a command. Randolph was panting, pushed to his limit.

"Help Sacha," he said.

Griswold yelped and raced ahead. Randolph broke into the quickest run he could maintain on the overgrown path. Soon, Griswold's growls mixed in with the other's snarls.

Sacha had come upon the killer eating. Blood splattered the brush, grass, and trees. She recognized both the killer and the meal at once. She also recognized the smell, familiar, and yet strange. It was Goar, but yet not Goar.

Hugh had not made it home. Goar had circled back and attacked the farmer. Sacha could not believe he was capable of such savagery. Her own mate!

"Goar." She spoke softly. "It's Sacha. Do you know me?"

He looked up, snarled, his white muzzle coated in blood and bits of flesh.

"Why?" she asked. "Why did you do this?"

His only response was to roar and set upon her with fury. His powerful body soared the distance in a single leap. His attack caught her off guard. She was almost pinned in the first rush. He bit into her back, opening a large wound as she wriggled free. Crimson blood splattered her white fur.

When Griswold arrived the two white panthers were tumbling, snapping and clawing. Goar tried to disembowel his mate; Sacha tried to stay alive. Griswold did not hesitate. He leapt, sinking his fangs into the haunch of their enemy. Goar whirled to meet this new assault.

As lupa and panther battled, Sacha dragged herself free. In addition to the loss of blood from her back, there were numerous cuts and bites on her stomach, chest, and neck. She staggered to her feet. She hoped desperately that Randolph was not far behind. As wily as the lupa was, he could not stand long against a larger and stronger adversary.

Griswold fought bravely, but was soon bleeding from many wounds as well.

"Leave." Sacha growled at Griswold. "Get your master. Goar is too large." She hoped he understood the tone of retreat, if not the words.

"You, leave, too," said Goar, as he and the lupa leapt apart, circling each other for an opening. "You are both fools to fight me. I will kill this pup in the beat of a glowbug's wing."

Griswold growled low in his throat and then lunged. He ripped the cut in Goar's haunch deep into the bone. The panther roared and grabbed the lupa by the back of the throat. His fangs sunk deep into the fur, deeper into the flesh beneath. He clenched the back of Griswold's throat and crushed the spinal column. Sacha heard the sound of snapping bone. She whimpered in despair as Goar flung away Griswold's body.

Blood gushed from Goar's shoulder as he slowly padded toward the trembling Sacha.

"Goar, why are you doing this?" She whimpered. "It's me, Sacha. Your mate. Think. Remember."

Goar stopped, a puzzled expression on his face. "Sacha?"

"Do you recognize me?"

Goar shook his head. "I don't know you. I thought for a moment I did, but it wouldn't matter anyway. I must kill you. Kaie commands, and I must obey."

"Goar, no. You can't do this. I—"

At that moment, the panther leapt.

Randolph had heard the silence and feared the worst. As the roars resumed, he listened hopefully for Griswold's growl. When he entered the clearing, he saw why he heard none. Kneeling beside the bloodied lupa, he rested his hand on the damp, soft muzzle. There was no breath. With a moan, he stood and unsheathed his hunting knife.

The two panthers were now more red than white. Randolph realized Sacha was the smaller one, and not faring well. As he went forward, the larger cat screamed in agony. The wound in his shoulder was bare to the bone. Muscle and vein protruded, a hunk of flesh flapped. A glistening, black stone fell from the opening with the next rush of blood. Goar screamed again.

As Randolph reached his side, Goar collapsed to the earth. "Sacha," he whispered. "Who has hurt us?"

Sacha looked into his eyes and saw recognition. "Goar? Do you know me?"

"Of course, I know you. But why are we here?" he asked as Randolph raised his arm for the kill.

"No!" Sacha roared.

Randolph hesitated and then clenched his muscles for the plunge. Sacha leapt. Randolph had no time to change his movement in response to hers. The blade descended. Sacha covered Goar's body with hers as the knife plunged inward. Randolph tried to pull back, but the blade sank deeply into her already ravaged body. She sounded a cry of pain and despair.

"Sacha!" cried Randolph. "No! No!" He yanked out the knife and tried to stem the fountain of blood with his sash. Goar eased out from underneath.

"What is happening?" Goar growled at Randolph. "You've stabbed my mate. I will kill you for that."

Randolph looked confused. "I try save her. You kill her. Like you kill Griswold."

He pointed to the lupa's body. Goar hesitated.

"There will be no more killing," whispered Sacha. Goar licked her face. "Randolph tells the truth, my love."

"This can't be," said Goar. "I would never hurt you. I don't understand any of this or how we came to be here. The last I remember was fighting the red and black giant who had clubbed you into unconsciousness."

"When I awoke," said Sacha in a strained voice, "you were gone. He took you prisoner. Since then, you have been a servant of Kaie. Her killer."

"No!" Goar said. "Why would I do these things?"

"Something about the stone," she whispered.

"Stone?"

"It came out from the wound in your shoulder." Sacha's voice rasped. "Then you remembered yourself. Randolph?"

"Yes?"

"Search for the stone. Black. The size of an eye."

Randolph walked around the bloody battlefield. He spotted its dark glow in a crimson pool. When wiped clean, its blackness glistened hypnotically. He brought it to the panthers and dropped it between their faces. Goar cringed, a shudder passing through his body.

"Take it away." Goar's voice rumbled. "It's evil. It hurts. I remember intense pain, insanity."

"Where from?" asked Randolph.

"I don't know, but it frightens me," Goar said.

"I think I do," whispered Sacha. "It is Kaie's weapon. It was inside you." She paused, panting. "It's how she controlled you. It is like the crystal on Anastacia's bracelet, only much larger."

"Anastacia?" said Goar.

"Later. We need Misty's help. The healer."

"Is Misty here?" asked Goar, his voice also fading.

"Close behind. She is our only hope," said Sacha as she rolled over on her side, breathing heavily.

Randolph spoke. "I go for her. First, I bandage you better."

"No, Randolph," said Sacha. "Not enough time or bandages. Go."

Randolph nodded, gave a sad glance in Griswold's direction, and ran. If the lupa had still been alive, Griswold could have raced ahead, bringing help in half the time.

Sacha lay on her side, panting rapidly, her blood making red rivulets in the dirt. She knew Randolph did not understand how Goar, the killer, could have so quickly become Goar, her mate, but she was of his pack now and he would accept her word. She only wished Griswold had stayed behind with him as she had ordered. His death was a huge loss.

Kaie checked the potion and smiled. It was ready. Perhaps she should test it? No, it would give too much away to have people beating at the exits to the outer world. She did not want anyone to know what was to come until the day of destruction. She had faith it would work.

The crystals, too, were near completion. A day or two at most. Kaie sighed and rubbed her temples. Why didn't her success ease the pain? Or the nightmares? Last night the woman in white had spoken to her, pointed an accusing finger, and she, great wizard of Dawn's End, had trembled at the confrontation. She had fallen to her knees and wept.

Kaie clenched her teeth. If this was some foreshadowing, she would prove it wrong. No woman would bring her to her knees. In fact, she would have great joy in pressing Anastacia Newman into that position. Imagine, an outworlder challenging her! The daughter of the Esteemed Nicole and Alaric Morrel. Pah!

Kaie spat. She wished she could have challenged *that* Esteemed Lady of sweetness and light. If Nicole had minded her own business, Dawn's End would not be the annoying place she was bent on destroying. But, no. The legendary woman had stopped Nightfall, brought back the sunshine to Dawn's End, and made it a sickeningly charming place to live. And now her daughter planned on saving it again. By challenging Kaie's right to rule. Not while there was breath left in her body.

Kaie steadied her trembling. She needed to focus. There was work to be done. Everything she had done up to now had been a diversion from her true goal.

Randolph raced through the forest. The others were not far behind.

"Come. Fast. Sacha hurt. Need Misty."

Quickly, they followed. Winded, nerves frayed, trying to hold his grief at bay, Randolph's pace slowed. Anastacia and the others kept up easily.

Kent stayed close to Randolph, ready to track should it be necessary. When the two men emerged into the small clearing, they stopped abruptly. Randolph from exhaustion and emotional fatigue, Kent from shock.

It looked like a slaughter house. Randolph stumbled over to Griswold's body, knowing the others would care for the panthers. The travelers watched with dismay as he stroked the dead body of his friend, and then threw back his head to howl.

"Damn," muttered Isabel.

Anastacia felt chills down her spine. Not Griswold. That beautiful animal.

Goar's sob roused them into action.

"Sacha!" Misty rushed forward.

"Wait!" Kent shouted. "The other panther. Who is he?"

Isabel saw the partially eaten body of the farmer and screamed. "It's the killer. Look!" Her arm trembled as she pointed. She fumbled for an arrow.

Durward unsheathed his sword, striding forward to help Kent kill their enemy.

"No kill!" Randolph jumped to his feet.

"What?" said Durward. "This animal is Kaie's. He murdered the farmer, the tracker, and Griswold, and injured Sacha.

"Sacha say no kill. She protect."

Anastacia stared at the panther. He looked like a larger version of Sacha. His face was filled with pain.

Not just physical pain, emotional. Grief. She knew that look. She saw it for months whenever she looked in a mirror. But why would he harm Sacha if he loved her?

"Didn't he kill your lupa?" Durward asked. "Didn't he hurt Sacha?"

Goar said, "Sacha is dead. I killed her as well. You took too long in coming."

"Savage!" Durward raced forward. Goar lay apathetically, waiting for the execution.

"Stop him!" Anastacia yelled.

Kent obeyed immediately. He grabbed Durward's arm wrestling for the sword.

Durward cursed. "Let me go! He's a murdering beast."

"And so will you be, if you kill him," said Anastacia as she came to his side. "Look at him. He has lost so much blood he can't even stand. He's not even moving to defend himself. There's more to this than meets the eye. Besides, I thought you people didn't believe in vengeance."

"He killed Sacha," muttered Durward.

"I helped," Randolph said.

The group gasped.

"It was an accident," said Goar. "She threw herself between us and took his stab that was meant for me."

"This is crazy," said Durward. "Kill him. He's dangerous."

"He's not dangerous now. He can hardly move," said Kent.

"Maybe he can tell us about Kaie," Isabel said.

Durward hesitated. "Alright, I'll question him first. Then Misty will assess if he will live if we leave him to his wounds."

Kent released his arm. Durward put up his sword. They all stood staring at the panther. Goar crawled closer to his mate and licked Sacha's massive, limp head as it lay in the dust.

Durward spoke through clenched teeth. "Don't touch her."

Goar looked at him with baleful eyes. "I can't help you. I remember nothing about Kaie. Sacha explained about your quest. If I could help you, I would. Kaie took my sanity, my honor, and my mate. My life means little now."

"You can't be her mate," Durward said. "Sacha was my friend. She told me about her mate. He would never have done the things you've done."

"No, he wouldn't. But I am he. Sacha freed me. We talked, and Sacha helped me pieced together what happened. Kaie . . . . "

"What did she do?" asked Anastacia, as the travelers gathered closely around the panthers. Misty knelt down and began to clean Goar's wounds.

"I was captured . . . huge beast of a man . . . black and orange, hairy, hideous. He left Sacha unconscious . . . don't know why . . . took me to Kaie . . . . She cut open my shoulder, put a piece of a black crystal inside."

"Black crystal!" Durward said.

Misty took out her curved needle and thread.

"Yes . . . Sacha said the same as Anastacia's . . . Who is she?"

"I am. This is the bracelet," she said, pulling up her sleeve to reveal the band. The gold shone brightly.

Goar winced as the sunlight caught the crystal in the embossed panther's eye. He growled. "That is evil."

Anastacia looked worriedly at Durward.

"Don't listen," said Durward. "Next, he'll be telling you to get rid of it. It's all some plot of Kaie's."

"I don't think so," said Misty as she tied off a row of stitches. "I believe him. Where is the crystal now, Goar?"

"Under Sacha's paw."

Durward bent down and gently lifted the massive paw. A blackness sparkled underneath. He gasped and picked it. Kent flinched.

"Look," cried Durward. "It's even bigger than Anastacia's." He wiped the blood on the grass and then polished it with his sleeve. "With this stone in my bracelet, I could defeat Kaie. I could win! I could control her!"

"Don't count on it," said Goar softly. "I remember more of those stones."

"That's impossible," Durward said.

"Then where did that come from?" asked Anastacia.

Durward glared at her in exasperation and shoved the stone inside his pouch. "I don't care. But I'm certainly not going to waste the chance it gives me. Let's go. We'll go north to the panther village tonight and find a blacksmith. The sooner we set this stone in the panther's eye, the sooner we have a weapon against the wizard."

Anastacia was surprised at this surge of confidence and assertiveness. "What about Goar?" she asked.

"Leave him. He'll be no use to the wizard now. I doubt if healing is one of her powers."

"It is one of mine," said Misty, as she untied her flute.

Durward grabbed her wrist. "You're not going to heal him. He'll just start killing us off one by one again. Kaie never releases her slaves."

"Let me go, Durward." Misty stood. "I believe he is freed of the wizard. I also believe that Sacha loved him." She pulled her wrist free of his grip.

They paused in their argument as Randolph set fire to the brush he had piled on top of Griswold's broken body. The flames leapt upward drawing their attention.

"Look," said Durward. "He is responsible for that funeral pyre. He is a bringer of death."

"And I am a bringer of life." Misty sat down beside Goar and put the whistle to her lips.

Goar closed his eyes and did not respond when Misty blew her first notes. Durward turned away, tight-lipped. He helped the others bury the farmer. Misty played on and on. The panther's breaths were short and shallow.

Anastacia watched Misty blow a few more notes without response. "What is it?" she asked. "Why are you stopping?"

"He is withdrawing. He has no will to live."

Anastacia tried to coax the panther. "Open your eyes, Goar. We want you to live. Don't let Kaie be responsible for another death."

"Sacha would want you to live," said Misty.

Goar's large eyes slowly opened, met hers, and closed again. Randolph approached. He crossed his arms and looked down his nose at Goar.

"He no care for Sacha. She die for him. Not fight hard. I stab, she take wound. All for nothing. Worthless mate. He quitter."

Goar opened his eyes and glared at Randolph. "What do you care? I killed your lupa. Sacha said he was your companion and her friend. I deserve to die."

"Kaie deserves to die," said Anastacia. Misty shot her a disapproving glance. "That is, if anyone does, it's her. You can help us stop her from hurting anyone else."

"How?"

"Take Sacha's place," said Anastacia. "She joined us because she believed in the quest. You must do it. For her."

Goar closed his eyes again. The three people waited quietly, unsure what to do next. Randolph shrugged and went back to the cremation. He chanted a few words in a language no one else understood as flames consumed Griswold's body.

Anastacia sighed with relief when Goar opened his eyes once more.

"All right," he said. "I will take Sacha's place. But, be sure, Kaie *deserves* to die, and die she will."

"Then I cannot pipe," said Misty.

"What?" said Anastacia. "You're not going to let him die because of a difference of opinion?"

"I'm not going to save him until I have his word. Goar, you must promise me this. If Kaie can be stopped without killing her, then you will not kill her."

Goar sighed. "I am to live then, but not have vengeance. This will be a great punishment for my guilt. My penance for failing my mate. Sacha followed you, and so must I. I promise."

Misty raised the pipe to her lips.

Chapter Eleven—Seduction of Power

Kent seemed to be the only one in the group not altered by the previous day. He was as outgoing as ever. His equilibrium convinced Anastacia that his adventurous stories had probably been true. They walked side by side, their paces matching perfectly.

"The rest'll come around in a while," he said. "This group has lived a pretty quiet life up to now. I imagine the past few days have been as much a shock for them as for you."

Anastacia nodded. "Just being here is a shock."

"Is it so different from your world?" he asked.

"I couldn't begin to explain." Anastacia paused to climb over a fallen tree. The forest was growing increasingly dense as they traveled. "This land is like living in the back of a mirror, a fun house mirror. I can't be sure if what I see is really there."

Kent chuckled. "Disorienting I imagine. In spite of that, you're holding up very well. I knew you would—not the type for hysterics."

"I guess not. I generally keep my feelings to myself." She paused. "Unless I'm ticked off. Then everybody knows. I don't say anything. Just go outside and shoot hockey pucks against the garage door. There's some impressive dents."

"That's not always best either. Feelings may need to be shared."

Anastacia glanced at him. His blond curls were limp with the heat, and his moustache could have used a good grooming, but he still looked like a model for business suits. No doubt about it. Her interest in boys, well, men really, was reawakening. "Now I'm sure I'm in another world," she said. "A good-looking, masculine man who's also sensitive!"

"You don't seem to have much of an opinion of men. Watch you don't become as bitter as Isabel," he whispered. "Have you ever tried sharing your feelings with one?"

"I can't say I really know any men appropriate for that."

"Then you must keep looking. Any man would be glad to be your confidant."

Anastacia smiled and shook her head. "I see why you're so popular with women. In my world, they'd fight over you."

Kent laughed. "I genuinely like women. All people, for that matter. I don't deceive the women who like me. I don't make false promises, in word or unspoken. I say exactly what I mean. "

"Even that you'll be gone in the morning?" They paused as a gray squirrel raced across the path, its little feet moving as fast as a sewing machine.

"Of course. They decide whether to continue based on the truth."

"And none of them hope for more?"

"Some, but I usually spot the type and end our encounter before she gets too hurt."

"Like the blonde in the village?"

"The blonde made incorrect assumptions. I simply took her home before she drank herself blind."

Anastacia smiled. She was heading into the wizard's den and yet felt actually happy that this Romeo spent one night alone. She must be crazy.

The trail narrowed, making conversation more difficult. Anastacia dropped behind. She enjoyed watching Kent's broad shoulders flex below his snug, gray shirt.

When they stopped for a rest in a small clearing, Durward was in high spirits. He gave orders now instead of requests and began to talk of his plans when Kaie was defeated. Whenever Misty offered a suggestion, he interrupted. Repeatedly, he took the shining, black stone from his pouch and stroked it.

"Look at the size! So beautiful! Incredible!"

Ellsworth and Isabel quietly discussed events in their village. They avoided Durward's conversation, seeming to take comfort in talk of ordinary things. Isabel remarked how impressed she was with Lissa's sewing skills.

"She has to be, what with all the children," he said. "But, she is a remarkable woman in many ways. I hope I don't leave her widowed."

Their conversation stopped.

Randolph had not spoken a word during the day's travel. He avoided sitting near Goar, but he did not demonstrate animosity. When Anastacia attempted to speak with him, he nodded and kept eating. His despondency affected the others.

As they gathered their things up, Anastacia whispered to Misty, "Randolph won't speak, and I understand why, but everyone else is depressed as well. This isn't a healthy attitude when we need to feel confident about ourselves."

"Durward has enough confidence for all of us," said Misty grumpily.

"He has been acting rather odd since he found the black crystal," said Anastacia.

"I'm concerned," Misty said. "This is so unlike him. He always blurted things out without thinking, but now he's so sure everything he says and does is right. He's closing himself off. He seems so . . . ambitious. That is not the Durward I know."

He's certainly taking command of the situation, thought Anastacia. *You have to admire that.*

Anastacia found herself walking behind Goar. She reminded herself that their numbers had dwindled because of him and he had taken the lives of her special animal friends. But Goar did not give her the feeling of a cold-blooded killer. It almost felt like traveling with Sacha again. The white panther was as subdued as Randolph, but Anastacia knew he needed desperately to be accepted and forgiven. When the path widened slighted, she stepped up beside him.

"Have you remembered any details about your time with Kaie?" she asked. "You never know what might be helpful."

"Shadows," he growled. "Bits and pieces. No weaknesses."

"Tell me what you can remember."

"I recall best when her control on me was least. Sometimes, when she was busy with her potions and spells, she had no need for me. I would start to remember myself. But always she called me back before I became strong enough to rebel."

"How did she do that?"

"The black crystal. She makes it give blinding pain."

"That's how she controlled you? Fear of pain?"

"If it had only been the pain, I might have had a chance. After the agony comes a draining of will, of self. It was like I was no longer alive, no longer in existence. I had no memory, no hopes, no fears, and no love. I simply obeyed. I had periods of total blackness in my mind after she seared me with the crystal."

"She did this to punish you?"

"Sometimes. Other times to ensure my quick, blind obedience to her orders. She used it just before I attacked your companions, before I killed my own . . . . " His voice choked.

"Sacha understood. I know she forgave you."

"Yes, and for her and my other victims, if not for myself, I will succeed."

"Kaie's victims. I believe you must have free will to have guilt. Only those who choose to be with Kaie are deserving of her fate, whatever it will be."

Goar glanced up at her. "You speak as though you understand guilt."

"After my mother died, I was angry with myself for all the time I had wasted arguing with her over stupid things, even though I know she understood that it was just normal adolescence. Then I felt guilty that I couldn't be happy for my stepdad's sake." Anastacia did a small hop as she adjusted her pack.

"But it is not up to you to erase the world's pain."

"You're right, yet I find myself furious that I can't ease anyone's, even my own."

"Is that exactly what you're doing here? Trying to erase Dawn's End's pain?"

Anastacia looked thoughtful. She watched the muscles flexing in Goar's haunches as he walked. His body was covered in scars and stitches. Misty had decided to leave them for a while since the wounds were freshly closed. "I didn't think of it that way. I hate not knowing why I'm doing things."

"The most difficult challenge of all is to understand ourselves."

"Yeah, I guess. When stuff gets to me, I go off by myself and have an adventure. Shoot white water in a canoe or something. I love the feeling of fighting for control and winning."

Goar's head drooped. "I've been fighting for control and losing. The power of the stone is unstoppable."

"That sucks. Being so totally under Kaie's control. Does she hold others like that?"

"I remember a friend was there. A good woman. Kind. Gentle. But, whenever I think of her face, I see flames and hear the screams of death."

A demonic face rose in Anastacia's imagination. "What does it mean?"

"I don't know," Goar said. "But I feel no hate toward her."

Anastacia realized this information could be valuable. In his relaxed mood, Goar seemed to be remembering things better. "Who else is with Kaie?"

"The giant who took me and many others prisoner. I feel prickles of disgust when I think of him. Another woman. I am unclear about her."

Carefully, not wanting to stress or pressure him, she casually asked, "Who else?"

"I remember no one else."

"Surely there are others. She could have an army."

He snorted. "I don't think she needs an army."

It doesn't make sense, thought Anastacia. "Why have anyone then?"

"I suspect we amused her."

Anastacia grimaced. "Not a comforting thought."

"There is nothing comforting about Kaie. She is beyond your worst nightmare."

Kaie would have been pleased with this description. But she wasn't pleased with Lachish's report. She sat on a dusty willow chair, threaded with spider webs. Her servant kneeled at her feet, trembling. She was in an anxious mood.

"What do you mean Goar is traveling with them?" Kaie asked. "How is this possible?"

"I don't know, mithtreth. He killed one of them, pluth a lupa, and another panther. There were thigns of a fearthome battle." He scratched his chest, puzzled.

"Why would he diminish their numbers and then join them? And why is he not responding to my call? He should be begging me for mercy by now." She stamped her foot.

Lachish lowered his bulky head. "I don't know, mithtreth. He looked thtrange."

"Be clear!" Kaie set her hands on the arm of the chair and pushed herself into a standing position.

Lachish flinched. "The animals put up a fight, but he had no fresh cutth on him. Just stitches on closed wounds." He looked up at her. "How can that be?"

"I'll ask the questions, idiot!" Kaie paced, thinking. "No cuts . . . . It must be that disgusting piper. But she couldn't free him. Unless, no! If the stone has been removed from his shoulder."

She fingered the stone on her bracelet staring into space. She shook her head. "One stupid animal is of no value. But the stone, the stone . . . . "

She strode toward Lachish and grabbed his matted, orange-brown hair. Jerking his head back and forth, she leaned down and screamed into his face. "I will call our spy to speak to you instead of Goar." She released his hair and pushed him backwards. "Find out what happened to the stone! Now!" He fell onto his back, hands braced by his sides.

"Yes, mithtreth," he said, crawling backwards like a crab out of the room.

Anastacia's group reached the crossroads early the next day. The right-hand path led toward Kaie's caves; the left-hand toward a village.

"We will go to the village," insisted Durward. "There, I can have the stone embedded into the bracelet."

"Perhaps we all should decide this," suggested Misty.

"There is nothing to decide," he said. "Continuing on would be foolish. She has diminished our numbers too much."

"If you feel that way," said Anastacia, "then why did you take us on this mission in the first place?"

"I did not know the devastation just one of her henchmen could do. If Goar could make us lose half our group single-handed, what could her entire army do?"

"She doesn't have an army," said Anastacia. "Goar says there are only a man and two women besides Kaie."

Durward sneered. "And you believe that traitor?"

"Durward!" said Misty. "Goar is free of Kaie now."

"So *he* says," Durward said. "Even *if* she's alone, we need the best weapon we can get. Anastacia has hardly shown us that she's our savior." He pointed his thumb toward his chest. "I'm the best chance."

Dismay swept the group. Kent and Anastacia exchanged uncomfortable looks.

"We can't waste the energy to bicker," Kent said. "And I could use a bath and a spot of ale while the bracelet's being worked. Anyone else like a night in civilization?"

"I would," said Isabel.

"I'd like some fresh supplies," said Ellsworth. "And I think we ought to let people know what's happened to the others."

Misty nodded. As the group veered left, Anastacia reached out and stroked Goar's head. He jumped.

"Sorry, Goar. I didn't mean to startle you."

"You didn't. It just reminded me of someone. The woman of fire. But, I also had a flood of images when you did that. One of them new."

"What was it?" asked Anastacia eagerly.

"Me talking to a man," he said.

"The ugly giant?"

"No," Goar said. He spoke slowly, remembering. "Pleasant looking. With a sword."

"You mean there's another man with Kaie?"

"No. Yes. I don't know. It doesn't make sense." He paused. "I see him with her, and I see him with you."

"*Me!*"

"Shh." Goar's voice lowered. "I suspect Kaie has an ally we don't know about."

"Not someone in our group," whispered Anastacia.

"I hope I'm wrong. I can't see his face clearly. It's just an impression. This man spoke to me. Told me things to help Kaie."

"My God, Goar." Anastacia clenched her fists in frustration. "Do you know what this means? That's how she knew our movements."

Goar nodded his powerful head. "I came right to the edge of your encampment. People were still awake. We met and talked in the darkness."

Anastacia groaned. "It also means we could be heading into a trap."

Kaie gloated. "So. Durward was successful. Soon, I will not only have my stone back, but it will be mounted in another bracelet."

Lachish bowed and smirked. Today, bearing good news, he stood in front of her chair.

"Now we wait. They will be here soon. You can have some time to enjoy yourself with the captive." She waved her bony hand. "But I want to question him first. The hunter seems an aware man. Not aware enough to get home safely once he abandoned the others, though."

"Thank you, mithtreth."

Kaie picked at a broken nail, tearing off a piece into the quick until it bled. She stuck it in her mouth and sucked. She took it out, looked at it, frowned, and then said, "Send the hunter to me while he is capable of talk. And also Beora. I don't want her to be inspired by Goar's escape. She balked at my command to caress that bandit with her fire. I shall test her obedience today in preparation for our visitors. Go now." She waved a dismissal.

Lachish rushed off. He felt torn with excitement. What a decision! To watch Beora cook the hunter alive or to tear him limb from limb himself. Life with Kaie was a whirlwind of delight.

Anastacia was enchanted by the village of the panther people. It was built of white marble and laid out neatly with a courtyard in the middle. Her first encounter with a true panther man was startling; he was more feline than she had imagined.

This is how my father looked!

His body was covered with short, straight, brown hair. Tapered, black eyes held the same white diamond as did Goar's and Sacha's. He dressed in a simple tunic and breeches and stood barefoot. His pug nose was barely noticeable in his bearded face.

"Welcome to our village, Misty," he said, greeting her as old friend. Misty introduced him as Fortune. It was his turn to be surprised when Anastacia was presented.

"The highest honor," he said, bowing. "I will request food for you all," he announced to the group. "Will you be staying the night?"

"Yes," replied Misty, "if you have room and it is not too much inconvenience."

"Of course. I will make sleeping arrangements with the villagers. How many wish to be bedded together?" he asked, glancing around the group.

"None," Durward said firmly.

Misty bit her lip to keep back the tears while the others shuffled uncomfortably. Fortune lifted an eyebrow and then nodded.

"I will also need to use a smithy," said Durward. "And I want everyone to meet in the square before nightfall."

"As you wish."

The arrangements were completed quickly. Panther people of every feline shade brought a variety of food and drink. Some stared wonderingly at Anastacia, the only descendant of the legendary Alaric Morrel and the Esteemed Nicole Newman. The group was split up among the hosts, graciously provided with warm baths, and shown their sleeping quarters.

Misty placed her hand on Durward's arm. "Why do you shun me, my husband?"

"You're a distraction," he answered, barely looking at her. "I have important things to accomplish. I must concentrate." He straightened his shoulders. "I must ready myself for the glorious battle to come. Please do not be a hindrance."

Misty nodded, bewildered.

Durward convinced the blacksmith to let him use his tools unsupervised. He asked Anastacia to stay with him so that he could periodically check her bracelet to be sure he was mounting the stone correctly. She perched on a tall three-legged stool out of range of the fire and anvil.

He worked feverishly, occasionally stopping to take deep breaths and steady his trembling hands. At last, the huge stone glistened vigorously in the gold band. He snapped it on to his wrist, held it tightly to his chest, and smiled.

He spoke aloud to himself. "Until this moment, my life has been worthless, empty. There is but one small step left before my power becomes without limit. Kaie is doomed."

He strode past Anastacia as though she didn't exist. She jumped off the stool and followed him. They entered the town square where a long table had been set up. The panther people were feeding and chatting with the travelers.

"Most of you do not know me," he shouted. "I am Canice Durward, bearer of the panther bracelet and last of the great magicians."

Anastacia heard whispers from the villagers, "Why does he not acknowledge himself as the husband of Misty? She is a piper and a woman of worthy lineage."

Misty looked at the ground. Anastacia edged to her side and placed her hand on her arm.

Durward continued. "I travel with the daughter of the Esteemed Nicole Newman and the legendary Alaric Morrel. Together, Nicole and Morrel saved Dawn's End from eternal darkness. Now, I travel to save our land from the darkness of evil. Anastacia possesses a perfect bracelet. I had an imperfect one at my command, and, now, I hold the most powerful panther band of all!"

He raised his arm to reveal it, newly repaired. The enormous black stone covered the head of the embossed leopard. It glittered ominously in the fading sunlight.

The villagers muttered among themselves and shook their heads. Finally, Fortune spoke. "Why do you tell us this? What is it you want?"

"Is it not obvious? I want your people to join us on our quest. You must witness me crush Kaie and earn your place in history. With Canice Durward as your leader, Dawn's End will enter a glorious new sunrise!"

"No stranger leads us," said Fortune. "You are welcome to our hospitality as long as you need it. But no one will follow you on this venture."

"Do you speak for all the villagers?" asked Durward.

"Fortune is right," said a panther woman from the crowd. "No one will follow you. We have kept ourselves separate from men with good reason. Now, we see another example of the rightness of this action. You come here and treat your wife as a non-bond for all to see. You shout of power and destruction and expect to rally us. We are not so gullible as that."

Fortune said, "Our people surrendered the bracelets to your magicians in order to stop their insidious control from further altering us. We have remained as we were in spite of the other world corruption brought about by the use of these bracelets. This vainglorious battle is of your making. We will have none of it."

"Fools!" shouted Durward. "Kaie cares not for your separateness. She will destroy you like she destroyed the lilyvern. Like she destroys all of Dawn's End. You are nothing but a pack of cowards." He spun on his heel, pushed past his companions, and headed off into the woods.

There he spent the night encamped alone, refusing to have anything to do with the villagers, but also separate from Goar and Randolph.

After the table had been cleared and most of the villagers had gone about their business, Misty apologized to Fortune on behalf of her husband.

"He does not understand us," said Fortune. "You have more of our blood and are more familiar with our ways. He and we are neither wrong nor right. We simply are what we are. We do not judge."

"Thank you," whispered Misty.

"We will provide you with everything you need for your journey and wish you all safely returned. But we cannot become involved in the struggles of men."

Isabel drew Anastacia aside. "This is so unlike Durward. He has always adored Misty, and I have never seen him be forceful or rude to anyone."

"He does seem different," said Anastacia.

"Men. As soon as you trust them, they change for the worst," said Isabel.

"The villagers might have helped the old Durward. He came on too strong and arrogant," said Anastacia. "They seem to have a soft spot for Misty. It might have even been better to have her appeal to them."

"How many men do you know who'd allow a woman to lead?" asked Isabel.

"I've never waited for them to 'allow' me anything," said Anastacia. "I just make myself indispensable."

Isabel laughed and punched her shoulder. "My kind of girl."

"I suppose, as cousins, you've visited Durward's village often," said Anastacia.

"Yes," said Isabel, "and, for most of my childhood, I lived in their village. We used to play together. Durward was always unsure of himself. My brother didn't help, I'm afraid."

"Your brother. Where is he?"

"He died a few years ago, in a foolish accident. He was always a daredevil. The opposite of Durward, and forever mocking him."

Anastacia frowned. "What for?"

"Durward could never keep up. My brother was larger, stronger, faster, and very foolish. He made Durward look weak by comparison. Durward worshipped him, in spite of the teasing. Can you imagine being called 'clumsy' and 'bungler' by someone you admire? Constantly?"

"I don't think it would do much for his confidence," said Anastacia. "I hate guys like that. I've had words with more than a few."

Isabel grinned and nodded. "Misty was always there to smooth things over. He was an empathetic boy, kind and forgiving, so he accepted the teasing without malice, but I think it still stained him."

Deep in thought, Anastacia tucked a strand of her black hair behind her ear. "I'm glad you told me, Isabel. I think I understand a little better now. Good night, and sleep well. Tomorrow's going to be a hell of a day."

Chapter Twelve—Traitors and Heroes

The walk from the village back to the crossroads went too quickly for Anastacia. She had misgivings about the group. Randolph walked alone. Goar spoke only to her; everyone else avoided him. He told her his memory was improving steadily. Talking with her had helped.

Isabel and Ellsworth again talked quietly together. Kent bounced back and forth between Durward and Misty trying to smooth relations between the estranged couple and lighten the dreary mood. He winked at Anastacia. She felt a surge of warmth for him, knowing his feelings for Misty.

Without a word, Durward went southeast to the wizard's caves. They had no chance of surprise and no coherent plan.

When they stopped for their evening meal, Ellsworth made a suggestion. "We should camp here. We don't want to reach the caves at night."

"Don't be ridiculous," said Durward. "If we camp a stone's throw from her cave, they'll pick us off one by one in the dark."

Ellsworth clenched his teeth. Misty looked on the verge of tears.

"I suppose it is best to get it over with," Kent said. "How far now, Goar?"

"An hour."

"If everyone's up to it, then we should snack as we go. There'll still be some light in an hour."

"I'm not hungry anyway," said Anastacia.

"Me neither," said Isabel.

"All right," said Kent. "Those who want to eat will. Everyone else will eat later." He squeezed Anastacia's hand in passing.

"Right," said Durward. "Let's press on then."

"I'll lead," Goar said. "I can sense if anyone's in waiting."

"No, thanks. *I'll* lead," Durward said. He forced his way past the panther and took up a quick pace. Anastacia gave Goar a glance of apprehension.

Twilight crept in, threatening their last threads of security. An uneasy quiet settled over the forest. A night bird called. The light was fading. Footsteps grated on their ears. It was worse than waiting in the dentist's lounge for her first root canal. Waiting for the door to suddenly open.

Isabel and Ellsworth silently brought up the rear. The path wound through rough bush and rock until it reached the cliff side. They progressed along the bottom, searching for an opening. It was impossible to walk quietly with broken slate underfoot. There was a continual sound like the shaking of a box of broken china. Anastacia stepped carefully, trying not to slip on the flat, sliding rock.

Anastacia's chest seized and her muscles tensed as Goar surged past Durward with a roar. They were all startled for a second and then raced forward.

In front of a large cave, Goar battled with an enormous, hairy man. The group edged closer, forming an arc around the duo. No one interfered.

Anastacia scorned their immobility, took a deep breath, and unsheathed her dagger. If no one would help the panther, then she would.

"No," said Kent, grasping her arm. "Don't interfere. Goar seeks this confrontation. He wants to prove himself."

Anastacia realized Goar was holding his own and in no immediate danger. The giant was fast for his size, but the cat was quicksilver.

"Dung licking animal." Lachish cursed as his club thudded to the earth. "Keep thtill."

Goar twitched as if the sound had started a recording in his head. "I know you . . . Lachish. You serve the wizard for pleasure. You're as evil as she."

"Thank you." The man shouted as he swung in vain. After three more futile clubbings, Lachish began to tire. "Kaie!" The giant bellowed. In a flash of light, he disappeared.

Goar leapt and sniffed the area. He growled. "Black magic. Kaie's doing."

"You gave him too good a fight," Kent said. "The coward ran back to his protector."

"I didn't even see him." Durward spoke for the first time since the confrontation had begun, a touch of his old self-doubt in his voice.

"Neither did I," said Goar. "I smelled him. He always did reek, the boar."

"We breached her first defense," Kent said. "But I think we should keep a lantern lit while we enter the cave."

The others agreed and removed their packs. Twilight was giving way to darkness. Inside the cave, nothing would be visible. Misty silently lit and passed a lantern to Durward, who looked hesitantly into her eyes, and then entered.

The smell was a combination of slaughterhouse, chemistry lab, dingy basement, and despair. Anastacia wet her lips, keeping her breathing shallow in a futile effort to screen out the stench.

They crept along a narrow passage. Durward paused when they reached an entrance, lifted the lantern high into the air while the others crowded around and peered in. The cave opened into a large underground gallery with various entries. The damp walls glistened in the lamp light. A soft platt, platt, platt echoed through the blackness.

At the end of the cavern, figures appeared. Lachish stuck a torch into a niche in the wall, while he rested his club on one shoulder. Six steps to his left stood a hideous woman. Her ravaged body made Anastacia shudder.

"Beora," said Goar. "She is my friend."

"Good," said Kent. "I wouldn't want to fight a woman who's already been through that. What happened to her?"

"Fire. But you *will* have to fight her," said Goar. "She depends on Kaie and obeys her commands, though sometimes hesitantly. Her last resistance was dealt with severely. I wouldn't count on her to show mercy. She is a formidable threat. Without Kaie, Beora will spend the rest of her miserable life in agony."

"What could a poor wretch like that do?" asked Ellsworth. "I don't know how she can even move, much less fight."

"Whoever touches her is consumed in flames. Stay at least ten steps away from her."

The band looked at Beora with deference. As Riva entered behind the human torch, the group gasped. Riva wore a skin-tight, low-cut, cobalt-blue bodysuit, knee-high black boots, and nothing else.

"Kent," Ellsworth said, "here's someone along your avenue of expertise."

The adventurer did not respond. He stared at Riva, slack-jawed.

"Don't look so thunderstruck," said Ellsworth, "or we'll all think you've met your match. Who is she anyway, Goar?"

"Riva. She has no special powers to harm us."

"I wouldn't say that," Anastacia said. "It looks like she has already subdued both Durward and Kent.

Durward flushed and looked away, but Kent continued to stare, a furrow forming on his brow.

"The question is," said Misty, "where is Kaie?"

"Here, less than woman." Kaie stepped into view, her face and body hidden by her black cloak. Durward stepped forward. The others followed him into the subterranean room and spread out in a semi-circle.

Kaie snapped her fingers. Beora moved about the room, lighting torches mounted on the cave walls with the touch of her finger.

Kaie mocked the companions. "What a pity to travel so far just to die."

"No one has to die today," said Durward.

Kai hissed. "Stupid, stupid. What do you think is going to happen, pretend-wizard?"

"We have come to help you find yourself," said Misty. "To restore both you and Dawn's End to their former beauty."

Kaie laughed a high-pitched, choking sound. "Idiots. None of us wants that. I am what I choose to be, and so is this stinking land. You dim-witted crusaders have simply provided a bit of entertainment. But I grow annoyed with you. You have cost me the loyalty of my panther. I don't like interference. I will reclaim what is mine."

Her allies stood stiffly in anticipation. A glow shimmered from under the cowl of her cloak. Riva smiled mockingly at the group and Lachish stroked his club, while Beora stood expressionless.

Anastacia shifted her feet. *What did Kaie mean?* Everyone waited for the first move. Shockingly, it came from their side. Kent jumped forward pulling Anastacia with him. He held his dagger to Anastacia's throat as he pulled her backward toward Kaie.

"What are you doing?" Anastacia gasped and pulled at Kent's arm. Adrenaline surged through her body. She couldn't understand what was happening.

"Bringing you to me, because he is mine," answered Kaie.

Hostage. I'm a hostage. "No." Anastacia choked. "No! Not Kent."

"Who did you suspect, outworlder?" asked Kaie. "The half-cat?"

Anastacia pulled on his arm bound tightly across her chest and stamped on his feet. He seemed oblivious to anything she did. "Kent! Let me go!"

Kaie droned on. "The pretentious Durward? The monosyllabic lupa tender? Surely not one of the pathetic tradespeople?"

Anastacia blinked hard fighting back tears. *I suspected one of the villagers, even Durward lately, but not Kent. Please, not Kent.*

"Let her go," said Durward. "I have the more powerful bracelet." He raised his arm.

"Oh? Really?' Kaie's voice was high and excited. Her eyes bulged, and she grinned maniacally. "Then use it to free her."

Durward hesitated then stepped forward. He raised his arm, closed his eyes and concentrated. Kent stopped halfway between Durward and Kaie. He slowly lowered his arm. The group emitted a soft sound of relief. Kaie laughed. "So gullible." She raised her arm and said, "Keep her."

Kent's dagger flew back to Anastacia's throat, and his grip tightened.

Durward opened his eyes. "Join me, Anastacia. Use your bracelet."

"Yes, Anastacia, join him." Kaie laughed. "Become one with Dawn's End. With *your* end."

Anastacia struggled, but then relaxed and closed her eyes. *Focus,* she thought. *Get in the zone. Find that moment just before I shoot the puck. The moment where I know exactly how I'm going to move, exactly what is going to happen. Where everything disappears but the puck, the net, and the goalie. Nothing but me and the bracelets, from mine to his.*

There was a blinding flash of light surging between the two bracelets.

Get away from me, Kent, she thought.

Kent flew against the cave wall like a Frisbee. He slumped into unconsciousness, limbs askew.

Anastacia gasped and then raced back to her group. Isabel met her eyes in recognition; they were now both victims of betrayal.

Kaie screamed and pandemonium broke out. She aimed her bracelet at Durward. He dodged in anticipation, but the seamstress was caught off guard. Instantly, Isabel dissolved into a pile of sand.

"Isabel!" cried Anastacia, reaching out as though she could pull the disintegrated body back together.

The group scattered, trying to shield their bodies with boulders or place one of Kaie's henchmen between themselves and her deadly bracelet.

Anastacia stumbled, her thoughts a blur. *Kent was the wizard's pawn! He lied to me. Mr. Honesty. Durward said no one would die. Isabel, dust under our feet. Shit, shit, shit.*

She banged into Misty and clutched her arm. For a second, no one moved.

Kaie laughed loudly. "What useless warriors you are. Below disdain."

Beora edged closer to Ellsworth, who scrambled behind large stalagmites to escape her touch. He peered around the gnarled stone. Kaie smirked, raised her arm, and shot out a wave of purple light. He turned into a bat and flapped chaotically away.

Goar charged Kaie, knocking her down, sinking his claws into her shoulder. Lachish clubbed him from her back, like a golfer teeing off. Goar tumbled away, coming to a shaky stand beside Beora.

"Burn him," Kaie said.

Anastacia screamed in horror as the ravaged woman slowly extended her hand.

Randolph whirled his sling. The stone struck Beora in the shoulder, knocking her to the floor. Goar leapt away.

"This is suicide," muttered Misty. She grasped Anastacia's arm and pulled her to the exit. The group retreated with them. Lachish rumbled behind, and Goar was forced again to engage the brute. Riva assailed them with a barrage of arrows.

Damn, we sure could use Isabel right now, thought Anastacia as she scrambled to safety.

Kaie waited, arm raised, for the women to expose themselves between the last boulder and the exit. As they stepped out, she screeched. "Interfering outworlder!"

Anastacia turned. Kaie's hood fell partly back, revealing her colorless, uncanny eyes. Shocked, Anastacia stopped, staring.

As tiny darts of light shot from Kaie's band, Misty shoved Anastacia to the floor and threw herself on top of her. The darts stabbed at her repeatedly.

Durward saw the darts slice Misty's arms and clothes into the flesh below. The silken hair he had caressed so often burned away. Still, she protected Anastacia. Always protecting, caring, and helping. Like she protected him from the anger of others when he blurted out words without thinking. Like she helped when he felt confused. Like she cared for him when he was ill. Like she comforted him when his father died. Love flooded over him like an incoming wave.

"No!" Durward bellowed. He raced to place himself in the path of the light knives. Using his bracelet, Durward managed to rebound many of them back to Kaie, while a few pierced his flesh.

Randolph flung one last stone in Riva's direction, smashing her bow and injuring her arm. He then jumped to aid Misty and Anastacia. The three of them stumbled out of the entrance.

Goar raked Lachish across the forehead, and, as the blood ran into his eyes, the panther dashed out after his comrades. Outside, darkness reigned as well, but moonlight weakened its grip. They regrouped, touching each other for comfort. Misty moaned softly.

"We have to help Misty," said Anastacia.

"We get to safety," Randolph said. "See her wounds."

"We can't leave Durward behind," Misty said.

Goar growled. "Take them to safety. I'll go back and help hold them off."

"Not necessary," said Durward, as he stumbled from the exit. "Stand back."

Light soared from his bracelet to the roof of the tunnel entrance. The stone groaned and shifted. A glow appeared in the cave, bouncing toward them.

"Hurry," whispered Anastacia. "They're coming."

Durward cried out. "Help me!"

Randolph increased his support of Misty as Anastacia stepped away and placed her arm by Durward's.

"What do I do?" asked Anastacia.

"Concentrate on what you want to happen. Envision it. Just like you did with Kent."

Anastacia closed her eyes. She raised her bracelet, focusing the power. Light crackled as the two beams merged. The entrance exploded in a cascade of rock. The ground shook as the group huddled together for stability. Dust mushroomed out of the twilight zone, stinging their eyes. Anastacia and Durward sagged with exhaustion.

Durward turned, trembling. "Lead the way, please, Randolph. I'll carry Misty."

They plodded on until Misty spoke. "You must rest, Durward. I'm not a light load. I can feel you shaking."

"You are no load to me, Canice Misty. But we must stop to treat your wounds. I feel your blood on my hands and soaking through my shirt." He was fighting tears with every step.

"Your blood as well, my love." Her voice was soft and warm.

Soon they found a suitable spot. Randolph lit a small campfire. Durward removed his pack and examined his wife. Rage soared through him.

"That damnable wizard! You're cut in a dozen places. Next time, I'll kill her! I—"

"Hush." Misty placed her fingers across his lips. "The Canice family does not kill. That is, if we are a family."

Durward lowered his head. The tears flowed.

"Of course, we are. I'm sorry, Misty. I don't understand what happened to me. I had no reason to treat you like that." He rubbed ointment on her wounds and bandaged the worst.

"It's the stone," said Misty. "It's corrupting you."

"It's my own weaknesses. I felt useless, clumsy, until I realized the power in this bracelet. With the black panther mine to control, I could be someone of importance, of respect . . . of value."

"You've always been of value, and no one could be more important to *me*."

When Durward finished, Randolph silently passed around the water skin.

"I respect you," said Anastacia, when Durward passed her the container. "Even before you saved our lives in the cave. You have great courage and a deep sense of what is right. But why didn't you teach me to use the bracelet before we attacked? I was next to useless. I could have made a difference."

"I was afraid the practice might corrupt you." Durward smiled in chagrin. "That much power can be seductive."

"Me?" said Anastacia. "What about you? You seem to be going through some changes."

"Yes. I thought I could handle it, but I was probably wrong. All I could feel was anger and power, a dangerous combination. I think I was right keeping you innocent for as long as I could. This group didn't need two tyrants."

"I get it, I think," said Anastacia.

"I led them into a slaughter." Durward passed his hand over his face. "If I hadn't been so bull-headed, Isabel and Ellsworth would still be alive."

He tried to wrap a bandage over the deep cut on his left arm, but it became tangled. Anastacia gently removed his hand and repaired the wrap.

Everyone was silent, remembering the optimistic man and the quietly courageous seamstress.

"My poor sister, now a widow." Misty sighed. "But it isn't your fault, Durward. There have been many deaths. We all knew the risks."

Durward nodded, unconvinced.

Anastacia cleared her throat. "We must get Misty to the village and then return, just Durward and I."

Goar growled. "What?"

"You were an amazing fighter, Goar. Our spearhead. Randolph and Misty were indispensable as well. But Durward and I are the least vulnerable. I understand the bracelet now. When I helped the rock fall, it became clear to me. I won't hesitate next time. Together, we will smash them to the wall, like Kent. When they're unconscious, we'll take their weapons and the bracelet."

"Randolph can take Misty to the village," said Durward.

"No!" cried Misty. "We must stay together. You both need rest. Durward needs his cuts properly tended, and, although Goar has not complained, I see him favoring his left hind paw. Please, Durward."

"Very well, my love." He took her hand and gently kissed it. "I've treated you so badly; I can't bear to argue with you. We will rest for a day in the village. But just a day."

He met Anastacia's eyes and nodded.

Chapter Thirteen — Beora

When Anastacia and Durward were rested and refurnished with supplies, they prepared to leave the village again. Misty was resigned. She focused her energy on supporting Lissa. Ellsworth's destruction had come as a great shock. Bedad tried to comfort her, but he was grieving himself for Griswold.

Their departure, however, was delayed by two startling events. As the companions said their goodbyes, a visitor was announced. Anastacia jumped back as Beora entered. Both she and Durward raised their arms in defense.

"Stop! I didn't come to harm you."

"What trick is this?" asked Durward.

"Must be a message from Kaie," said Anastacia.

"Neither. I come as a friend." Beora looked from one disbelieving face to another, stopping at the panther's. "Do you not trust me, Goar?"

"I don't know." He sniffed. "Why would you leave Kaie? How will you manage the pain?"

"I have enough potion for at least a week." She pulled a small vial from her pocket and held it up. "I have been stealing it, a little at a time, as well as holding back a few drops each morning. It has added up. Today, I took what was left since I had decided to leave." She returned the vial to her pocket.

"Why are you here?" Anastacia asked.

"I want to help." Her voice was earnest, pleading.

"But *why*?"

Beora straightened and took a deep breath. "I hate Kaie and her servants with all my heart. She did this to me. She should have let me die." She pointed to her face.

Goar growled. "But when the potion is gone?"

"I doubt very much if Kaie will allow me to live that long. She is plotting her vengeance on you, as well. We are both doomed." She held her hands out, palms up. "I prefer the quicker death anyway."

Goar nodded, and then, forgetting, padded forward to be petted.

"Stay back!" She tucked her hands into her sleeves. "Now that you are free of the black crystal, I can't touch you."

"You knew of the crystal placed in my body?" Goar's eyes narrowed.

"Yes, but I didn't know where," she said. "I couldn't remove it. I would kill you trying. I was afraid to tell you while you were under Kaie's spell. You might have betrayed me. We both kept secrets from each other." She slumped, eyes downcast.

"How do we know you won't betray us?" asked Anastacia. "You could be a spy, like Kent."

"Kent could no more help it than you, ivory panther." Beora looked at Goar, then back at Anastacia. "Kent holds a crystal in his body."

"How could she have done that?" asked Anastacia doubtfully.

"Lachish captured him traveling to the cottage of the Canices. At first, I thought he would be given to Riva to poison. I was terrified I would have to burn him. Such a beautiful man."

"Yeah, I know," Anastacia said tersely.

"Instead, Riva drugged him, and Kaie inserted a black stone under his skin. That is how she controls him. When she ignites the crystal, he has no will of his own."

Goar's voice rumbled. "I remember now. It was Kent with whom I spoke to gain knowledge of your plans. He was the infiltrator. We would meet on the outskirts of your campsites. And, yet, it didn't seem like Kent. That was one reason why I couldn't recognize him. When under the wizard's power, he was devoid of all personality."

"Please," said Beora, "let me join you. Lachish and Riva cannot harm me. I can protect you. I am a fearsome ally."

The comrades looked at each other and then nodded, one by one.

"But Anastacia and I were just leaving to face Kaie without the others," Durward said. "It would be best if you stayed here with them."

"You can't fight her," said Beora. "She is planning to take the other crystals and embed them in her bracelet. She dared not try this before for fear she would damage it and lose all power. But now she's decided to risk it."

"That's insane," said Durward.

Duh, thought Anastacia.

"Riva has been working on her," said Beora, "driving her to take great risks. Pushing her to greater evil. It seems to have worked. Riva has become reckless and Kaie maniacal. There is more involved than you realize."

Anastacia sighed. "You mean it gets worse?"

Beora explained Kaie's plan to control the people with drugs and the crystal, causing them to storm the doors into the outer world, which would yield to such great pressure. Then they would ravage whatever they found on the other side.

"By my estimate, she should be ready any day now," Beora said.

"My God!" cried Anastacia. "We must stop her."

Beora shook her head. "The two of you will be no match."

"How many stones does she have?" asked Durward.

"Originally she had four. One was placed in Goar, which you now have. One was placed in Kent and, as far as I know, it is still there. That leaves two."

"Plus the one on her band," said Anastacia. " That makes three. Three crystals to our two."

"Three against three," Beora said.

"Pardon?"

"Three. That was another reason I came. I was not sure Goar would remember about the other bracelet."

"What other bracelet?" asked Goar.

Beora turned to him. "Kaie told you once about another band of power. I was listening from an adjacent tunnel."

"Tell us!" Durward urged her to continue.

"Goar is a talking panther," said Beora, "a he-who-once-was."

"Once was what?" asked Anastacia.

"Human," said Durward.

"Goar was human!" Anastacia looked quizzically at the panther.

"Not Goar personally," said Durward. "His ancestors. His family descended from people who used the bracelet so extensively that it changed their descendants eventually into panthers. Like your father, Alaric Morrel."

Beora nodded.

Anastacia lifted her wrist and stared at her bracelet with horror. "You mean, if I keep using this, my kids will be panthers?"

"No," said Durward. "It must be used repeatedly over generations. Besides, you are already of the panther blood, and no one could even tell."

Misty interrupted. "The people like Fortune are panther-people. They were altered and then no longer used the bracelets. They stopped changing and so remain as they are today. Goar's people continued to call upon the power of the crystal until they reached the form they are now. They can alter no further because they can no longer use the bracelet. It will not respond to one with so little humanity."

"I'm half-human only," said Anastacia. "Am I the best to control the bracelet?"

"Yes, now that you know how to use it," said Durward. "But Kaie is more human, although there may have been an ancestor we don't know about."

"You didn't tell me I would be altering my children by using the bracelet," said Anastacia. Her blue eyes flashed with anger. "You deceived me."

Durward looked at the ground for a moment and then met her stare. "I thought you would use it only twice. The effect would be as slight as a single black hair on your child's body. Much less than what you have already inherited."

Anastacia crossed her arms, legs apart and shoulders back. "And now that I'll be using it repeatedly?"

"It will still be so slight as to be unnoticeable," said Misty. "As long as it is not used for generations."

"You can't be sure. My parents always said my reflexes were as fast as a cat's. I'm much stronger than any other girl in my school. It hasn't hurt me, but I won't use this bracelet." She turned away. "Now, Beora, tell us about the other bracelet."

Kaie was in a rage. Riva had picked at her doubts until she was in a whirlwind of fury. Losing Goar was more than she could tolerate, but Beora's rebellion and subsequent desertion angered and confused her.

First, she sent Riva, Lachish, and Kent off in search of the woman of flames. Then she called Kent back, doubting her control over him. Angry with the way things had gone, and looking for a scapegoat, she took her anger out on Kent. When he passed out from her torment, she turned on Fulke, the hunter, who had revived.

Riva and Lachish returned without Beora. Kaie screamed and stamped her foot. Unable to control her anger, she transformed Fulke into a frog. Cursing, she stomped him into the dusty cavern floor, his guts bursting through his green skin.

"Bring me the peddler," she screeched.

"He's dead, mistress," mumbled Lachish.

"Shit! I forgot. Why did I order that? Am I to have no amusement?"

She yanked a clump of matted hair from her own head and swallowed it.

"There's still Kent of the Lake," said Riva, as she tucked back her own hair.

Kaie kicked his prostrate body.

"Yes, there is. Bring water to revive the puppet."

Anastacia, with Durward, Randolph, Goar, and Beora, entered an area of Dawn's End unlike any she had seen before. They had been traveling steadily north and now entered a tropical forest. At least, that was the closest description she could devise. The palm trees, vines, heavy undergrowth, and brilliant blue, sapphire, and purple flowers were spaced out neatly, almost like a cultivated garden.

"We're close now," Beora said reassuringly when she heard the sound of running water.

Anastacia gasped when the forest opened on a small stream crowned by a splashing, fifteen-meter-high cascade. The banks of the river were marshy, dotted with bright, silver lilies.

"It's beautiful." Anastacia breathed in deeply.

"My ancestral home," said Goar.

"We'll find the bracelet above the falls," said Beora.

"Right," said Durward.

But they were slow to move, hypnotized by the idyllic view. The river divided above the cascade. On the right, it formed a small stream. On the left, it broadened into a quiet pond. On either bank of the pond sat a panther, one white as the breast of a dove and the other as gleaming black as a raven. They sat, immobile as statues.

Anastacia turned to Goar. "Perhaps you should question them."

The beast nodded and padded ahead.

"Brothers. We need your help. An evil force is choking Dawn's End. We have come to free it."

The great cats did not move.

He roared. "I am Goar. I travel with Canice Durward, wizard; Anastacia Newman, outworlder, daughter of the revered Nicole Newman and Alaric Morrel; Beora, woman of fire; and Randolph of the lupas."

No response.

"Durward and Anastacia are wearers of the panther band. We seek the third bracelet. The evil wizard, Kaie, knows it is under your protection. She may come for it. We wish to claim it first."

The felines did not even blink.

"Can you help us?" asked Anastacia.

"No." The black panther's voice rumbled.

"They *can* talk," she said, then louder. "Why won't you answer Goar?"

"He asked no question," said the white leopard.

Anastacia laughed. "That's true. Well, here is our question. Will you give us the other bracelet so that we can defeat Kaie?"

"No," said the dark panther.

"Why not?"

"It is ours to protect from the foolishness of humans and half-humans."

Durward interrupted. "But you don't understand. I will begin at the beginning."

Kaie snarled. "A son of a wizard has escaped me, and the fools care for him. Where is he now?"

"W-with Canice Misty's sister." Kent of the Lake stammered through bleeding lips, his face badly bruised and one eye swollen shut.

"And is there a husband with this sister?"

Once again, Kent took too long to respond. Lachish punched him jaw, lifting him off the floor. Kent collapsed.

"The more you hit him, the longer this takes," Riva said in a complaining tone.

Kaie hissed. "Do I detect a note of sympathy?"

"No, mistress, just impatience. Lachish will kill him before we learn anything. He has a habit of overdoing it."

The giant curled his lip into a snarl.

"Answer me!" Kaie pressed a barbed needle into Kent's hand.

"Stop, stop! Why are you doing this? I'm telling you everything I know."

"Because you bore me. I itch to crush those who waste my time. Speak fast, fool, before I have Lachish rip your arm out of its socket like a turkey drumstick."

Kent looked at the hairy brute, who grinned crookedly and muttered, "Gobble, gobble."

"Do not delude yourself into thinking I would not allow you to bleed to death. With Lachish's strength and my magic, we can turn you into a limbless lump. Leave you propped against the cavern wall, like so much bat droppings."

For the first time in his adult life, Kent felt tears of fear and frustration forming. He swallowed and coughed. "I know where the boy is."

"I am Reason," said the white panther when Durward had finished his story. "You have met my requirements. I recognize your right to the band of power."

"Wonderful!" Anastacia said. "Where is it?"

"I am Anger," said the black panther. "You have not met *my* requirements."

"What are they?" asked Durward.

"Reason must be persuaded by reason, but Anger must be persuaded by anger. Durward was the champion who placated my brother, but who will satisfy me?" demanded the dark panther as it paced sleekly toward them.

"What do you mean? How?" asked Anastacia.

"Who is your champion of anger?"

"Anger?" said Durward. "I don't understand."

"I am!" Goar roared. "I understand your challenge, and I accept it."

"You must defeat me," said the black panther, "utterly, in order to win the bracelet. It will not be given to fools or weaklings."

"No," said Anastacia. "You can't fight. We're on the same side."

"Wait," said Beora. "Let me fight him. He won't stand a chance."

"This is my fight." Goar coiled his muscles and sprang.

"Damn!" screamed Anastacia. "Not again!" She raised her bracelet and shot a wall of light between the leopards, knocking them apart.

The dark cat gasped. "You will never get the bracelet without my information, and I will not tell you until my challenge has been met."

"Are you hurt?" asked Anastacia, rushing to Goar's side. He lay sprawled on the embankment, panting for breath.

While her attention was diverted, Beora edged slowly toward the black panther. She extended one finger close to his paw. The cat shrieked and leapt up into the air and backwards. He frantically licked his singed skin.

"That is just a taste of what I can do," said Beora. "I don't want to hurt you, but I will if I have to. You will die, so easily. I've done it before, with much less motive, and, this time, I will not hesitate."

The panther glared. "I am no match for black magic. Anger was meant to challenge the strength of others. Not their evil."

"I am not evil."

"You are a demon." The panther roared and leapt. As he sank his teeth into her neck, his fur burst into flames.

Anastacia screamed, even as she raised her bracelet. Durward reacted as quickly and their beams joined, driving the two apart and flooding them in a cool light. Beora sat, her hands to her throat, the blood running through her fingers. The panther's body was blackened by fire. He dripped blood, raw, red flesh glistening in the stillness.

Beora moaned. "Oh, no. I didn't mean to kill him. I was bluffing."

Randolph rushed to her side. "Bandages. Hurry."

"Don't touch me!"

Randolph stopped, bewildered. "But you're bleeding."

"It doesn't matter. Find out where the bracelet is before the panther dies."

"It's too late." Durward whispered, as he bent over the charred body.

Anastacia dropped the bandages beside Beora. "Can you do it yourself? You've got to stop the bleeding."

Beora wrapped her hand in her cloak and then picked up the bundle. She touched it to her neck. Fire flared up and transformed the bandages into a pile of ash. Beora shrugged weakly and lay back on the grass. "I've lost control of the fire."

"Beora!" cried Anastacia. "She's bleeding to death! What can we do?"

The two men looked helplessly at each other.

"Why have you done this?" Goar roared as he raced around the pond toward the white panther guard.

"It was not I."

"You must help her."

"Yes. It is reasonable to do so. You have met all the requirements. The bracelet may be able to save her."

"How?" asked Goar.

"With it, perhaps she can focus her own flames on the wounds. Control the fire to stop the bleeding. Cauterize them."

Durward quickly removed his bracelet and set it by the pile of ash. "Use mine, Beora. Try."

She lay back on the ground. "I must not touch it. The panther was right. I *am* evil. I can't control the fire anyway."

"Please, Beora, try," said Durward. "I don't believe you're evil."

"None of us do," Anastacia said.

Goar raced to her side. "If you are evil, then I am twice as evil. I put you in Kaie's power. You killed strangers, I killed Sacha. If you die now, it will be because you fought my fight. I can't live with any more guilt. If you understand guilt, then you must know how I'm feeling. Please, save yourself."

"What for? To live my life as an outcast? A freak with a shameful past. In eternal pain." She rolled onto her side and covered her eyes with one hand. "Dawn's End will be glad to see me pass to ash as I was meant to when my home caught fire."

"It didn't catch fire," said Goar. "It was lit."

"What? Who would do such a thing?"

"Need you ask?"

They both said, "Lachish."

"I saw him do it," said Goar. "I waited until he was gone and the flames diminished before digging you out. Kaie did not arrive by accident. She was checking his handiwork."

Beora moaned. "They did this to me. They killed my family."

Goar spoke quietly. "There are those who do not want to see you die, Beora. I'm one of them."

"So am I," said Durward.

Anastacia nodded, her throat was too tight to speak.

"Clayton deserves to know what happened," said Goar.

"No!" She rolled over and sat up. "He must never see me like this."

"Don't you realize every minute Kaie wreaks havoc on Dawn's End, people like Clayton lose their chance for happiness?" said Anastacia. "Help us defeat her so that no more young couples will be destroyed. No more families burned in their beds."

Beora clenched her teeth and reached for the band. The blood flowed freely down her neck, blending with her scarlet gown. She snapped the band in place, lay back, closed her eyes, and concentrated. A wisp of light, like a golden thread, wriggled from the black crystal. It wove its way up her arm and encircled her throat. There, it twirled, faster and faster, a hissing halo.

Anastacia sank her hand into Goar's fur and gripped him tightly while they watched. Suddenly, Beora fell back. The light retreated in a flash.

They all spoke at once. "Beora?" "Are you alright?" "Can you talk?"

Beora slowly opened her eyes and smiled widely, the first time Anastacia had seen her smile.

"I'm better than alright," Beora answered, sitting up. She rubbed her throat and looked wonderingly at each of them. "The pain is gone."

"Your throat doesn't hurt?" asked Anastacia.

"No, it doesn't." Her eyes were bright with delight. "But it's not just that. Nothing hurts, anywhere."

"What do you mean? I thought Kaie's potion stopped the pain," said Goar.

"It did. If I used it full strength. I put myself on half potency yesterday, so it would last longer. The pain has been barely tolerable. But now it's gone. Completely."

"That's wonderful!" Anastacia could barely restrain herself from hugging the woman. Instead, she buried her face in Goar's musky fur and wrapped her arms around his neck.

"Is good," Randolph said.

Beora removed the band and dropped it at Durward's feet. He bent to pick it up, but then quickly snatched back his hand.

"Ouch! It's too hot to touch."

"I can tell you where our bracelet is," said the panther of Reason, his voice rumbling as he joined them.

"Why would you do that?" asked Beora. "I killed the other panther."

"He died as he wished. It is far more complicated than you have time to hear. You have mastered both Reason and Anger and are entitled to the bracelet."

The group watched the great white panther dive into the reedy pond. Bubbles broke the surface, ripples spread and died, and the silence waited. Anastacia absently stroked Goar as they observed the placid surface. Goar's sensitive paws felt the tremor first. He gave a warning.

"Something moves."

As the rumble increased, the group fidgeted anxiously. Slowly, a bronze shape broke the surface, an enormous paw, claws extended. The statue rose into view, a snarling panther, in fighting position, one powerful paw raised to strike. As the water poured off the figure, the object of their search was revealed. Encircling the standing front paw was a bracelet.

"There it is!" shouted Anastacia.

The white panther emerged on the other side of the pond and trotted out of sight, without a word.

"But how do we get it?" asked Durward.

"Swim, of course."

Durward picked up the cooled wristband from Beora and snapped it into place. "Perhaps I could use my bracelet to bring it here."

"What for? That's risky," said Anastacia. "It's only ten meters. It's a warm day. Just watch out for the reeds."

Durward rubbed his bracelet with his thumb, avoiding her eyes. "I can't swim."

"I only little," said Randolph.

"I can swim like a fish," said Anastacia, as she removed her shoes.

She waded into the quiet water. When it deepened, she front crawled to the statue, and climbed upon the base. She unlatched the bracelet and snapped it onto her other wrist. As she prepared to dive back in, a large, pale tentacle emerged from the pond. It was quickly followed by two more thick, exploring arms.

"Don't move!" Durward said. "It's searching for you."

He raised his band to strike, but the arms sank out of view.

"Not gone," said Randolph. "I feel it waiting."

"So do I," said Durward.

"I'm going across," called Anastacia. "It can't harm me with two bracelets."

Durward shouted to her. "No! You could be attacked by surprise. It isn't safe."

"I can't stay here," she said. "We're wasting time. I'm coming across."

But, before she did, Beora suddenly disrobed and raced into the water.

"I'm coming for you. Nothing alive can touch me." Beora pulled off her gloves, boots, and robe. Underneath, she wore a gray tunic and shorts.

She dove in. When Beora reached the base of the statue, tentacles rose from the water and flung themselves upon her small figure. In a flash, she disappeared below the surface.

The water boiled and two bulging eyes in a sickly, white face surfaced. An agonized screech tore from the creature's beak-like mouth. It rolled on its side, floating lifelessly on the surface, its tentacles now burned to a curl. There was no sign of Beora. The pond around the dead creature slowly cooled.

Anastacia dove in to search. Durward hopped from one foot to another while Randolph stared intently as she disappeared from sight. She found Beora lying on the bottom. Anastacia grabbed her tunic and pulled but it was too difficult to handle Beora without making contact with her bare arms, legs, or face. She swam to the surface.

"Beora's unconscious," she shouted to the others. "She's too hard to lift without touching her skin. She's drowning!"

"Use the bracelet to make an air bubble," called Durward.

"Of course." Anastacia dove.

"If she ever wakes," said Durward. "She may need resuscitation or medical care. I wish Misty were here. She'd know how to help her."

Chapter Fourteen — Potions of Death

As Kaie cut the black crystal from the most vulnerable place in his body, Kent thought he was dying. Then he remembered his treachery and hoped he would die.

"You can have him now," she said to Riva and Lachish. "I'm finished with him. Take him away and dispose of him in whatever way you like. I have a more important guest to attend to."

Kaie left.

Tossed aside like a dog chew toy, Kent drew inward. He ignored the taunts, neither begging for mercy nor responding with anger. Pain, humiliation, and shame filled him. Riva and Lachish took turns ravaging his body, like dogs fighting over a bone.

"Aren't you aloof?" Riva mocked him. "I wonder if your buddies will be so stoic. It will be especially interesting to watch Lachish destroy the outworlder."

Knowing his betrayal had weakened his friends, Kent allowed the tears to roll silently down his face. Riva screamed with laughter, but when Kent offered no further response, she became bored.

"Let's leave him where others will see, as an example of our power. Then we'll look for his friends. It's time to end this."

Lachish carried him to the path leading to the caves and lashed him to a wide, white birch tree. Riva dipped her fingers in blood and wrote in the white bark above his head.

After Beora regained consciousness, she found Anastacia sitting close by. They were surrounded by an enormous air bubble. She was too weak to swim to shore.

While she regained her strength, Beora shakily told Anastacia how much she regretted becoming Kaie's servant.

Anastacia pressed her lips together and shook her head. "You are as much a victim as anyone, Beora. I can't say I would have done anything different, except probably lost my temper and been killed."

"Maybe, but you're tougher than I."

"I've never suffered like you," said Anastacia. "You're a courageous person, Beora. To turn against Kaie, knowing her so well, to face the pain, to risk your life with the panther and again with the water-creature. I admire you. What is it? Why are you crying?"

"I've hated myself for so long, it stuns me that everyone else doesn't." She buried her face in her hands, sobbing.

"None of us hate you, Beora. If you would allow it, I would like to be your friend." Anastacia waited while the other woman sobbed.

Finally, Beora nodded. "You must forgive Kent as well. He had even less choice than I."

"You said he was under Kaie's control," said Anastacia. "Like Goar, I guess. How did she get the crystal into the panther?"

"Kaie fired a crystal-tipped arrow into Goar's shoulder. It was designed to break off, leaving the stone hidden when the wound healed. Whenever she used her bracelet, she controlled him totally. The stone also kept him docile. When she ignored him, he would be more like his old self, but unable to leave her without permission. She put a binding spell on him. Sometimes I think it was worse, when he was most like his true self and knew he was trapped."

Anastacia considered how horrible it would be to jump like a marionette under Kaie's control. "Did she fire an arrow into Kent? Wouldn't that kill him?"

"Kent was not a physical danger to her. Goar would have killed her. Instead of an arrow, Lachish subdued Kent. Kaie performed a small operation to place the stone under his skin."

"Why didn't Misty notice when she treated his wounds."

"Because of its placement. Somewhere he did not allow Misty to see. A very private and hidden place."

"Oh!" Anastacia winced and looked away.

"Kaie's clever," said Beora. "She did not want Kent to become involved with a woman. It could complicate her plans. He could become infected with Riva's disease. He could fall in love or create a child, powerful forces against her control. By placing the stone where she did, he was rendered impotent. Struggling against the impotency would be physically painful."

Anastacia's eyes widened. "That explains the pain when we kissed."

"You kissed Kent!"

Anastacia covered her mouth and nodded.

Beora smiled. "He's handsome, charming, and far less the philanderer than he pretends. You could do worse."

"Yes. I thought so," said Anastacia. She wiped her forehead with the back of her hand. The air bubble was as hot as a sauna. "I was shattered when he betrayed me."

"If you forgive me, you must forgive him."

"I already have. The zombie who held a knife to my throat wasn't Kent. I just hope I didn't damage him when he hit the wall. But I haven't been completely honest with him either. I never told him my age."

"Which is?"

"Sixteen."

"Oh, oh. Kent does many questionable things, but he does not take advantage of girls."

"It's legal in my world."

"Legal has nothing to do with it. He's ten years older than you and would not have kissed you. You know that, or you would have told him."

Anastacia sighed. "Yeah, I know. I'm not perfect either."

"It is good Kaie does not know your age. Somehow, she would use it against you. She is an expert at taking away all hope."

"Oh, Beora. I can't imagine how you feel, but you mustn't give up. Dawn's End appears to be a land of endless possibilities. Look what miracle has occurred today. You are no longer in pain."

"That's true," said Beora. "But Kaie infects everyone around her like a running sore, making us unable to be close to others. She made me unable to return to Clayton, my fiancé. She kept Riva untouchable. She separated Goar from his mate. She made Kent impotent. This united little group is the most challenge she's ever received."

"She's tried to isolate us from each other, too," said Anastacia. "Even that strange business with Durward and the new stone. I wonder if she wasn't, somehow, responsible for the change in his personality. When I met them, he and Misty were like two sides of the same coin. They are reunited, even though he still wears the bracelet. Goar has lost Sacha, but he is himself again. There is hope for Kent as well . . . . And you."

Beora smiled sadly. "I'm feeling stronger, now, Anastacia. I think I can swim now."

"I wish I could hug you, Beora."

"Me, too."

Durward and Randolph were waiting anxiously on the shore. When Beora's and then Anastacia's faces popped into view, Durward let out a relieved breath. Randolph clapped his hands together and shook them.

The women crawled onto land. Anastacia removed the new bracelet and handed it to Durward. He turned it over and over in his hands, thinking.

"I want you to wear it, Beora."

"I can't."

"Yes, you can. You controlled mine to stop the bleeding, so you are able to work it."

"I'm not worthy." She turned her face away.

"None of that." Anastacia was insistent. "You've proven yourself."

"Take it," said Durward. He held it out insistently.

Beora looked at Randolph who also nodded.

Anastacia felt pumped, determined, and nervous during the return hike, the kind of feeling she had when her hockey team made the playoffs but had a couple of team members injured. She was traveling to face an insanely violent, powerful woman who held the odds in her favor, yet Anastacia had an urge to whistle. She felt confident, more in control than she'd ever felt. She'd stared death in the face today and lived to talk about it. Beora, too.

Randolph was his usual silent self. Beora seemed reborn, and Durward had found a healthy balance between embarrassed incompetence and arrogance. Everyone was changing, often through pain and loss, but with hope for the future.

Lunch held little conversation but many comfortable smiles. Beora beamed at their gratitude when she warmed the fruit drink. It was late afternoon when they heard the first laughter.

Goar growled, deep in his throat and lunged ahead of the others.

"They've come to meet us!" Durward shouted. "Are you ready Anastacia? Beora?"

They nodded.

"You help Goar with her servants," Durward said to Randolph. "We'll get the wizard."

"Right."

They surged forward. Where was the wizard?

"She's not here," said Anastacia. "Just her henchmen."

Again, Goar battled the giant. Randolph and Riva slipped from tree to tree, exchanging stones and arrows. Riva's injured arm had been fully healed by Kaie's wizardcraft. Beora joined Randolph, turning the incoming arrows to ash while he concentrated on aiming his sling. Durward used his sword to help Goar. The three of them moved away from the tree, deeper into the woods.

Anastacia decided to help the person lashed to the tree. She cut the ropes from behind, her dagger finally useful, and caught the man before he fell. She lowered him gently to the ground and tipped back his head.

Shock hammered through her body. "Oh, my God, Kent!"

He did not respond. Anastacia quickly checked the cuts and bruises around his face and chest. Opening her pack, she searched for the first aid supplies. His chest was bare and crisscrossed with jagged cuts, and his trousers were stained with blood. Taking a deep breath, she cut away the fabric from his groin and began to pack the ugly, ragged wound.

Suddenly a knife appeared at her throat. It was Riva.

"I'll kill the outworlder," she said.

Anastacia took one look at Kent's drawn, bruised face and willed Riva away. Her wristband tingled. Vibrating light flooded Riva. She screamed once and staggered back.

"Guard Kent and Anastacia," Beora said. "I can take care of this doxy myself."

Randolph moved into position by Anastacia.

"Well, well, sister in sin." Riva mocked Beora as she circled warily. "You have, at last, become the enthusiastic killer Kaie predicted."

"There is no sisterly bond between us, Riva. You have no bonds with anyone. You are less human than I."

Riva tossed her blonde hair back and sneered. "I almost feel sorry for you, Beora. You know nothing. Isolated from reality."

"You're the one who's isolated," said Beora. "A pitifully empty life and an empty soul."

"Don't waste your pity on me. I can touch a man without him bursting into flames. In fact, I have touched men even you would desire, Miss Righteous. One in particular. A rather melancholy character named Clayton."

"Liar!" Beora reached for her tormentor, but Riva nimbly twisted away.

"Yes, Beora." She stuck out her tongue. "Your *precious* Clayton. You didn't think he'd wait for a scrawny bit like you? Even if you hadn't been turned into a smoking lump of disfigured flesh, you'd never be able to deny him my beauty."

"No, he loves me!"

Riva laughed. "Loves you! If he ever saw you, he'd run screaming into the forest to vomit. He'd sooner bed Kaie."

"Shut up!" Beora lunged at Riva, who drove forward her dagger. It would have driven into Beora's chest if not for the bracelet. Beora raised her arm to fend off the knife. It glanced off the hard metal, rerouting the weapon up over Beora's right shoulder. A look of terror filled Riva's face as she stumbled. The torch woman took a step forward, her face grim as she clutched the taller woman.

Beora hissed through her teeth. "Now, you will feel my beauty."

Riva screeched and writhed as her arm shimmered in flame.

Beora stepped back as Riva fell to her knees. She looked up with a grateful expression, holding the burnt arm. She whispered. "I can finally feel something other than hate."

"What?" said Beora.

Riva's eyes filled with tears, the first Beora had ever seen her shed. "You were right about it burning me from the inside. I am empty."

Beora frowned. "Is this some kind of trick?"

"I've become like the women I hated," said Riva. "I'm a monster, and I don't know how to stop. By all that is sacred, there was a baby. A baby."

Beora knelt in front of her. "It's possible to change," she said softly. "Look at me."

"You're the true beauty," whispered Riva. She stumbled to her feet and threw herself onto Beora. Screaming, she knocked Beora to the ground and lay on top. Beora struggled, but Riva did not release her until her own body was black and lifeless.

Horrified, Beora pushed off the charred corpse and crawled away. She turned and saw Anastacia staring, mouth open, cradling Kent in her arms. Randolph looked away.

"What the hell just happened?" Beora whispered.

A guttural scream drew their attention as Goar tore open the throat of the giant. Lachish stumbled into view and fell to his knees.

"Kaie." Lachish's voice gurgled in his throat as he collapsed face down.

The forest was suddenly quiet. Anastacia unrolled another bandage, her hands trembling. She was glad Misty was absent. The healer would be horrified. Anastacia wondered how one told the good guys from the bad without a program.

The others joined her. Oddly, Beora was shivering. She exchanged an anguished look with Goar.

Ever practical, Randolph lit a fire to heat a broth for Kent.

"I don't think he can drink it," said Anastacia. "He's very weak."

"Maniac," muttered Beora.

Anastacia wasn't sure whether she meant Riva or Kaie, but she nodded anyway. Beora placed her hand in front of the tree where Kent had been tied, facing the bark. Anastacia glimpsed the word 'traitor' written in blood before Beora singed it away. She bit her lip and wiped Kent's chest.

They carried him to the village in a stretcher made from branches, boughs, and spare clothing.

Durward was overjoyed to see Misty recovered but bewildered by her near hysteria.

"Bedad had a horrible vision!" she cried, wringing her hands.

"A vision?" said Durward.

"It is the onset of the farseeing gift," she said. "Then I had nightmares. Horrible things happening to you all."

"Kent *is* badly wounded, but, with your help, he may yet recover. Beora has become our dear friend and ally, and the bracelet has cured her of incessant pain. Anastacia escaped the many-armed water-creature. Randolph and I are alive and well. Your worries confused your dreams." He smiled and took her hand.

"But what of Bedad?" Her gray face was creased with worry.

"Bedad? What do you mean? Is he not well?"

Misty face filled with anguish. "He has been missing since breakfast."

"What do you want with me?" Bedad's voice was high-pitched and tremulous.

"Cheese in the trap," said Kaie. "Now, shut up, or I'll gag you." She giggled. "I'll stuff a rat in your mouth. A dead rat. Or maybe a live one." She giggled again.

Terrified, Bedad watched Kaie increase the fire under the enormous cauldron. It was large enough to boil an ox and encrusted with brown scum.

Periodically, she stood very still. A light glimmered under her hood while she chanted softly.

"Where can they be?" she muttered. "What is taking so long?"

Finally, Bedad could stand it no longer. "Who are you waiting for?"

"What?" Kaie turned and toward him as if she had forgotten he was there.

"Who are you expecting?" He repeated.

"Never mind!" Kaie screeched, flailing her arms and coming toward him. "They'll come. They wouldn't ignore me. Then you'll wish they had. Yes, you will. Yes, you will."

Tied to a tall stalagmite, Bedad shrank from her foul breath as she towered over him.

"I'm not alone, you know," she said, spittle flying from her mouth. "Not alone. I can raise an army anytime I want. No one can resist my command."

"I could," whispered Bedad.

"What?" She jerked with surprise.

Bedad shouted. "I could. You're a hideous, old wizard, and no one in their right mind would follow your command."

"I'm not old," she said, puzzled, ignoring the rest of his outburst. "I'm still a young woman. I have a long life ahead of me."

"Long and happy, I'm *sure*."

She held her hand to her head as though in pain.

"Happy, happy? No, that stupid woman in white is happy. She'd better not be coming here. I'm ready for her. She won't get away with anything. I wish she would leave me alone."

"What woman in white?" asked Bedad. Kaie turned away. Bedad shouted. "What woman in white!"

She returned to her cauldron and added grisly ingredients from the jars and boxes tossed about the cave. Bedad looked away, his stomach lurching, when she removed rings from a rotting human hand, before adding it to the brew. The vomit rose when he realized it was the peddler's.

Misty calmed herself when concentrating her energy on Kent. She redressed the wound, stuffing it with unguents, stitching it closed, and lightly rubbing it with the last of the lilyvern cream.

She smiled at Anastacia who had helped throughout. "You did a fine job patching him for the trip. Why, you're gray as ash! How did you ever manage alone?"

"I didn't have time to think, then. Most of it was covered in blood, but now that I can tell how bad it is . . . . " Anastacia bit her lip.

"Don't worry, Anastacia. In my opinion, and I've been doing this most of my life, he'll survive. I've given him meatvine to build his strength, herbs to stop infection, lilyvern cream to speed the healing."

"Then he'll be just like before?" asked Anastacia.

"I can't be sure, especially concerning such a trauma. He may have sustained permanent physical or emotional damage that will prevent him from performing sexually as a man. These things can be tricky."

"That would be a living death for Kent!"

Misty shrugged slowly. "We just can't tell yet." She gathered her things, patted Anastacia's shoulder, and left.

Anastacia sat on a chair beside the bed and watched Kent's shallow breathing. She brushed his matted hair off his forehead. *He needs his hair washed,* she thought. She rounded up some wet cloths and wiped his face and hair as well as she could. Kent blinked and opened his blue eyes.

"Kent! Can you hear me?" She raised her voice to a shout.

"I'm not deaf," he whispered, hoarsely. "My ears are about the only thing they didn't try to ruin."

Anastacia buried her face into his neck and began to cry. "I didn't believe Misty. You looked so awful. I thought you were going to die."

"Water, please."

Misty had left a pitcher and a jug. Anastacia wiped her eyes, poured the water, and held his head while he drank a few sips. He pushed the cup away.

"Might have been better if I had died," he said.

Anastacia set the mug aside and sat back in the chair. "Don't say that. Misty believes you'll be well again."

"Where she cut me . . . . " He closed his eyes tightly and swallowed. "I remember . . . . "

Anastacia interrupted. "Misty is the best. You'll be well before you know it."

Kent turned his head, looking away. "What I did. I'm a traitor, a weakling."

Anastacia leaned forward, took his chin in her hand, and turned his face back. She held him, looking into his eyes. "You're not either. This entire affair has been an absolute nightmare — "

Just then, Beora walked in to check on Kent.

"Anastacia, my sword." Gasping, Kent tried to rise. "Get behind me."

Beora stepped back, realizing he thought she was about to attack.

"No," said Anastacia as she pushed him back down. "She's one of us now."

Kent looked at the two of them, bewildered. Beora gave a tentative smile and stepped closer to the bed.

"That's just what I've been trying to tell you," said Anastacia. "Kaie's magic is most destructive when she turns people against each other. Beora is no more evil than you or Goar. They have both shown their true alliance once freed from her control."

She patted his arm. "I've learned a lot from her, Kent."

He looked at her questioningly.

"People in your world have fought so hard to keep control over their own lives," said Anastacia. "And me, I didn't work at establishing control over my own life when I had the chance. I just pushed my grief down and ignored it, let it push me into being an adrenaline junky. Taking stupid chances, like leaving my cousin's and wandering around Lucerne in the dark. Though, I think, in that case, it had something to do with the bracelet."

He licked his lips. "Why did you feel like you had no control?"

"When my mother died, I felt so angry. I didn't remember my dad, and now I had wasted the last years with my mom being a pain in the ass to her."

"I'm sure she didn't think so," said Beora.

"She should have; I *was* a pain in the ass. But she loved me anyway. I was so angry when she got sick again. If you beat cancer, it's not supposed to come back. That's a battle you shouldn't have to fight twice."

Kent squeezed her arm.

"My stepfather was powerless," Anastacia said. "He and my stepbrother seemed to share their grief with each other. I think they tried to include me, but I didn't want to deal with it. If I just kept myself distracted, I thought it might fade away."

"I'm so sorry," said Beora. She touched Anastacia's shoulder with her gloved hand. "I know how you feel. I lost my whole family to the fire. I haven't had the chance to grieve properly. That's one of the many things I'm going to have to face now."

Anastacia nodded and squeezed the hand on her shoulder.

"By the crystal," said Kent. "We've all been through a lot. I think we should be extra kind to each other and to ourselves."

Beora smiled and nodded.

Slowly, Anastacia nodded too. "Unfortunately, that will have to wait." She looked up at Beora. "There's a wizard to catch, if that's even possible."

"It's possible," said Beora firmly.

They paused in silence. In a small voice, Kent said, "Can you forgive me, Anastacia? Durward told me I threatened your life."

"As did I," said Beora.

"Goar would have killed any one of us as well," said Anastacia. "But he's free of the wizard now, like you. We have to unload all this anger. It will kill us as surely as Riva. Of course, I forgive you. Willingly."

Kent turned his face to the wall, his shoulders shaking. Beora nodded to Anastacia; the two women left quietly, without speaking.

Chapter Fifteen — The Last Attack

"She's captured Bedad," said Durward. "I pray Misty's dream about him being boiled alive was wrong. The poor child. What a life he's having."

After Kent had eaten and fallen asleep, Anastacia had joined the others for their evening meal in Lissa's kitchen. The room smelled of herbs and fresh, baked bread. The group now sat with Lissa discussing Bedad's whereabouts.

"Searched everywhere," Randolph said. "No tracks. No sign. Disappeared, like magic."

"Kaie's magic," Beora said. "She leaves no trail. She probably brought him to the cave. She must have opened the rockslide. We must get there as soon as possible. Before she tries to disperse the drug."

"We'll leave at first light," said Durward.

"You can't wait until morning," cried Lissa. "He'll be dead by then, just like my Ellsworth."

"Traveling at night is too risky," said Durward.

"For Bedad, waiting is too risky," said Beora.

"Why she take him?" asked Randolph. "Boy no threat."

"Bait," replied Anastacia. "I don't think she'll harm him until we get there."

"How can you be sure?" asked Lissa. "She's not rational."

"I understand what she's up to," Anastacia said. "I understand strategy, getting inside your opponent's head. She uses us against each other and against ourselves. Betrayal and hostage-taking is her style. She wants us to rush in, unprepared, tired, and vulnerable, in the dark. Then she will kill Bedad. Believe me, he'll be in his greatest danger the minute we step into her cave. We need to be our strongest to rescue him before she has time to act."

"Blast her." Lissa paused. "Do what you feel is right. I need to go for a walk and collect myself." The group watched her leave.

"I didn't want to say it in front of Lissa," said Beora, "but there is another side to Bedad's captivity. She will be bored and irritated until we arrive. Bedad will be subject to her brutalities until that time. I have seen her amuse herself with captives. She may plan on keeping Bedad alive until we arrive, but he does not need to be whole or sane."

Misty choked and set down her food. Anastacia, too, had lost her appetite remembering her shock upon seeing Kent tied to the tree.

"We should leave before first light," said Durward. "She'll expect us to either rush over now or wait until morning. We should attack just before dawn, when she least expects it."

"Yes," agreed Misty.

"Not you, my love." Durward squeezed her hand. "Only Anastacia, Beora, and I will go. Her henchmen are gone. We will fight bracelet against bracelet."

"But—"

"He's right," said Anastacia. "No one without a bracelet can stand against her. Remember Isabel and Ellsworth."

Poor Ellsworth, she thought. *I wonder if he knows how to catch bugs and hang upside down.*

She was suddenly grateful her mother had taught her to respect bats and treat them with kindness.

Kaie became increasingly distracted as the night wore on. She removed black crystals from a metal box and turned them over and over in her hands, put them back, and then did it again. Periodically, she checked the huge, bubbling cauldron in the middle of the cave floor and added logs to the fire underneath.

She muttered to herself, startling Bedad into wakefulness whenever she burst into wild chants. His head ached, and he was exhausted from fear.

"I need a blacksmith," she muttered. "If I could mount all the stones in my bracelet . . . . But, maybe that would kill me. It's never been done." She paced, waving her hands and pulling out thatches of hair. "I need a blacksmith. Who will find me one?" She stopped, placed both hands over her face and rocked side to side. She dropped her hands and screamed. "Traitors! Traitors all!"

She stopped and in a calm voice said, "What a fool I've been. I don't need a blacksmith. I can use magic." She clapped her hands like a child about to open a birthday present. "I can do it myself."

She took the stones from the box and left the chamber. Periodically, Bedad heard crackles, saw flashes of light, and smelled melting metal. Kaie cursed wildly throughout. Finally, she staggered back into the room. On her wrist she wore a misshapen bracelet containing three black stones. She collapsed on a stool, stroked the bracelet, and rocked back and forth, singing the first two lines of a common nursery rhyme over and over. "Don't cry, baby, morning comes soon."

In the early hours of the morning, she looked up at Bedad. "Are you still here?" She stood and added a few more ingredients to the cauldron. Bedad closed his eyes, not wanting to see what they were.

"Why are you still here?" she asked.

Bedad did not know how to respond. If only he could get at the jackknife in his bag.

"Everyone else is gone," she whispered.

"If madam could untie my ropes . . . . "

"Untie your ropes, no, no, no," she muttered, pacing. "I can't do that." She looked almost sorry for a second. "But, soon, the cauldron will be ready." She straightened her thin shoulders. "Now, it will render senseless those who touch it." Her voice strengthened. "When I add the last ingredient" — she smiled and traced her finger down Bedad's cheek — "it will melt flesh on contact. I thought I might need an extra weapon. Now that I am so close to completing my plan, I can't have any one interfering."

The pungent aroma filled the cave, making Bedad nauseous. Kaie stopped pacing and stared straight into his eyes. She walked over, yanked the pouch from his neck, and stuffed it in her pocket.

"It begins," she said.

Bedad stiffened and leaned back into the stalagmite.

"They come," she whispered as she cut Bedad's bindings and pressed the dagger against his throat. "Walk to the cauldron."

Bedad took two hesitant steps. She shifted behind him and pressed the knife into his back. As he stepped forward, a torch light entered the cave, distracting Kaie. Bedad turned quickly and flung her to the ground. Although she was slightly taller than he, she was as light as a stalk of corn. He involuntarily shuddered when she crashed to the rock floor.

In the gloomy half-light, his heart pounding, Bedad raced for the exit. Eight more steps, and he would have made it . . . .

"Stop." An arc of light soared from Kaie's bracelet like a lasso, halting the boy in mid-stride. Durward, Anastacia, and Beora entered the room. Beora held a burning flame in her bare hand. The trio paused, seeing Bedad frozen in flight.

It was all Kaie needed. A thin sliver of white coursed through the beam, knocking Bedad unconscious. As he sank to the floor, she released him and turned her magic on the intruders. Lassos of light pulsed from her band. The attackers were dazzled. They struggled, individually, to release themselves with the power of their own bracelets, but Kaie's voice filled their minds, overwhelming their concentration. Using her tripled power, she spoke to her three enemies simultaneously.

"Durward, you fool, why do you mock everything your father stood for? You think an artist can wield the power of the magic bracelet? Your cousin was right about you, clumsy, stupid, boy."

Durward's power shrank and withered with each word.

"You are not fit. Unworthy. Weak, dependent upon that pathetic, disgusting half-she-cat —"

Durward felt a surge of protectiveness. He was released from his bondage as he thought of Misty's wounds, the death of Isabel, and the transformation of Ellsworth. Innocents all, depending on him to stop the horror. He raised his arm and met her stream of light, strength for strength.

The subjugation of Beora continued.

"I know why you are here, torch woman," Kaie said. "You seek revenge."

Beora envisioned the wizard begging for mercy and then torn to bits.

"See. It is as I say. You are no better than I. Bloodthirsty, stained with the death of innocents, corrupted by power. Joining them is but an excuse to kill for personal pleasure. You don't care for the others, just as they don't care for you."

Anastacia's smiling face entered Beora's thoughts. She remembered the bottom of the pond. Alarmed, she watched as her new friend stood, still as a cave rock, at Kaie's mercy. She knew the concern was reciprocal. She had to save Anastacia. Had to start making up, somehow, for all the lives she'd taken while under Kaie's control. She was no longer Kaie's puppet.

Beora's bracelet surged and repelled the black magic.

Anastacia still stood, captivated by the small wizard's spell. She felt as though she was buried in cement.

"Why are you here, outworlder?" Kaie's voice rang in her head. "This is not your battle, not your land. You owe these people nothing. I can kill you with a snap of my fingers. Is your life so worthless you would throw it away for strangers?"

Anastacia shifted stubbornly. Kaie changed her tactics.

"They are using you, just like they used your mother. Yes, your mother, the Esteemed Nicole Newman. She was as foolish and ignorant as you. As an apprentice magician, I was told all the secrets of Dawn's End. I know the truth about her death."

Anastacia shivered, while Beora and Durward fought to disarm Kaie's control. Kaie spoke aloud again.

"Your friends don't know, but they wouldn't have told you anyway. Dawn's End killed your mother. They used her and left her to die, just as you are being used. Dawn's End poisons outworlders. You know that's why she had to leave after you were born. But she didn't know that every time she used the bracelet, the poison intensified. She only used it four times, but it was enough to kill her. To give her an incurable disease. How many times have you used it, Anastacia? How many?"

Anastacia groaned and felt her resolve weaken. She remembered her mother, pale and fragile, hairless, scarred from the surgeries and tubes.

Kaie droned on. "Are you angry, little Stacey? Angry because there is nothing you can do to stop the deaths? Because you are a powerless nothing? Did you believe your father had died? Because he did not. He was alive and well in Dawn's End while your mother lay dying in your world. He could have gone to her. Comforted her. But he didn't. He could have gone to you."

Stop! Anastacia begged in her mind.

She remembered her anger at her mother's death. Why hadn't anyone done anything? Why hadn't her stepfather found a doctor who could cure her mother? Anger with her brother who continually told her to follow the rules, to be safe, to be a good girl, when she knew it made no difference. Death came for you no matter what. Such anger. She had driven it deeper, down inside herself where she no longer recognized it.

Bedad moaned and blinked open his eyes, He lifted his head from the floor and saw Anastacia's face filled with pain and streaming with tears. Durward's shirt was soaked with sweat, his teeth clenched. Sparks shot from Beora's skin. Kaie laughed triumphantly as Anastacia fell to the floor.

Silently, little by little, Bedad crawled to the cauldron. He seized the ladle, scooped, and flung the contents toward Kaie. The scalding liquid splattered on her back.

Kaie screamed, staggered, and released Anastacia, Beora, and Durward. She turned on the boy.

"Die, interfering brat!"

Beora and Durward interrupted her triple spear of light, holding it in check a meter from the boy's face. It slowly shuddered closer and closer to him.

Beora shouted. "Run!"

Bedad jumped back and ran in a half-circle around Kaie. The light surged forward.

"Anastacia!" shouted Durward. "Help us. We can't hold her."

Anastacia lifted her head from the floor and licked her lips. She watched Bedad dodge the ribbons of light.

"Quickly!" Beora was pleading with her. "She'll kill the child."

Anastacia stumbled to her feet. Swaying, she looked questioningly at the other two.

"Is it true?" she whispered.

"Help me!" shrieked Bedad, when the light narrowly missed. "Please!"

She's going to kill him, Anastacia thought absently. *Like the others. I'm already dead. I feel nothing. Without anger, I am empty.*

"Anastacia." Bedad sobbed, his eyes big with terror. So helpless. "Why won't you do anything? You can save me. I thought we were teammates."

Anastacia shuddered and then lifted her arm. "Triple overtime," she muttered. Light surged forward from her bracelet, repelling Kaie's in a mighty whoosh of strength.

Kaie staggered under the onslaught as the trio focused their powers upon her. Anastacia felt, rather than heard, an agonized scream. One second, Kaie was standing, a horrible vision of fury; the next, she crumpled to the floor, like paper caught in a draft.

They edged forward, tentatively, bracelets ready, but Kaie did not move.

"Is she dead?" asked Bedad, his voice both hopeful and horrified.

Durward kneeled beside the tiny body. Kaie looked like an abused rag doll, thrown to the floor. He took her wrist. "No. There's a pulse."

"I can fix that," muttered Beora, as she raised her bracelet.

No one moved to stop her as she stood over the prostrate, black figure. She held her trembling wrist over the body and smiled, her eyes glittering.

"Are you going to kill her when she's unconscious?" asked the boy. He looked uncomfortably from one to other. Anastacia walked away from the group and leaned against the cave wall.

"No," said Durward. "She won't." He removed Kaie's bracelet.

"Step aside, Durward."

The young man shook his head slowly. "You mustn't Beora. You'll be no better than she is if you do."

"You know nothing! She's dangerous. She'll never stop. Step aside."

Anastacia turned toward them. Her voice was soft and remorseful. "If we fill ourselves with anger, there is room for nothing else."

Suddenly, Durward drew back as a small, black shape fluttered across his face and landed on Kaie.

Bedad cried out. "A bat! Is it hers? Is it dangerous?"

"I don't know." Beora hesitated. "She never had a pet when I was with her."

The bat flexed its claws into the fabric of Kaie's coat and screeched in turn at each of the watchers, protecting her.

"Those brown eyes seem familiar," whispered Durward.

"Ellsworth?" said Anastacia. "It can't be. Why isn't he ripping her to shreds?"

"I doubt he believes in mindless vengeance. That's what this would be. She's totally defenseless."

Beora lowered her arm. "Shit. Now what?"

"We have Kaie's bracelet, as well as our own. Perhaps we can change Ellsworth back to a human. If we wield them together, it might work."

"But there's only the boy to wear Kaie's," said Beora. "Is he old enough to control the power of three crystals?"

Bedad drew himself up proudly. "I'll be thirteen on my next birthday, and I'm a wizard's son."

"I wish you had an older brother, just like you," said Anastacia with a smile.

Bedad held out his fist for a bump. Anastacia chuckled.

"You can be on my team anytime," she said.

Durward helped him snap on the bracelet.

The bat flopped along the floor away from Kaie. Durward, Beora, and Bedad joined hands in a circle around him.

"What about Anastacia?" the boy asked.

Durward shook his head, Kaie's message echoing in his thoughts. "We owe her too much. We can do this without her."

Chapter Sixteen — Partings and Pardons

Her face was white, skeletal, a gaunt reflection of death. Her long strings of hair were so badly knotted and filthy, they would have to be shaved. Her skin was covered in sores, teeth rotten and missing, eyes crusted. The black robe clung to her prone body, outlining her emaciated figure. Anastacia felt both revulsion and pity.

"What will you do with her?" she asked the group as Durward picked Kaie off the floor and carried her to a stone bench.

"She'll be tried by the villagers," answered Durward. He brushed a clump of hair off her face.

"Will they kill her?" asked Anastacia.

Durward shook his head. "We do not have capital punishment."

Anastacia nodded. "Good."

He continued. "We have to clean her up. She's not fit to undergo a trial, but I doubt they will care. She's malnourished as well. I think all her strength came from the bracelet."

"You take care of her," said Beora, "I'll burn the potions."

"Good idea," Durward said. "I'll help Randolph prepare a meal. You all must be hungry. I know I am.

"Not in here." Bedad was nearly begging. "I couldn't eat in this grisly place. You can't imagine what I've seen here."

"I can," muttered Beora. "Take everyone outside. I will burn all her ingredients and then collapse the entrance for good. The fresh air and sunshine are just what everyone needs."

They laid Kaie on the sweet-smelling grass. After Durward cropped the worst lumps out of the wizard's hair, Anastacia tried to wash away some of the grime. She pushed the wet hair back off Kaie's white face.

"Durward! Look!" She stepped back and pointed to Kaie's forehead.

"What is it?" He rushed over. "An old wound. It's healed completely over."

"But what is it? It looks like someone struck her with a hammer in the front of her forehead."

Beora frowned. "She used to get terrible headaches. I wondered if that's why she was so crazy."

Durward examined the divot carefully. "There's something odd about this."

Durward placed the hand with the bracelet above Kaie's forehead and concentrated. A flash surged from her skin to meet his.

"What the hell was that?" asked Anastacia.

"A crystal, responding to the one in my bracelet."

"A crystal in her forehead," said Anastacia. "Why did she do that? Did it increase her power? I thought crystals inside a person made them vulnerable to control."

"So did I."

After Beora had concealed the cave and they had all eaten, Durward raised the topic again. "I think I understand what happened to Kaie's forehead. If it's true, we may have to rethink our opinion of her."

Beora snorted. "Fat chance."

"I don't believe she put the stone there herself," he said. "It was projected into her body by another force, just like the stone that was shot into Goar."

"By who?" asked Beora, startled.

"Not who," said Durward. "What. It entered her forehead when the original crystal exploded. We were not sure if she was present at the meeting when the black crystal killed the wizards." Durward paused, remembering the shocking deaths of friends and family members.

The group nodded, listening intently.

"I think she was there, but she didn't die," Durward said. "A piece of the stone smashed into her face. Somehow, she survived, I can't imagine how. But the crystal changed her. It contained all the darkness and all the evil the magicians could force into it. The piece that entered her body carried the darkness. As long as she holds that stone within, she will be filled with wickedness."

"We must remove it," said Bedad.

"Yes, but how? We don't know how far into the brain it has gone. We could kill her."

"Do it the way you freed me," said Ellsworth. "Use your bracelets to remove the crystal without damaging her."

They smiled at him, repeatedly amazed at his total recovery.

Durward turned to Beora. "Are you willing to try? You must do so without reservation for our efforts to be effective."

"I never knew her before she changed. It's hard to believe she could be anything other than a monster," said Beora. "But, then, I was a monster as well . . . . "

"Please," Durward said. "It's the only way to end it."

"Not the only way," whispered Beora. She lifted her arm and looked at her gloved hand. There was silence. Bedad gave a small whimper. She looked up into his desolate eyes. "All right, I'll help."

"Anastacia, give your bracelet to Ellsworth," said Durward.

Anastacia looked startled. She closed her hand over the band. "He won't know how to use it."

"I'll figure it out," said Ellsworth.

"How will I get home without it?"

"We'll open the door," Durward said.

"Help me put it on," said Ellsworth.

"No!" She stepped back. "You can't have it. My mother gave it to me, and it's all I have of my father."

Ellsworth looked anxiously at the others.

"Be reasonable," said Durward. "It's nothing but a curse for you. The sooner you remove it, the sooner it stops harming you."

"No! It's mine!" shouted Anastacia, her face contorted with anger.

"She'll never give it up." A strained voice was whispering.

Bedad shrieked. "Kaie's awake."

"What do you mean, 'She'll never give it up'?" Beora asked.

"She has used it too much," said Kaie. "It's part of her now. The crystal never releases those who fall under its spell."

Beora nervously stroked her band, and Bedad looked at his with horror, while Durward met her gaze thoughtfully.

"She's right, you know," he said. "I felt the loss of control once before. We must remember the stone's history. Originally, the crystal was used to control the elements. Then something went wrong. The wizards lost control and darkness began to dominate Dawn's End. Anastacia's mother, Nicole, and Alaric Morrel stopped it, and the stone, once again, was under the wizards' control. So they thought. It worked their magic, but no one knows why the explosion occurred. Except, possibly, Kaie."

"But the wizards weren't evil," Ellsworth said.

"They almost never used the bracelets," said Durward. "Except in the direst circumstances. Then they surrounded themselves with protective magic and purifying rituals. They were able to resist being altered or poisoned. Being a stubborn fool, I didn't learn those magic protections. We've been using a power we don't fully understand, without invoking the safeguards, and paying a price. Anastacia may have paid the heaviest price of all."

"These things are evil," cried Anastacia. She yanked off the bracelet and flung it at Durward's feet. He snatched it up, as Kaie tensed.

"No, not yours," he said. "It's still clear."

Anastacia threaded her hands through her dark hair. "Power is seductive enough, clear or not."

Durward nodded and held the bracelet out to Ellsworth. "Put it on. We will use it only twice more. To free Kaie and return Anastacia to her home."

No one expected so much blood. It spouted like a pierced water hose when the stone burst out of Kaie's forehead. She sat up, screaming. "No! No! The woman in white! I *am*." Then she fell back, unconscious.

Bedad swallowed repeatedly, trembling. Anastacia hugged him, while Beora cauterized the wound.

"Poor Kaie," he whispered.

"You are some amazing kid," she said.

"I'm not a kid," he grumbled.

"No, I guess not."

Anastacia admired his compassion. She would have been flooded with anger. From now on, she would have to balance anger with other emotions, like this special boy did. He had lost as much as she did, suffered more, yet, somehow, he kept his true self intact. She looked at his pale face with wonder. She hoped Kaie would recover, if only for his sake.

Ellsworth placed the stone from Kaie's forehead into his pocket. Durward bandaged Kaie, muttering how he hadn't expected such a big hole. Kaie's eyelashes fluttered open, but she didn't seem to focus.

"The woman in white," she whispered. "She came for me after all."

"What woman?" asked Durward.

"The woman in white. I remember now." She gave a shuddering sigh. "She was me. From before."

She slipped back into unconsciousness.

"She's awfully small to lose so much blood," said a worried Bedad.

"She was a small lady before," Durward said. "All these years of malnutrition have reduced her to a stick. I doubt she'll live. I . . . . "

He caught Anastacia's glare and stopped, chagrined. "Misty would scold me for that."

"Misty could help her!" Bedad's voice rose in excitement. "She has all sorts of medicines."

"Don't worry," said Anastacia. "We'll get her there in time."

Reuniting with Ellsworth and Bedad left Lissa giddy with joy. She hugged them repeatedly and clutched their hands until she realized she needed to keep her own hands free in order to feed them.

"Sit down, sit down," Lissa said. "Everyone sit down."

"Kaie needs a bed," said Durward, carrying in the small, limp figure.

"Kaie!" Lissa hesitated for only a second. "In the back."

"I'll come with you," said Misty, as she hugged her husband's arm.

"Bring your medicine," he said.

News spread through the village of their return. Everyone had to hug Bedad and pound Ellsworth on the back. Lissa finally moved the whole noisy crew out to a table in the square. Kent shocked the entire village and disappointed more than one woman when he raced up and kissed Anastacia, hard, on the mouth.

"Kent! I—"

"I know. You're leaving, my brave Ana. I'm just so crystal glad you're alive, I couldn't help myself. I won't kiss you again."

"Too bad," she said, kissing him back. His lips were soft, sweet, and warm. His tongue trailed along her bottom lip and then met hers. A wave of heat and desire threaded through her body. She felt her nipples harden in response. She slipped her tongue between his teeth. His finger threaded into her hair, holding her gently.

He pulled away and then hugged her hard.

"There's no hope, you know," he whispered. "You have to leave. I've heard the food here isn't good for your people." He pulled back, holding her by the upper arms, looking deeply into her eyes. "But, you know, I just might be willing to risk going to your world."

"There's something I haven't told you," she said, looking embarrassed.

He furrowed his brows. "You'd better not be married. I'm not that kind of guy."

Anastacia laughed. "Far from it. I . . . . I'm only sixteen-years-old."

"By the crystal!" Kent's eyes widened in shock as he released her and stepped back. "I thought you were just inexperienced." He ran his hand through his curls, studying her face. "I . . . . I . . . . "

"It's okay. You're a little much for me anyway."

He laughed and nodded.

Villagers quickly brought food to the outdoor table. Bedad ate heartily, smiling at Anastacia, who picked at her meal. Beora gathered food in her cloak and left to eat with Goar. Lissa fed Misty and Durward inside.

"I hear you brought the wizard with you," the bricklayer said to Anastacia. "I'll be glad to see her punished. We all knew at least one of her victims, and some of us had relatives she killed. It's times like this I wish we had the death penalty. I wouldn't mind stringing her up myself."

Bedad smacked his glass down, the milk sloshing over the top. "Oh, you're real brave now, when she's helpless. Where were you when Durward needed fighters?"

Startled, the bricklayer blushed and stood up. "You're too young to understand, and much too young to talk to your elders like that."

Bedad glared at him and opened his mouth, but Anastacia silenced him with a touch on the arm.

"It's not worth it," she whispered.

The bricklayer left. Others soon followed, muttering.

"Mob mentality is an ugly thing," Anastacia said.

"What's that?" asked Bedad.

"It means Kaie could be in grave danger. I'm going to talk with Durward. You stay here and have another helping. I'm sure you'll find room. Don't look so worried. It'll be okay."

Anastacia walked into Misty's home. She shut the door tightly behind her to keep out prying eyes and big ears.

Kaie had regained consciousness and was sobbing into her pillow. Anastacia scarcely recognized her voice, now soft and frightened.

"I can't believe it, Durward," Kaie said. "I don't remember clearly, but when you tell me details, I know them to be true."

"It was the same with Goar and Kent," said Misty. "Look, here's Anastacia, come to see you."

Anastacia blinked in surprise at the small, pale face that peered fearfully up at her.

"I remember you," said Kaie. "You were in the cave."

"Yes."

"Thank you for stopping me." She stared at Anastacia. "I remember a boy . . . oh, Dawn's Light, I tried to kill him. I'm a monster."

"You *were* a monster," said Durward. "But you're just Kaie once again."

"I have images of other things. They can't be true. They can't be true." Kaie wailed.

Misty patted her shoulder as she sobbed. They waited until she could speak again.

"I'll be tried for my crimes," she whispered. "Won't I?"

"Don't think about that now." Misty's voice was soothing. "First, we're going to get you well."

"That's what I came to talk about," said Anastacia. "Misty, could you come in the other room?"

As Anastacia explained the villagers' anger at the wizard's presence, Kaie eavesdropped.

"I think you should take her out of the village before their anger grows," said Anastacia. "A lot of people hold grudges. I know something about anger. Isabel, Hugh, Fulke, and Steevin didn't make it back. Those who didn't join our battle may feel they have something to prove. It could get nasty."

Kent entered, shadowed by Randolph. "We came to say goodbye," said Kent.

"Goodbye!" Anastacia said. "Where are you going?"

"Now that Kaie has been captured," said Kent, "the group can disband. Randolph is returning to the lupas. I wish to resume my traveling."

"Safe journey to you both," said Misty. "Visit us when you can, Kent." She hugged each in turn. "Thank you for joining us, Randolph. We will never forget Griswold."

"Goar will be a good uncle," said Randolph.

"Goar?" asked Misty.

"Goar with me now. He waits by forest. Will be pack member and take duties of Griswold."

"Will the pack accept him?" asked Anastacia.

Randolph shrugged. "He comes despite risk. Asks us to say his goodbye."

"I'll miss him. I'll miss all of you." Anastacia touched Kent on the arm. "I'm glad you're recovering so well. You have most of your color back. Where will you go?"

"To Sida," said Kent.

"Sida! Why?" asked Anastacia.

"Misty and I discussed it while you were gone," he answered. "She feels my plan may work. I was ready to toss the idea if you were willing to give us a go, but I know now this was meant to be."

Anastacia nodded, a lump in her throat.

"We must go now, while there's still daylight enough to travel. Take care, Anastacia. I'm glad I met you."

Anastacia stood in the doorway until he vanished from sight.

"What did you discuss with Kent?" Anastacia asked Misty, her voice strained.

"It's rather personal," said Misty.

"He's so subdued," said Anastacia. "Unlike himself. I can't understand what he'll do with Sida, a dying species."

"He feels he owes her," said Misty. "The root saved him twice."

"I know, but he can't help her. It's so futile."

"I see I'd better explain," said Misty. "Kent may be able to provide what she desires most, the chance to continue her species."

"He's going to . . . . But that's not possible. How?" Anastacia was stammering.

"There are legends of men falling in love with lilyvern before," said Misty. "I'm not sure if they ever mated successfully, but, because of the location of Kent's injury, he has drawn the essence of the lilyvern within his maleness. I think the crystal has affected him, too, although I can't say how. He fears mating with a human because of his experiences. This may give him a sense of wholeness again."

"I couldn't see Kent spending his life without touching a woman," said Anastacia. "For him, it would be worse than death."

"Yes, much of his spirit would die," Misty said. "Sida may not be a human woman, but she has her own beauty. Her mystery will be a challenge to him. If he succeeds in creating a lilyvern child, it may help to ease his shame."

"Considering how widespread Riva's disease is becoming," said Durward, "taking Kent out of circulation may be the best thing for him. Being a voracious lover is risky business these days."

Anastacia laughed.

Beora entered the room. "I've just decided to leave with Goar and the others. I don't relish the thought of coming to Kaie's defense. The villagers are talking about stoning her. I am working on forgiving her, but I fear they will ask me questions and my experiences will only make them angrier."

"We understand," said Misty, as she squeezed Beora's bare hand. Anastacia snatched it away in horror. They both examined Misty's unharmed hand. Beora laughed.

"Wonderful, isn't it? I don't burn anymore unless I wish it. Somehow, using the bracelet again has affected me in a positive way. Now I can control my fire completely. This means I can wear regular clothes, be bare-handed, and, best of all, I can touch animals and people again."

"Clayton?" asked Anastacia.

"I could touch him, if he still lives," said Beora, "but Riva ensured he couldn't be intimate. That path is best left untraveled. Still, you did say life in Dawn's End holds endless possibilities. I have much to atone for as well."

She hugged Anastacia. Anastacia flinched, but then relaxed and hugged her back.

"This is wonderful, Beora. The magic has helped you twice now."

"Yes. No pain and the ability to control myself. I suspect my skin is healing as well." She held out her hand. Anastacia took it, examining the back and the palm. "There have been small improvements, though it might be too soon to tell."

"You must keep the bracelet, then," said Durward. "For some reason, it doesn't harm you to use it."

"It's because of the fire." Kaie gasped as she swayed in the doorway.

"Kaie, you shouldn't be out of bed." Misty scolded her, rushing to her side.

"I had to tell her. I couldn't face the others. I've brought them so much pain, Beora the most pain of all, and now I must help her."

"Help me." Beora snorted. "Now that's a switch."

"I don't blame you for not trusting me, Beora, but I have knowledge to give you. I know one of the protective substances against the negative powers of the bracelet. It is fire. Whenever you feel the bracelet start to influence you, purge yourself with fire. That will subdue the bracelet's negative powers. The magicians regularly laid their bracelets in the forge until they knew they were safe to wear."

"If this is true," said Durward, "then we can all use them safely."

"It's true," whispered Kaie. "Unfortunately, I do not remember how often it needed to be done, or if the intervals were decided by how often the bracelet was used. Beora may be safe if she uses her flame often. I wish you all the best, Beora, and I truly hope you finally find happiness."

Beora stared into Kaie's eyes, which now had black pupils and green irises, and then turned away. She squeezed Durward on the shoulder and left.

Misty helped Kaie back to bed.

Anastacia and Durward sat in the kitchen and discussed the future.

"I know you have a high opinion of your people, Durward," said Anastacia, "but I believe Kaie is in grave danger. You and Misty may be as well for protecting her."

"I agree." Durward nodded. "We'll be leaving in the morning. We'll take her home with us so I can try to get her through the trial."

"She won't be ready by morning," said Misty, as she entered the kitchen. "I've given her a sleeping draught. I can't imagine her walking as far as the courtyard and back. She's more dead than alive."

"What about a cart?" asked Anastacia. "I've noticed your people use some ox-like animal to pull cart loads of food in from the fields."

"Of course. Our people do not ride on animals or use them to pull us when we could walk, but we do use them to gather food," said Durward.

"And we use them when moving supplies or homes," Misty said. "It would be perfect. We can make a bed for her in the back."

"Will the villagers lend you one?"

"My sister will," said Misty.

"Good, then everything is settled," said Anastacia.

"Except for you," said Durward.

"We can bring Anastacia home with us," Misty said. "The door isn't far from our home."

"That's not what I meant," said Durward. "Kaie told us something in the cave, about the bracelet."

"You could hear her when she spoke to me?" asked Anastacia.

Durward nodded.

"What was it?" asked Misty, her gray nose wrinkled in worry.

"Anastacia has been poisoned every time she used the bracelet. Her mother, the Esteemed Nicole, died early because she used it twice."

"No! You mean we've caused her death!"

"Not you," said Anastacia. "It was my choice to join you, and my mother gave me the bracelet. No one but Kaie knew the damage on outworlders. I guess it was something the wizards figured out before the explosion."

"I refuse to accept this." Misty's voice was firm. "I will consult with other healers. We'll travel to the Pond of Lilyvern. Kaie may know more. We won't let you die!"

Chapter Seventeen—Settling

Goar and Randolph hesitated by the Pond of the Lilyvern.

Turning to Kent, Goar growled. "You sure you want to do this, Kent? It's so quiet here, empty, not like you're used to."

"Be sad, no pack," said Randolph, his brow wrinkling.

"No, I need the silence. It will give me the chance to know myself. Who I am now."

"If it doesn't work out, join us. The forest can be quiet, too." The panther's voice rumbled.

"Thanks," said Kent. "I'll remember."

"May all your hunts be easy," whispered Randolph.

"And yours."

The pond was more peaceful than he recalled. A gentle breeze blew the surface water into little ripples. Frogs croaked, and dragonflies flitted. Kent sat by the reeds and stared at the white blossom.

"Sida, it is Kent of the Lake. I want to talk with you."

The flower remained still, the only movement a soft breeze stirring weak ripples.

"Sida, I have something important to discuss with you. It is important to both of us."

The silence throbbed.

"Very well. I'll wait here until you're ready to listen." He stretched out on the grass, looking up at the clouds, and relaxed. It felt wonderful not to worry about enemies creeping up on him or plans gone wrong. He watched the clouds shape and reshape.

"I'm still here," he said when it was time to eat.

When a day and night had passed, Kent admitted to himself that Sida's patience was stronger than his.

"Si-da," he called in a singsong voice. "Kent here, in case you've forgotten. Will you not grace me with your beauty for just a few moments?"

A small insect buzzed by and landed on the lily. Kent stared, fascinated. Was she pollinated by bugs? He hadn't considered how much of a plant she might really be. The bug crawled deeper into the white petals. The flower twitched, and the insect zipped away.

"You show more kindness to that little insect than you do me," he said. "At least he was given a response."

The flower rose, bubbles broke the surface, and a petite, green face appeared.

"I have no more root to give to travelers for a while." The lilyvern sighed.

Kent knelt, leaning forward on his hands. "I did not come for root, nor am I any longer a traveler."

"Why did you come then?" She tilted her head in puzzlement. Her lips were full and wet. Kent wondered how they would taste.

"I'm lonely," he said.

"Oh." She blinked her yellow eyes and nodded.

"What will happen to Bedad?" asked Anastacia.

"He'll stay with us, of course," answered Lissa. "I couldn't bear to lose him again. He's part of my family now. That is, if he wants to be."

"Good," said Anastacia.

Lissa continued. "I guess, now that Kaie's subdued, it would be safe to travel. He could go somewhere else if he wanted. But I don't know why he would." She reached out and tidied one of his wild, dark curls.

Bedad studied Ellsworth's expression and then asked, "How do you feel about me being here?"

"I'd be right honored to have a son who showed such courage and cleverness these last few days. If it weren't for you, I'd still be flapping around, eating bugs, and sleeping upside down."

"Ugh! Don't mention it." Lissa shuddered. "I'm not letting either of you out of my sight for at least a year." She pointed at one and then the other.

Misty laughed and squeezed her sister's shoulder.

"Well, now, a year might be a bit too long," said Ellsworth. "I was thinking Bedad might like to go fishing at the ridge. We'd be gone a couple of days."

"What?" said Lissa.

"It wouldn't be right away, dear. He hasn't had time to settle in yet."

"I'll say. He needs to get to know his new home, the other children, the neighbors, his . . . . "

"Hold it, hold it," said Ellsworth as he raised his hand. "That'll be enough for a start. We'll go in two weeks."

"Two weeks! All the sewing I've still got to do. I'd better start right now. Bedad, you run to the linen shop and pick out what colors you like in shirts. Tell the storekeeper to set them aside. I'll be there before closing to buy the lengths. Well, don't just stand there, hurry!"

Even Anastacia laughed as Bedad leapt to his feet and headed out the door. He was back in an instant. "I haven't said goodbye to everyone. Will they be here when I get back?"

"You have to learn not to let her rush you, son," said Ellsworth. "Say your goodbyes first. The store'll still be there when you're done."

Lissa began to stammer. "Well, of course it will. I didn't mean to not let him say goodbye. You've thrown me for a loop with your impetuous plans."

"Now, dear, you know I always take the young ones overnight alone at least twice a year," said Ellsworth. "I'm sorry I flustered you."

Bedad hugged Misty. "I'll be seeing you," she said. "Lissa and I visit often."

Then Bedad shook Durward's hand solemnly. "Ellsworth gave you his bracelet, I see. Do you want mine too?" He held out his small wrist.

"No," replied Durward. "I think the bracelet belongs with the son of a wizard. You wear it. But promise you won't use it without my supervision."

"You mean you'll teach me?" His brown eyes lit up with excitement.

"Whenever we visit. And I'd like you also to spend some private time with me. If that's all right with Ellsworth."

"As long as it's not when the leapfish are running," said Ellsworth.

Durward paused and then laughed.

Misty smiled. "Why Durward, you didn't take him seriously!"

"I intend to be a lot less serious from now on. Except about you."

Misty beamed. "Five weeks from tomorrow is the youngest child's birthday. We'll visit then, and Bedad can have his first lesson. Do you think you can wait that long?"

"Are you kidding?' Bedad said. "I've seen what these bracelets can do. I'm not messing around with it by myself."

Anastacia pushed back her chair and walked to the window. The others exchanged glances.

Bedad watched her. "As soon as I become a wizard like Durward, the first thing I'm going to do is cure Anastacia."

Anastacia turned and smiled, her eyes bright with tears. "You mustn't say that Bedad. You set your sights too high."

"No. Durward will help, and Misty. Even Lissa has special skills. And Kaie. I've been talking to her. She'll help too. You'll see. It'll be all right." He nodded reassuringly.

Anastacia smiled. "I'm sure you'll do your best. Now, give me a hug goodbye, and go pick out your shirt cloth."

They hugged, and then Bedad held out his fist. Anastacia laughed and gave him a bump.

After he left, she turned to the others. "I must leave as soon as possible. My family must be frantic by now. I only hope my stepdad hasn't flown to Lucerne to look for me. I've probably ruined Julie's wedding."

"Maybe not," said Durward. "Time flows differently in your world than ours. Days here are but hours there."

"But the more food and water I drink, the more I may be poisoned."

"Early tomorrow, then," said Durward. "I'll take you to the door. I must go now. I have been summoned to speak at the trial."

That evening, Durward announced the trial was complete.

"Already?" said Anastacia. "It would take months, maybe years, in my world."

"She has been sentenced to forty years in prison," Durward said. "And no visitors for the first five years. No speaking with the guards. Total isolation."

"That won't do her state of mind any good," said Misty.

"What about parole?" asked Anastacia. "Do they let prisoners out for good behavior?"

"Good behavior? How hard is it to be good when someone is restricting your every move? Forty years means forty years."

"She'll be an old woman when she gets out," said Anastacia with a pang of sympathy.

"Almost seventy," said Durward. "But I doubt if she'll make it that long. Her spirit and her body are broken. She'll never be strong again. Few people could survive five years in isolation. It's an outrageously cruel judgment."

Anastacia turned away. *That wizard caused so much pain and death,* she thought. *She was the reason I used the bracelet. Now, I'm going to die. Why should I care? Why? I'm a damn fool but I keep thinking about the young girl in the white dress she spoke of, the one she used to be. I'd be more comfortable with some good old-fashioned anger right now instead of all these complicated feelings.*

"I can hardly bear to say goodbye," said Misty. "You feel like family to me now."

Anastacia wrapped her in a huge hug. "You will always be family to me."

When Durward opened the door to her world, Anastacia ran through, but, because she did not wait for him to stabilize the passage, she felt as though she was running through an electrically charged field. When she emerged on the other side, she stumbled and crashed onto the cobblestone courtyard. It was daylight. Just before she lost consciousness, she heard a woman exclaim something in alarm and a man respond.

"I've gotten permission to unearth Kaie's books of magic and go through them for useful information," said Durward. "Bedad also shows an uncanny talent and, in time, will be a help as well."

Misty had prepared a delicious salad of garden greens and vegetables while Durward was consulting with the village council. They sat together, enjoying the calm, as they ate in the kitchen. She relished these moments of peace.

"You're not going to use those evil books?"

"They will be carefully screened. I must summarize each page to the council, and they will decide its fate. If the spell has no potential for good, it will be burned immediately. A copy will be made of all the other pages, to ensure I do not become an imbalance of power. They will be given to different people to memorize. No one will know all the people who have the information."

"Seems prudent."

"There is a new member on the council," said Durward. "Did you know? Someone close to us all."

"Ellsworth?" asked Misty.

Durward shook his head.

"Randolph?" But, even as she suggested it, Misty didn't think it possible.

Durward snorted. "Beora."

"Beora!" Misty dropped her fork.

"She'll be a power to be reckoned with. She's taken the job of Runabout."

"Amazing," said Misty. "Beora is to travel around, settling civil disputes."

"Yes," said Durward. "She holds the power to pursue and arrest lawbreakers, and, in certain situations, deal out the punishment herself." He ran his fingers through his hair, worsening an unruly cowlick. "Can you imagine anyone fighting her? I predict most people will come peaceably."

"Yes, I would imagine so," said Misty as she picked up her fork.

"I hate to leave you alone with all this work," said Durward. "But I'll be leaving tomorrow to help dig out Kaie's cave."

"Do you think there will be anything worthwhile there?" asked Misty. "I can't imagine Kaie collected cures for warts or incantations to make the crops grow."

Durward smiled. "Most of Kaie's magic came from the wizards of old. They were benevolent. She twisted the power to evil. It can be straightened again."

"You just be careful." Misty pointed her fork at him.

"I will," said Durward. "The hardest part will be deciding what to teach Bedad and what not to teach him. I begin to understand the responsibility the old ones had when they chose apprentices."

"Which is why they chose you."

"Yes, there was a wasted opportunity," said Durward, as he put on his hat. "One that I am doing my best to correct."

He left to prepare for his journey.

Misty cleared away the dishes, smiling, pleased by Durward's increasing poise, skill, and hopeful attitude. He seemed to be developing a healthy, balanced confidence. He might never become a truly great wizard, like his father, but he would be a good, and probably wise, one. Teaching Bedad would bring Durward pleasure.

She picked up a basket and headed out to the garden. In spite of all Bedad had been through, he was a loving child. She knew when she first met him that he could not have come to kill Kent of the Lake. There was something about him. He had gifts they must nurture carefully, as well as his body and spirit.

Anastacia woke in the emergency ward of the Lucerne hospital. Julie was sitting in a chair beside her bed.

"You're awake!" Julie exclaimed.

"What happened?" asked Anastacia.

"I was hoping you would tell me," said Julie. "When I came back from running my errands, the apartment was quiet. I assumed you were sleeping and went to bed. I didn't even realize you were missing until the morning. I'm so sorry."

"No, I'm sorry." Anastacia reached for a glass of water beside her bed. Julie snatched it up and brought it to her. She took three sips. "I should have stayed in the apartment. I couldn't sleep, and I thought a walk would help."

"I spent the day looking everywhere for you," said Julie as she took Anastacia's hand. "I called the police that evening, but they said it was too soon to file a missing person's report. I called everywhere I could think of and then finally realized I should call the hospitals. You were here. You had been found unconscious."

Anastacia pushed her black hair out of her face. "Could you help me with the pillows?"

"Of course." Julie fluffed and stacked the pillows so Anastacia could sit in a comfortable position.

"Can you tell me what happened?" Julie leaned forward, studying Anastacia's face. "Did you faint or get mugged or what?"

Anastacia frowned. She rubbed her forehead in thought. "I have no idea. I just remember getting lost and seeing some statues in a courtyard. Then I woke up here."

"Well, don't worry. We'll get to the bottom of this." Julie patted her hand. "I have to phone Mom and tell her you're awake. And I will tell the nurses too. They've been checking on you regularly."

"Oh, Julie, I am so sorry." Anastacia pulled the sheet up to her chin. "This is the last thing you needed just before your wedding."

"Don't worry about it. I'm just glad we found you and you seem to be okay."

"Why are you really here, human?" Sida asked Kent of the Lake. It was a cool autumn evening, and a threat of frost hung in the air.

She had not questioned him since the first day. He had built a hut with an open lean-to facing her pond. Their days had slowly blended together.

Kent coughed. "I told you. I was lonely."

"So. Why here? Why me?" Her gestures were slow, fluid. "I remember your stories the night you were injured. You have no trouble finding company — of any sort."

Kent nodded. "That was then. I'm not the same man now, am I?"

Her white hair was dry, standing straight up on her head, like dandelion fluff. "What do you mean?"

"Because of my injuries."

"Did my root not heal you?" She tilted her head in puzzlement and concern.

"Yes. The first time, it was miraculous. But there was another time. Another injury . . . . " He gestured toward his groin.

"It bothers you to speak of it."

"Yes. It bothers me." He looked over her shoulder to the multicolored forest beyond.

"I will listen quietly."

Kent glanced at her and then looked away. He plucked a blade of grass at the side of the pond and shot it into the water.

"For me to tell this to a woman . . . ." He shook his head.

"Then, tell it to a flower," Sida whispered as she sank below the surface.

Kent watched the white petal trembling softly in the wind. He took a deep breath and began.

Chapter Eighteen — Seeds of the Future

It was weeks before Kent dared tell Sida the rest. That he had hoped they could become lovers. He had cut an old pair of pants into shorts and stood knee deep in the water. Her response was unexpected.

"What!" Her yellow eyes opened wide. "Do not flatter yourself. I am lilyvern; you are a man." She gestured dismissively. "What makes you think we could ever be lovers?"

"I must seem an alien creature to you, just as you did to me," he said. "But being with you here has soothed my spirit. You saved my life twice, and I want to help you."

She sniffed. "I see. This is debt of honor then."

"I might have said that, before I knew you." He took a deep breath, and his facial expression softened. "But, Sida, I find you are as beautiful and alluring as any woman I've ever known."

Sida pouted. "I'm not entirely sure that's a nice thing to say."

"You don't have to answer me right away," said Kent. "Just think about it. At least we can be friends. We're both the only one of our kind."

Sida's yellow eyes studied him. "You *are* my friend, Kent-of-the-Lake," she whispered.

"Then there is a chance we could be more?" He smiled and raised his eyebrows.

"Nothing is impossible." Sida giggled and sank below the surface.

Kent expanded his shelter by the water's edge. He told Sida stories of his travels. She responded with equally amazing tales of the people who had come to the pond for roots. These stories had been passed down through generations.

"Now you are the only one I have to tell," she said softly. "You must remember, Kent of the Lake. When I die, they will be gone."

"They will never be gone, Sida. I promise."

When Sida rose the next morning, Kent was not cooking breakfast as usual. She sank back to the bottom. At midday, he was still absent. The blanket door on his lean-to flapped in the wind, an empty call. She remained above water, waiting, until the moon appeared.

"Where were you yesterday?" she asked as Kent cooked pancakes over the fire.

"I went shopping." He smiled mischievously.

"Shopping for what?"

"I needed some supplies," he said. He lifted the pancakes out with a fork and placed them on his plate. "The forest doesn't provide everything I need."

"It provides everything I need." Sida spread her arms expansively.

Kent poured the tea into his cup and smiled. "What about paper?"

"Paper. What is paper?"

He dug into his pack and pulled out several sheets. "You write on it. With this." He lifted a pen.

Curious, Sida examined the pen and paper. "It does not look as though paper would survive long in water."

"No," he said as he put the paper and pen back in his pack. "I don't imagine it would. Which is why I'll write, and you'll talk." He picked up his plate and fork and took a mouthful of food.

"Talk? I don't understand?"

He chewed and swallowed. "Your stories. About all the people who've come to the pond since the first lilyvern. I'm going to write them down." He pointed toward his pack with his fork. "I'm not going to live forever either, you know." He took a large bite.

"You are right. But what will you do with the stories when they are written down?"

"They will go into the archives."

"It will take years. There are many stories."

"I've got years." He waved his fork and then cut off another piece of pancake.

Sida smiled. "This is a wonderful thing you are doing."

Kent smiled back as he chewed.

"Still, it would be nicer to have a child to teach the stories," said Sida.

Kent swallowed, his eyes wide. "My offer is still open."

Sida laughed. The sound was a mixture of a woman's soft laugh and wind blowing through rushes.

"How lovely." Kent drew in a deep breath. "I've never heard you laugh before."

"I never felt like laughing before."

Kent made an indignant expression. "All this time with a clever wit like me, and you never felt like laughing?"

Sida shrugged. "I was too saddened by my loneliness."

"And now you're not so lonely?"

"No, not as much," she said. "But, yesterday, when you weren't here, I felt what it will be like when you are gone. That will make me sadder still."

"Gone! I'm not going anywhere." He waved his fork back and forth. "I've got all these stories to write. Years of them, you said. And did I tell you? I'm a very slow printer."

Sida laughed again.

"Dozens of them!" said Durward as he showed Misty the box of pages. "Almost all of them were suitable. The council has faith in my virtue. Beora spoke in my favor. It was thrilling. They destroyed only the last few pages, those in which Kaie devised her own spells. Oh, Misty, do you realize the possibilities?" He clutched the pages to his chest.

Misty laughed. "No, but I will listen eagerly to everyone. I missed you Durward."

He put the pages back in the box, shut the lid, and then kissed her.

"Will anything in the pages help Anastacia?" she asked.

"I'm not sure," said Durward. "There's a lot there. A few have possibilities. I'm going to give Bedad a few to study to speed things up."

"Is that wise? He's just a child."

"Yes, almost thirteen is still very young. But he's had to grow up quickly. I'll skim the pages I give him to make sure there's no danger. But wait!" He waved his hands and shuffled his feet in excitement. "The other good news. I still can't believe Beora supported me in this."

"What?" Misty laughed. "What is it?"

"They will allow me to consult Kaie on magic as long as I do not provide her with any materials, and I must remove my bracelets before I visit her."

"Oh, that's good." Misty smiled. "She shouldn't be alone so much, without purpose, and she may be able to help you."

"Of course, she will. With Bedad and Kaie working on it, we're sure to find a way to help Anastacia."

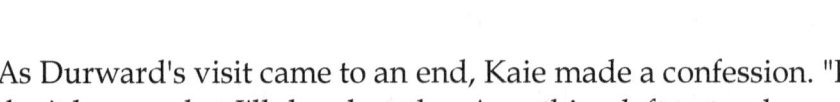

As Durward's visit came to an end, Kaie made a confession. "I don't know what I'll do when there's nothing left to teach you. I'll be alone again."

Her hair had grown in to a cropped chin-length. It was not the lustrous black it had been before the explosion, but it showed a marked improvement over its appearance in the days under the influence of the stone. The council had allowed a dentist to fix her teeth, and she had gained a little weight.

"I'll still come to visit," said Durward as he tidied his papers and returned them to the box. "What do you do in between my visits?"

"I've developed a passion for poems, reading good ones and writing bad ones."

"I should like to see them," he said as he latched the box shut and locked it.

"Why?" She suddenly seemed shy.

"Because you have gone through so much and you have insights no one else has. That is one reason I will continue to visit."

Kaie bit her lip. "Won't you become bored when I have no magic left to teach you?"

"No," Durward said. "We have a connection. You understand the bracelet better than anyone. Because we understand each other, I can talk to you, share my doubts, my fears, and feel no shame."

"Shame!" She studied him, puzzled. "Yes, I can see that. But beside me, all shame is like smoke."

"Don't talk like that, Kaie. Some have forgiven you. You know I have. You must forgive yourself." He paused to cast a binding spell, making the box impossible to open by anyone other than himself, Kaie, or Bedad. "There is rumor of reducing your sentence at the next festival of pardon."

"Pardon? Who will pardon the sentences I have placed on the others?" She bit her fingernail and stared at the floor.

"I have news of our little group. It should cheer you." Durward smiled.

"Yes?" She looked up hopefully.

"Bedad is growing well. Quiet and studious, but a clever wit. A natural gift for magic. Whatever you teach me, he learns in half the time."

"And Beora? Is she still trying to purge Dawn's End of outworlder influence?" asked Kaie.

"Beora the Bright. That's what they call her now. With her double powers of flame and band of the panther, no one can oppose her for long."

"She must be a fierce enforcer of the law," said Kaie.

He nodded. "But not merciless."

"Misty is well?"

"Wonderfully so," said Durward. "Her sister was right about adopting a child. Our home is filled with joy."

Kaie smiled. "I'm so glad. She's done so much for me."

Durward tucked the box under his arm. "I was nervous about fathering, but they both seem happy with me."

"Durward! Not still doubting yourself?"

He tilted his head and gave a one-shouldered shrug. "Sometimes, a little. Old habits die hard."

Kaie squeezed his arm. When he placed his free hand on top, she bit her lip and turned away.

"What is it?" he asked.

"I think that's what hurts the most about being here. The lack of human contact. I spent so many years repelling others. Now, when I need to be touched, I'm not allowed. You can't imagine what these visits mean to me, Durward."

"I know. I'm glad I can come."

Kaie looked into his eyes. "And Anastacia. Do you know if she survives?"

"No. I don't. But Bedad and I keep working on an antidote. I think we may already have a cure for the disease Riva spread."

Kaie looked away in embarrassment.

"There are new diseases from the outworld. We work on treatments for those as well. Perhaps you could help. I could ask the council."

Kaie's green eyes sparkled with delight. "That would be wonderful."

Kent put down the pen and flexed his fingers. He was not used to the life of a scholar.

"Tired?" asked Sida.

He uncrossed his legs and rubbed them. "Not of listening. Just of writing."

"I imagine you're not used to sitting so long either."

"No." Kent looked down the trail towards the woods.

"You need a horse," she said.

"A horse! I'm not going anywhere."

"Not to travel," she said. "Just to ride."

"Yes, that would be nice." He nodded. "But horses cost silver, and I'm afraid I'm all out." He smiled at her thoughtful expression. Sometimes, if he closed his eyes and listened to her talk, he would forget she was a lilyvern. She sounded so normal—and so lovely. He had begun to dream of her. Upon awakening, he would watch the white flower on the moonlit water, unable to sleep.

What an odd relationship they had. Yet he intended to make it odder. Lately, he doubted the possibility. How does a man 'sleep' with a woman who sinks into the mud at night? What does green skin feel like? Would she be slimy or coarse? Would her kisses taste like dirt? When he bent his head to her breasts, would it be like eating pond weeds?

"You seem so thoughtful," she said.

Kent started. She was perceptive.

"What were you thinking?" Sida asked.

"About a horse. Trying to figure a way to get one."

"I have an idea, if you can wait a month more."

Kent smiled. "How can you know so much? Where the best berries are? Where the ache root grows?"

"My body may be trapped by this pond, but my mind is as free as the insects who visit and the birds and animals that drink from the waters." She gestured toward the forest and pond. "They have much to share."

"You can actually understand the animals!" Kent sat up straighter, his mind buzzing with possibilities. "Sida! You never told me this."

Sida giggled. "Kent, there is much you don't know about me. The stories you write are about others, visitors to the pond. You seldom ask me about myself."

"You're right, Sida." He stroked his moustache. "I'm embarrassed to admit it, but I think I've made a lot of false assumptions about you."

She tilted her head in that charming way and made his heart surge. "Tell me one."

"Tell you one!" He ran his hand through his hair and looked away. "Dawn's Light, no. I might hurt your feelings."

"Then ask me a personal question," said Sida. "Something you really wonder. You've told me many private things about yourself. What do you want to know about Sida of the Lilyvern?"

Kent glanced toward the forest and then examined his hands.

"Well? I never thought a man with your reputation would be shy."

He stood, crossed his arms, paced back and forth, stopped, and looked her square in the face. "All right. I want to know how you feel. And how you taste."

Sida paused, studying his clear, blue eyes, so similar in color to her world of sky and water.

"Take off your clothes," she whispered.

"What?"

"If you are to touch and taste my body, is it not fair that I should do the same to yours?" She smiled, her eyes sparkling.

Kent grinned.

"Can you swim?" she asked.

"You bet."

"Then come to me. The water here is deeper than you are tall. I stretched my body towards the edge for Misty, but I can't hold that position for long. If you swim out to me, you can stand on my lower leaves."

Tingling with nervous anticipation, Kent shed his boots, jacket, and shirt. He touched a vivid scar on his chest and then hesitated on his privacy pants.

Sida giggled. "Shall I avert my eyes?"

"There is more scarring," said Kent. "No one has seen me there since it healed."

"Perhaps you feel more unclothed than I." The water lapped gently around her waist.

"I imagine you're not wearing anything but leaves, but you might as well be fully dressed from where I stand," said Kent.

"In that case, I should adjust my leaves." Her body twitched as the leaves peeled away. Kent gasped. He kicked off his last article of clothing and waded into the water.

Sida brushed a tousled section of white hair out of her eyes. The water was pleasantly warm as Kent carefully stroked toward the lilyvern. She reached out and guided his feet onto her broad leaves below the surface.

"Are you sure I'm not too heavy for you?" he asked.

"The water holds much of your weight," said Sida. "But don't be fooled. I'm much sturdier than you think."

What if he couldn't?

She drew him closer. Her bare arms encircled his waist, and her breasts trailed across his chest. There was a familiar response in his groin.

"You seem to have healed well enough, Kent of the Lake."

He smiled. "Thanks to you."

A flutter of wind blew her hair into his cheek. He rubbed his face in it. "So soft," he murmured. He looked into her face. "Your eyes are like sunshine."

"And yours are a peaceful sky."

He kissed her tentatively. She tasted mildly of sweet berries.

"I don't even know how lilyverns love," he said.

"Not so differently, so far," said Sida, as she ran her hands over his chest and back.

Gently, Kent cupped her right breast. "But how did they reach each other?"

Sida laughed. "I forgot I am the only lilyvern you've ever know. I didn't realize you'd never seen a male."

She rubbed her nose against his cheek. "Only the females are anchored permanently. The males float where they wish. I hold a few surprises yet."

"I'll bet." Kent's voice was a whisper.

Passersby during the next few days carried tales of wondrous singing heard near the Pond of the Lilyvern.

After the wedding, Anastacia returned home with new resolve. She had a lot of explaining to do to her stepfather who had received a frightening call from Julie. Fortunately, Julie had phoned again just before he and Ali were to leave for Switzerland, telling them Anastacia was awake.

I feel bad about worrying them, thought Anastacia.

They thought the accident, as they were calling it, had changed her personality. She was calmer and more in control. Anastacia still insisted she could remember nothing of what happened. She suspected it would be a long time before her stepfather allowed her to travel alone again.

If Kaie was right about the poison in my body, I don't know how much time I have, thought Anastacia, as she shot practice pucks in the driveway. *But I'm going to make the best of it. Look at the lilyvern. They only live for fifteen or sixteen years, and no one thinks it's tragic. If my mother taught me anything, she taught me how to die with dignity. But I'm not going to waste my life spinning in anger. I've been living angry since Mom died. She would never want that.*

She put the net and the hockey stick in the garage.

I need to follow that motto, she thought as she lowered the door. *What is it? Change what you can, accept what you can't, and figure out the difference. And, most of all, dump the anger.*

"Jamail, do you know why Mom named me Anastacia?" she asked her stepfather as she entered the kitchen. She wiped the sweat from her forehead on the back of her sleeve.

Her stepfather put down his sandwich. "She told me a story about the Russian princess."

Anastacia turned on the kitchen tap, pumped soap onto her hands, and washed them. "The one whose family was killed in the Russian Revolution?"

"Right." He nodded. "Some people thought Princess Anastacia survived. Nicole liked the romanticism I guess. She wanted to imagine you could survive, no matter what. She said you were spunky enough for the name. Now, of course, they know Anastacia didn't survive, but your mother didn't know that when she named you. She also said your father was some kind of village nobility, so maybe she thought you should be named after a princess."

"She always called me the full name, no nicknames. I guess that's why I always get angry when Ali calls me Stacey. It's like he's taking away the name Mom gave me." She dried her hands on a tea towel.

"Have you told him that?" asked her stepfather.

Anastacia shook her head and flopped into a chair across from him.

Her stepfather frowned. "No. You're a doer, not a talker, I guess."

Anastacia took a deep breath. "Ever since Mom died, I've been so angry."

"I was angry when I lost my first wife and family," said her stepfather. "I cursed the world and everyone in it. Then I met your mother. But I was afraid to love again. In case I lost her too. She changed my mind." He smiled.

Anastacia squeezed his hand. "I'm so sorry that you did."

"But I'm not sorry I took the chance. I wouldn't have had those years with her, and I wouldn't have you. I think everyone is scared of losing the people they love. But we can't stop loving. That would be worse. We must accept that everyone dies, and it will hurt profoundly. It is something we cannot change, so we must find happiness when we can."

Anastacia nodded. "I was scared and that made me more angry. I hate being scared. I'm always tough, and nothing can touch me." She wiped her eyes.

Her stepfather stood up, walked around to her side of the table, bent, put his arm around her, and drew her close.

"You have to let the good things, the good people, touch you, Anastacia, or otherwise you'll be a very lonely woman."

Anastacia nodded again, tears now rolling down her cheeks.

As Ali washed the dishes, Anastacia told him about her plans. She stacked groceries into the kitchen cupboards.

"I've decided to go to Confederation College after high school and take aviation."

"I assume you talked this over with Dad," said Ali, frowning.

"Yes, and he supports my decision," she said. "And it's mine to make."

"Well, of course," said Ali. "It's just that flying those little planes can be pretty risky."

"I'll live." Anastacia's voice snapped with irritation.

Ali flinched, dropping a plate into the sink. "If you're really sure, Stacey."

"I'm positive. And my name is not Stacey."

"I know." He picked up the plate, rinsed it, and placed it in the drying tray.

"I've asked you not to call me Stacey, and you still do it." She put her hands on her hips, her adrenaline rising.

"I didn't know it was such a big deal." He narrowed his brown eyes defensively.

"Well, it is. I hate being called Stacey." Anastacia's voice rose.

"Okay, okay," he said, raising his palm in a halting gesture. "You don't have to get so angry."

Angry. Anastacia paused, watching Ali rinse the plates and stack them to dry. Why was she so angry? *Think*, she told herself.

"That name is too little girlie for me," she said. "And . . . I get angry when it seems like you don't care about my feelings." She paused. Ali nodded, listening. "I — Mother picked Anastacia for me. It helps keep her alive to me."

He dried his hands on a towel and turned to her. "I'm sorry. I honestly didn't realize."

She felt the anger drain away. "Why do you call me Stacey anyway?"

Ali looked at his hands. "It sounds like a little sister, that's all."

"Why do you want me to sound like a 'little' sister? There's nothing little about me."

"Well, because . . . you're so standoffish and tough." He examined the palm of his hand, avoiding her eyes. "It was sort of a special name that only I called you. You don't give me much opportunity to feel like a big brother."

Anastacia touched his sleeve. "I didn't realize, either."

He looked up. She took a deep breath. She hadn't looked at things from his point of view before. His mother died, his father remarried, and then his stepmother died. Then his stepsister disappeared in Switzerland. His life had been tougher than hers, and yet he never lost his temper.

"You can call me Stacey if you want, just please don't introduce me that way. I'd like some people to call me by the name Mom gave me."

Ali smiled. "Sure. Only when we're alone."

Anastacia grinned. "Maybe you could ease up on the big brotherly advice a little, too."

Ali winced. "Sometimes I'm just scared that I'll lose you, too," he said, turning back to the dishes in the sink.

I'm an idiot, thought Anastacia. She hugged him from behind. *I wish I could tell you that you won't.*

That night, she woke up crying. She had dreamt of her mother. She had been standing outside Nicole's bedroom feeling small and helpless. She knew, on the other side of the door, her mother was very ill, and there was nothing she could do about it. She felt great, roaring anger. Anger at Dawn's End for luring Nicole to her death, anger at Nicole for endangering herself, anger at the doctors and her father for being unable to save her, anger at her stepbrother for accepting it all so stoically, and anger at herself for smothering her life in unreleased anger. For letting anger keep everyone who loved her at a distance. For letting anger surface in rebellion, risk taking, and callousness. It would take a long time to get out so much anger, but at least, now, she recognized its choking grip.

She remembered Bedad's vow to find a way to save her. He had been so determined, refusing to accept her destiny. Now, he was on the other side of the door, unable to help. She rolled on to her stomach and cried into her pillow. She cried for her mother, dead when she was still just a child. For her grandmother, killed far too early by a reckless driver. And for herself, destined for the same fate. But maybe not. Durward had promised to find an antidote if it was possible.

Durward smiled as Kaie tasted the windnut bread. She was as frail as ever, but his visits had given her life purpose. She kept her dark hair cropped short, which made her small face appear as petite as a fairy's.

"I really loved the last poems you gave me," he said. "I've had several printed and put into circulation. They've become quite popular."

Kaie smiled shyly. "I never expected that."

"Speaking of never expected, Kent and Sida have a son," he said.

"Another?" Kaie licked crumbs from her fingers.

"Yes, this one is a lilyvern."

"Is it healthy?" She took another bite and closed her eyes, savoring the sweet, nutty taste.

"It seems strong," said Durward.

"Kent will have his hands full caring for the human baby they had last year. I'm glad Sida has one of her own."

"Yes." Durward laughed. "I never expected to see Kent as the harried father."

Kaie set down the bread. "She has not been able to carry a blend to term still?"

"No. They know now the lilypeople, as they call them, will not survive. Still, they hope."

"I may be able to give them more than hope," said Kaie.

"How?" Durward leaned forward. Whenever Kaie got that thoughtful look, something amazing always followed.

"I've been working on the problem. I have some ideas for you to try."

"Kaie." Durward grasped her hand. "That would mean so much to them."

"*If* it works. What other news?"

"Bedad has become a young man. He'll be twenty-four next year. His powers are incredible. It is a good thing he has such a passion for fairness."

"How has Lissa adjusted to his independence?"

"There are two younger than Bedad to sooth her ache, and her oldest is betrothed," said Durward. "She'll have grandchildren before she knows it."

"Grandchildren. I'm sure Lissa will be as wonderful a grandmother as she is a mother." Kaie's eyes were wistful.

Durward watched her face, wondering whether his news hurt or helped. "Goar dropped in for a visit back to his own feline people."

"His self-imposed penance is served then?"

"Yes, he and Randolph have rid the forest of trappers and trophy hunters. Beora has severely punished everyone they've caught."

"She must miss the hunt, though, now that she is a judge."

"I've heard it is not above her to don her badge and rout the lawbreakers herself. Goar was considering joining her," said Durward.

"The criminal element is done for now!" Kaie gave a rare laugh.

Durward laughed as well. "I've had some interesting results with the creekstone and veilroot this last month. I would like to discuss them with you. I also have an idea about researching the lilyvern blends."

"Of course."

Durward smiled, his eyes twinkling with happiness. "I also want you to look at my preliminary test results. I've been working on antidotes for some of the new diseases brought in to Dawn's End."

Kaie's eyes filled with tears. He took her hands in his. "I'm sorry. I didn't mean to upset you, but this is good news. I'm making progress, and I think some of my initial experiments are promising. I may even be able to develop something to help Anastacia, should she need it."

Kaie wiped her eyes and nodded. Durward passed her his notebook. She opened to the first page and began to read.

~The End~

Other Adult Books by Bonnie Ferrante

Nightfall - Dawn's End Book 1

Outworld Apocalypse - Dawn's End Book 3

Bouquet - Short Stories with a Buddhist Scent

Inhale - Short Story Collection

Terror at White Otter Castle - young adult novella

My Ass - play on words humor

Learn more about Bonnie and her books online at BonnieFerrante.ca

Check out her author page on Amazon or Goodreads.

Follow (@Bonnie Ferrante on Twitter.

Connect on Linkedin, or Pinterest.

Follow her Facebook pages:

Bonnie Ferrante - Author

Bonnie Ferrante - Books for Children